# THE TELLING STONE

AMULET BOOKS
NEW YORK

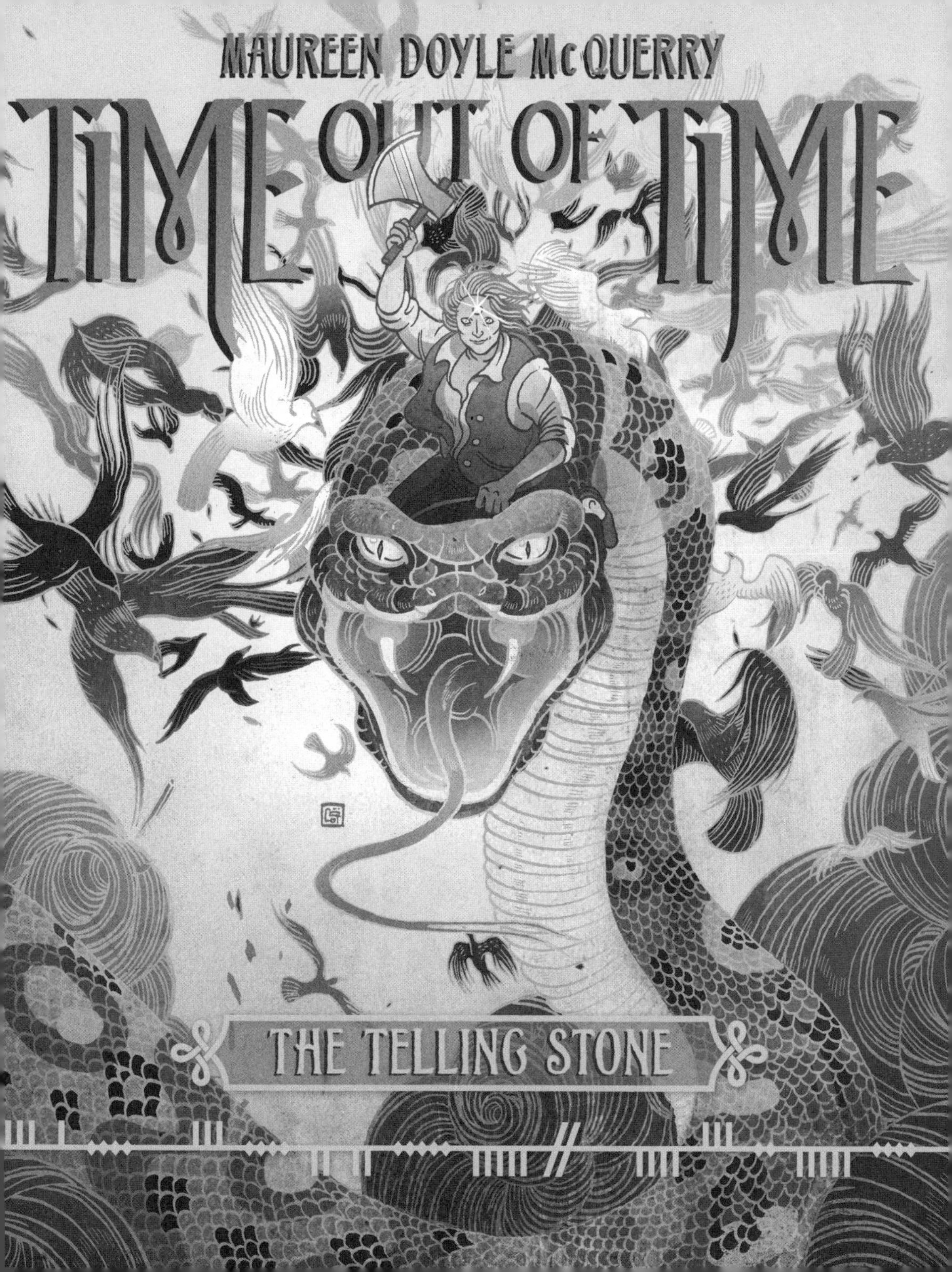
MAUREEN DOYLE McQUERRY
TIME OUT OF TIME
THE TELLING STONE

Library of Congress Cataloging-in-Publication Data
McQuerry, Maureen, 1955–
The telling stone / by Maureen Doyle McQuerry.
pages cm. — (Time out of time ; book 2)
Summary: Timothy James, his sister Sarah, and their friend Jessica race against time and an ancient Evil to save their mother and restore peace and harmony to the Travelers Market. Includes glossary and a map with a code for readers to decipher.
ISBN 978-1-4197-1494-8
[1. Adventure and adventurers—Fiction. 2. Brothers and sisters—Fiction. 3. Mythology, Celtic—Fiction. 4. Space and time—Fiction. 5. Magic—Fiction. 6. Animals, Mythical—Fiction.] I. Title.
PZ7.M24715Tim 2015
[Fic]—dc23
2014019618

Printed and bound in U.S.A.
10 9 8 7 6 5 4 3 2 1

ABRAMS
THE ART OF BOOKS SINCE 1949
115 West 18th Street
New York, NY 10011
www.abramsbooks.com

FOR THE BOYS FROM THE BASEMENT
WHO INSPIRED ME SO LONG AGO: BRENNAN,
JOHN, THE MICHAELS, BEN, AND BRENT

SEE PAGE 345 TO LEARN ABOUT THE TREE CODE USED IN THIS BOOK.

# PROLOGUE

INSIDE A BRIGHTLY painted caravan, Balor stared into the cracking flames of a woodstove and wondered whether the rat had killed the woman. His long golden curls fell forward, almost covering his face. Around him silver cages were stacked among traps and elegant snares. He warmed his hands close to the flames. The night was cold and strangely silent, the only noise the hiss and pop of the burning logs. After leaving the Market, he had traveled deep into the surrounding woods. Here nothing would disturb him except the hoot of owls or the rustle of night predators hunting for food.

He reached into the pocket of his tapestry vest and withdrew a small cobalt-blue bottle. Unstopping the lid, he sprinkled a fine gray powder into the fire. The flames leapt higher. Yes, he could see things quite clearly now. The boy, Timothy James Maxwell, was home tending to his mother. Somehow she had survived. Timothy had found a cure for the toxin that had entered her system when she was bitten by the rat. Rat-bite fever wasn't usually fatal, but this had been no ordinary rat. It had been sent as a warning to Timothy and a reminder of the Dark's power. The Dark didn't like to have its warnings ignored.

Balor blew into the fire. The flames shivered. He had done everything he could to bind the boy to him. He'd appealed to Timothy's sense of pride by offering to make him his assistant Animal Tamer. He had sickened the boy's mother and imprisoned his sister, Sarah Marie. Now he would use their friend, the curly-haired Jessica Church, as bait. When Timothy returned, Balor would own him. But first the Travelers' Market must be destroyed.

He opened the caravan door and walked down the folding steps. The sharp air bit at his face. He would search Timothy out just as he hunted his exotic animals. He was the Animal Tamer; he would catch Timothy, the Filidh by birth, a keeper of memories and wisdom. Timothy would have no choice but to lead him to the map he needed to find the Stone of Destiny. Once he had the map and the stone, he would have no further use for Timothy and his companions. If he eliminated the boy and his sister, no one else would remain of the true line of Filidhean. He, Balor, would rule without contest! The old stories would be forgotten. He would establish his own truth, and that truth would become the memories of the people.

An animal mewled. One of the snow leopard cubs was restless, its cries only a minor distraction from his plan. The Light wouldn't easily give up the Market and its Filidh. A defeat at the Market would tip the balance of power. It would put other worlds at risk. If it came to a battle, he would need allies. The sound of murmuring voices made Balor pause. But it was only the wind stirring up the leaves.

+ + +

The Greenman moved through the forest of old trees circling the Market, assessing his troops. The oldest, an oak, *Quercus robur*, had seen one thousand years. Its thick trunk was muscled like the torso of an aged wrestler. Even six men, arms outstretched, could not circle its girth. While the oak was the eldest, many of the trees in this part of the forest had lived through more than a hundred cycles of life: sap running, leaf budding, green unfurling, and color turning, golds and reds falling to the wind-rattled bare limbs of winter. Soon the trees would be awakened, needed for battle. He scanned the sky; it was a cloudless wash of blue.

There was a time beyond most human memory when the trees had rarely slept. When they had been the guardians of the earth, and humans mere caretakers. That time had long passed, and the Greenman grieved its loss, knowing it would never come again. He stretched, straightening his limbs; a bird flew from his branches.

He moved less stiffly now, though still more tree than man in appearance. In these next days the Market would be at risk. Balor would grow bolder now that Timothy was of an age to claim his title. The Greenman listened to the wind rising. It rustled his leaves as a breeze might lift the hair of a man or woman. The quest had been thrust upon Timothy Maxwell. But Timothy, he knew, was not alone. He, Cerridwyn, and Gwydon had known Filidhean throughout the centuries, and others had known them as well: Mr. Twig and Julian. Sarah and Jessica had their own roles in the story that was unfolding. Still, it would take time for Timothy to grow into his powers. Whatever the outcome, it would be witnessed by Electra, one of the Pleiad sisters come to observe this intersection of history, to bear witness to the events leading to the crowning of a new Filidh.

Timothy had escaped Balor twice, once from his workshop and once from a challenge in the Market. And Timothy had risked himself for Jessica Church even before she was his friend. The Greenman thought of the leaf he had plucked from his own branch. In Timothy's hand it had grown as hard as glass, and its color shaded from cool blue to hot red. It allowed Timothy to measure danger, to gauge whom to trust. The leaf grew warmer to the touch as danger increased. It seemed a small thing against the growing Dark. Yet, the Greenman knew, Timothy kept it with him always. For now the leaf and its ability to warn was his only defense.

# PART I

# THE BATTLE OF THE TREES

# THE GOOSE WOMAN

**N**O ONE HAD ever told Jessica Church how to rescue a girl who was enchanted. Yet here she was, alone in a strange market somewhere in time, trying to help her friend Sarah Maxwell, who had been turned into an ermine. Jessica sat on a bench away from the bustle of the Travelers' Market. A beautiful white ermine lay curled in her lap. The bench was hidden behind a cartload of apples, and she was glad for the temporary cover because she had stolen the long, sinewy animal from its cage when the Animal Tamer was distracted. Now she had no idea what to do next. As she worried, she absently stroked the animal's lithe body. "Don't fret. I'll think of something soon." Did ermines worry? She had no idea. "Sarah, can you understand anything I'm saying?"

A leg twitched. Did that mean anything? Jessica didn't know. She considered the animal's bright brown eyes. She'd never had a pet. She didn't particularly like animals; they were smelly, and many of them drooled. If only the Greenman was here to help.

A shout dragged Jessica from her thoughts. She startled, almost dropping Sarah. The ermine squirmed. A man's voice boomed, followed by a steady stream of curses. Jessica's fingers tightened around the ermine's narrow body. She could feel the rapid heartbeat, the small bones beneath the silken fur. The animal twisted in her hands, and Jessica loosened her grip, just a little. She didn't want to get bitten again.

"I'm sorry, but I don't know what else to do." It felt ridiculous apologizing to an ermine, even when that ermine had once been one of her friends. Jessica shoved the still-squirming Sarah into a burlap sack. The bag bulged and wiggled. Claws scrabbled at the fabric. She eyed the thumb her friend had bitten when she'd grabbed her from the cage. In no time at all Sarah would chew or claw her way through the sack. Jessica needed a safe place to hide her friend and fast.

The shouting subsided. Sarah stopped thrashing, and the bag on Jessica's lap lay still. Jessica brushed a curly strand of hair from her eyes and took slow, deep breaths. She needed to put some distance between herself and the scene of the crime.

Peering out from behind the apple cart, she considered her next move. Any minute now the Animal Tamer might find her, and then what would happen? Her memory replayed the Animal Tamer's laugh as he turned Sarah into an ermine and locked her away. Their friend Peter had tried to save Sarah. He'd caused a distraction so Jessica could get to the cage. And it had worked. But distraction hadn't worked so well for Peter. The last Jessica had seen of him was as a slinking brown ferret. She shuddered.

As Jessica watched the crowd, an idea unfolded. The Travelers' Market was bustling with men and women bartering wares, buying apples, filling their bags with green and gold squash, arguing over the price for a cheese. Her best hope would be to blend in with the crowd, a curly-haired girl carrying a dirty bag that might be full of a day's purchases. She'd get far enough away from the Animal Tamer's stall that she'd be able to think clearly and come up with a plan. Dusting off her skirt and with a firm grip on the sack, Jessica walked briskly into the crowd, looking straight ahead as if she had somewhere important to go. No one noticed how fast her heart was beating. It took great effort not to run.

Was it only a day ago she'd come to the Market with Sarah and Timothy Maxwell to find a cure for their mother, who was desperately ill with rat-bite fever? No, she reminded herself, they hadn't *come* to this market between worlds; they'd been led there through a portway by a scrawny little man called Nom, who looked like a rat himself. He had promised this was the place to search for a cure. And they'd be given an ointment, something that Timothy could take back to his mother. But nothing had gone as smoothly as Nom had promised. The Dark was already there waiting for them: Balor the One-Eyed disguised as the handsome Animal Tamer, and Tristan, the Master of the Market, who was his pawn.

Behind her something hissed. Jessica froze. Had she been discovered? Before she could turn, something pinched the back of her thigh right through her long skirt and twisted. Jessica screamed. She grabbed for her leg. The bag spilled open.

"Sarah!"

In a flash the ermine was out of the sack, a white streak winding away behind a barrel of grain. Jessica dove after her, but the ermine was too fast. It disappeared from sight. Jessica swore in frustration, then screamed as something else took a pinch of her backside. She swung around. A large white goose thrust its serpentine neck forward, yellow beak and shiny black eyes just inches from her nose. Spreading its wings, it hissed a threat. In response Jessica rose up to her full height. The animal thrust its neck forward.

"There, there, my pretty boy, leave the young lady alone!" A short gray-haired woman in a red bandanna tapped the animal's neck with a stick. The goose straightened up, head wobbling but still hissing. Then she rapped him again, more sharply this time. The animal turned and waddled back to its gaggle. "I expect you'll have a rare bruise there by morning." The woman turned to Jessica. "And you've lost your pet, too," she added with a cluck as she tucked her stick back under her arm.

"She's not my pet!" Jessica sobbed. Her leg stung like fury. Where was Sarah? She dropped gingerly to hands and knees, peering beneath tables of fruit and behind baskets of nuts. With every movement, she winced.

It was no use. Sarah was gone. Jessica collapsed in the dirt with her nose running, a waterfall of tears coursing down her cheeks. She wiped her nose with her sleeve, but the harder she tried to stop crying, the more she cried. She cried because she had lost Sarah and Peter, because Timothy was gone, but mostly she cried for herself, stuck in this miserable Market.

"Oh, my, this isn't good, isn't good at all." The old goose woman bent over and peered into Jessica's face. Her gaggle crowded close behind her, strutting and honking. "It can't be that bad, now, can it? Well, I suppose it can. But how can I help you, since it was my dandy boy who caused the problem in the first place?" The old woman took Jessica's arm and with surprising strength pulled her to her feet. "Suppose you tell me the whole thing, eh? Get *back* there, Minerva!" She wielded her stick at a big gray goose with a bulbous beak that was about to help itself to a barrel of grain.

Too miserable to resist, Jessica found herself being steered by the arm to a bench beside a large pen.

"You sit here"—the goose woman pushed Jessica onto the bench—"while I put my beauties away." With a series of clucks and a few well-timed taps of the stick, the old woman managed to corral the entire gaggle into the pen. The geese fretted and honked in protest for a few seconds and then settled down to drink from a metal trough in the shade of an oak tree. She dipped a long-handled cup into a wooden barrel.

"Here you go, Jessica," the woman said finally, wrapping Jessica's hand around a cool cup of water.

"How do you know my name?" Jessica asked between sniffles. She was sure she had never seen the goose woman before.

"So, you've forgotten me already?"

And as Jessica watched, the lines in the woman's old, round face softened, and her gray hair lengthened and cascaded into red waves around her shoulders.

*"Cerridwyn?"* Jessica gasped. Could this be the same fierce huntress who had led her, Sarah, and Timothy into their first adventure? The same woman who had once been disguised as Jessica's elderly great-aunt?

"Yes, it's me. Do you remember your first lesson? After the night of the storm when the Wild Hunt rode, you and I traveled together. Remember the first rule I taught you? Things aren't always as they seem."

"But I didn't know if I would ever see you again."

"I have had many names in many places. I told you that you would never see me again as I was in your world, your great-aunt Rosemary Clapper."

Nothing could have prepared Jessica for the events of the past few months: traveling through portways, fleeing from flying wolves, and discovering that her great-aunt Rosemary wasn't just an old family friend but Cerridwyn, a character right out of Celtic mythology. Now here she was, just when Jessica needed her! Cerridwyn would help her, would tell her what to do.

"It seems your friends have had a very difficult time of it."

"My *friends?*" Resentment sharpened Jessica's voice. "*I'm* the one having a hard time! Timothy's gone home with an ointment for his mother, and *I* got left behind to help Sarah. And even if I do find her, *I* don't know how to turn her back into a girl. And Peter tried to help, but—"

"Yes, he needs help, too. It can't be pleasant being changed into a ferret! Nasty, slinking creatures. Always stealing eggs." She glanced fondly at her gaggle, then turned back to Jessica with a solemn face. "I'm afraid things may get worse before they get better; they often do. But things won't get better if you keep thinking of yourself first."

Jessica's face flamed at Cerridwyn's words. It was hard to think about how her friends felt when she felt so alone herself.

Cerridwyn watched her with sharp eyes. "You are *not* alone."

How did Cerridwyn always know what she was thinking?

At Cerridwyn's urging, Jessica took a swallow of the sweet water. She wiped the back of her hand across her lips. "I think the Animal Tamer knows I've stolen Sarah."

"*Balor.* It's important to call evil by its true name. But here in the Market it might be safer not to mention it. You never know who might be listening."

Jessica looked over her shoulder. A prickle of fear ran down her arms.

Cerridwyn peered closely into Jessica's face. "Of course, we live in a world noisy with evil. History is nothing if not a story of the long battle between good and evil. So we shouldn't be surprised when we find it. Now, clean yourself up." She handed Jessica a handkerchief.

Jessica wiped her nose. None of this was reassuring. "But what can we do to help Sarah and Peter? What should I do?"

Cerridwyn held up one knotted hand. "I can't tell you what to do. What I *can* tell you is that the Market is on the verge of a great battle. News of it has been abroad for some time, and many are preparing for it even as we speak. Even Balor will be preparing."

The small hairs on Jessica's arms stood on end, and her heart beat faster. "A battle? Here?" She looked wildly around the Market, where people haggled and laughed, gossiped and sang. Already some merchants were putting away their wares, closing up their caravans for the day.

Cerridwyn's face remained grim. "Things have not been right in the Market for a long time. The balance of power has turned toward the Dark. But now something has happened that threatens that power, and the Dark will not stand for that."

"What's happened?"

Cerridwyn spoke carefully, as if weighing what she would say. "The next in the true line of Masters of the Market has come of age. As you've seen, Tristan is nothing but an imposter. He's controlled by the Animal Tamer. The true Master of the Market is always a Filidh, one of a long line of people who are keepers of the truth. And that is why a true Filidh is a threat to the Dark and to the lies it weaves."

Jessica thought about the stories of the Filidhean that she and Timothy had heard from Julian, the Storyteller at the Market.

Julian had told them, "The Filidhean are a race of poets, keepers of the word, keepers of wisdom. Only a Filidh by birth can rule the Travelers, the people of the Market. A Filidh fights in all worlds against the power of the Dark." And then he had added the most remarkable thing of all: All Filidhean shared a common ancestor with the name O'Daly.

Timothy had looked at Jessica and said: "My mother's maiden name is O'Daly!"

The very thought of Timothy Maxwell, a small brainiac, being in the line of the Filidhean was hard to believe, but maybe it wasn't any stranger than everything else that had happened to them.

Cerridwyn was still watching her closely.

"Julian said that the true Filidh has to find something to prove his birthright." Jessica furrowed her brow and squeezed her eyes shut, trying to remember. "A stone! The Filidh must find a stone that cries out and something else, something about four treasures."

Cerridwyn smiled. "You listened well. Yes, the rightful Filidh must find a very particular stone, but it will be a difficult quest."

"But it is Timothy, isn't it? He must be the Filidh!"

"Time will tell you that and more. Right now we must prepare for the coming battle."

"Is the stone here at the Market?"

"No, it's not in time out of time. This stone has a long history in your world. It's been part of the coronation of many kings."

Feeling as if the conversation were spinning out of control, Jessica pressed for an answer. "If there's a battle, what am I supposed to do? And what about my friends?"

"You will have help when the time comes. It won't be easy; battles for the Light never are. But the first thing you must do is get your necklace back."

Jessica's hand flew to her neck, her face flushing. "My necklace?"

Cerridwyn nodded. "The one I gave you with my trust."

"I didn't mean to lose it! I traded it for Sarah. Tristan wanted it, and the Animal Tamer said that if I gave it to him, he would let Sarah go."

"A noble attempt to help a friend, but the Dark never keeps its bargains. Don't you know that by now?" Cerridwyn laid a hand on Jessica's arm. "It's time you retrieved it."

"But how? Tristan's wearing it, and he's a friend of Ba—I mean, the Animal Tamer."

"You'll have to figure that out with help from another friend." Cerridwyn looked past Jessica's shoulder.

Had Timothy returned? Jessica swung around, only to see Nom standing there, cap in hand, looking as skinny and dirty as ever.

"But he's just a ratcatcher!" Jessica cried, her hopes dashed as quickly as they had risen.

"Rodent exterminator," Nom corrected her with a smile that showed too many of his yellowed teeth.

Inwardly Jessica fumed. So far, what had Nom done to help? He'd come to Timothy and Sarah's house when their mother was bitten by a rat. He'd trapped it, and then, when Mrs. Maxwell became seriously ill with rat-bite fever, he'd gotten them to this Market between worlds to search for a cure. But that was the last they'd seen of him. He'd abandoned them here when they needed him the most.

"Your first lesson again," Cerridwyn said. "Everyone is more than meets the eye. For example, I know a very brave girl who once did a terrible deed out of anger. But she is more than that one deed, is she not?"

Jessica blushed, remembering how she had once betrayed her friends.

"I think Nom will be of more help than you might expect."

Jessica looked again at the little ratcatcher in his baggy pants and shabby vest. He didn't look like anyone who could be of help. She didn't know why a necklace, even a necklace from Cerridwyn, was so important when her friends were missing and a battle was about to be fought. When she turned back to Cerridwyn, it was the old goose woman she saw, round-faced and smiling. The questions died on Jessica's lips.

"I hope that bit of a sit-down did you good. You're looking as fit as a fiddle! And now I have to get back to my geese and eggs."

White and brown eggs overflowed baskets. Others, painted with vines and flowers, were balanced on small wooden stands. The most intricate had entire rural scenes ringing the eggs. On one, a village nestled under a starry canopy.

"I paint them myself," the goose woman said proudly. "And we haven't been properly introduced. In the Market, my name's Brigit, and over there's my brother, Nom." She leaned close and whispered in Jessica's ear. "Black sheep of the family, but not a bad sort once you get used to 'im."

"Now, Brigit, don't be telling secrets on me." Nom's cap was back on his head at a jaunty angle.

"It wouldn't hurt you to help out in the stall occasionally, you know. But right now you can help Jessica retrieve her necklace."

"I suppose it's the one I've seen around Tristan's neck!" Nom took Jessica's arm in his thin, sharp hand. Jessica tried not to cringe at his long, dirty nails.

"Off with you, then. I've work to do." And the goose woman gathered a bucket of grain to toss into the pen.

"She's right—usually is," Nom said. "Now we'd best be off to see to that necklace of yours."

"But we can't go without finding Sarah first!" Jessica cried.

Nom scratched his head. "Oh, she'll be long gone by now. Not as smart as rats, but ermines is tricky in their own way."

And Jessica, not knowing what else to do, allowed Nom to lead her in the direction of the Animal Tamer's stall.

# ERMINES AND FERRETS

**S**ARAH WORMED HER WAY under bins of grain, behind baskets of apples. There were spaces in the dark that humans could not see, spaces she could fit through when her body was flattened to an almost boneless state. She passed like a white shadow, a whisper, through the Market, the black dot on her tail an eye that trailed her every move. She was looking for a suitable den, a holing-up-in hiding place to rest and sleep what was left of the day away. The old roots of a tree would be best, dry and safe from humans.

She was hungry, too, but it was not safe to hunt here, close to people and unprotected by anything but her swiftness and her thirty-four sharp teeth. She thought of rabbits and birds. An egg or two would make a fine meal.

She darted across the open meadow of the Market and into the forest. Now to find the perfect den. The first tree was too new, its roots buried deep in the earth, but the second was an old oak. Its twisted roots rose above the ground like fingers. If Sarah had looked up, she would have seen that the tree was occupied. A barefoot girl with long silver hair sat on a branch right above her.

But Sarah didn't look up. She began to scrabble in the soft soil, her claws efficiently cutting through dirt until there was a small opening, just big enough to ease her body into. And then she made her second fortuitous discovery: Tucked between the roots was a killdeer's nest, and in the nest were three eggs. She bit into one, sucking out the warm yolk, then consumed the second as well. The third egg she would save for later. She rolled it with her larger front feet into the small burrow under the tree roots. Once nestled into the dark, dry hole, she curled herself around the egg and slept.

+ + +

The Animal Tamer lifted Peter from the cage with one gloved hand. Squeezing tightly, he stuffed the ferret into a sack and fastened the top with a leather tie. "Don't want to waste one of the good cages on an animal no one wants. But I've got a red fox who would find you a tasty meal."

Peter clawed furiously in the burlap sack and bit at the fabric. The sack rocked wildly as Balor swung it through the air and dropped it onto a table. Peter heard the sound of voices raised in argument. His human thoughts were no longer clear and sharp, but his sense of smell was keen. He recognized the pungent scent of Tristan, Master of the Market, and he smelled fear as well. The ferret's instinct to escape was strong, and again and again Peter tore at the sack, working at the loose weave. Soon a small rip appeared in the fabric, and then the burlap began to unravel.

The hole was no bigger than a quarter when the ferret poked his brown furred head through the opening and sniffed the breeze. His quick eyes darted from side to side. Nearby, Tristan cowered in fear as the Animal Tamer shook with rage, his voice raised in anger. And in his anger, his handsome exterior melted away. Balor of the one eye grabbed Tristan by the neck of his shirt and shook him. Tristan spat and touched his forehead. The ferret caught no other scent of humans.

Peter pushed the rest of his sinewy body through the hole, worming his way out of the sack unnoticed. He slunk to the edge of the table and scrabbled down the rough wooden leg.

Metal cages of all sizes littered the ground. He dashed behind the nearest one, where a large bobcat slept. The animal carried the scent of a predator. The ferret's heart beat furiously, and he ran, using each cage as temporary concealment, toward the open ground beyond the Animal Tamer's stall. No one gave chase. Rounding the last cage, Peter smelled the wind for signs of predators. His way was clear. A distant elm stood just beyond the edge of the Market. He sped toward it.

A great shadow passed overhead. Completely exposed, the ferret ran faster. The shadow descended with a great flapping. The ferret's claws and teeth were his only defense, but they were formidable. He could easily kill an animal larger than himself by ripping its throat. But this creature, descending from the sky, grabbed his body in a fierce embrace of claws. No matter how he twisted his head left and right, he could find nothing to sink his teeth into.

As he rose, struggling furiously, into the air, the ground retreated in dizzying circles. Instinctively, he let his body go limp. Peter knew this was his end.

# THE RUBY NECKLACE

NOM MOVED THROUGH the Market, Jessica dogging his heels. He moved silently, his head thrust forward and his nose twitching as if he were smelling his way along. Jessica was quiet, too. She didn't ask Nom what he planned to do to retrieve her necklace. Her heart was still filled with fear for Sarah. Like a shadow, Jessica moved when Nom moved and stopped when he stopped. So when he paused, hidden behind a table stacked with bolts of cloth just a few stalls away from the Animal Tamer's, she paused as well, waiting quietly—which was not like Jessica at all. Beyond the stall a silver-haired girl in a long dress stood watching and listening.

Nom rubbed his hands together and smoothed them across his face—almost, Jessica thought, as if he were smoothing whiskers. The usual chatter and bustle of the Market were stilled. There were no shoppers about, no jugglers, no musicians. The silence enfolded them and made her scalp prickle.

"It will only get worse from here on," Nom said. "But we've got our job to do, hasn't we?" He shook himself all over, like an animal shedding water, and his pointy nose twitched. "Smells like trouble, and that's a fact."

"Where is everyone?" Jessica asked in a hushed whisper.

"Going or gone" was the unnerving reply. "They knows better than to wait around and be killed."

Jessica felt her courage unravel thread by thread. "What do you mean, k-k-killed?"

"There's not many can stand up to the Evil Eye. Not when it's looking right at you. I should know." Nom shook his head. "Oh, he looks pretty and talks a good line when he wants to, but he's evil all the way through, he is." Nom leaned against the nearest caravan. It was a deep orange, and with its windows closed and steps drawn up, it looked like a giant pumpkin plopped down in the middle of the Market. "Once I believed 'im meself. Wanted to be the Animal Tamer's assistant, I did. Wanted to be even greater than him. He promised me, he did. Said I'd outdo Brigit's magic. She's terrible powerful, Brigit is, and full of *draíocht*, magic. She's called Cerridwyn in your world, but it's all the same. She's powerful, and she's good. Animal Tamer said all I had to do was tell him where she was one night. Said he wouldn't hurt her, only wanted to scare her. Kind of a joke, see?"

Nom looked at Jessica with pleading eyes. "Should've known better, 'course, should have stuck with my sister. But I wanted to be stronger than her, wanted it bad. Tired of playing second fiddle. So I told 'im where she'd be. My own sister." To Jessica's horror, the little man began to weep. He shook his head from side to side, shedding tears, and wiped his dripping nose on his sleeve.

She put a hand on his arm. "I'm sure you didn't know any better."

"Oh, I did. Knew exactly what I was doing. Just didn't want to think about it. And when he came back, he didn't make me no assistant. He just turned me into a rat and tossed me into a cage. Hardly any food or water. In the cage for years I was, never knowing what happened to Brigit, watching him do horrible things to animals and people. Listening to his ugly plans."

Jessica didn't know what to say. "What did he do to Cerridwyn—I mean, to Brigit?"

Nom shuddered. The tears ran down his cheeks and dripped off his chin. "She was too strong for him to kill. He could only mark her. But burned her with his eye, he did. All over her face. But she never gave in. She kept telling him the Light would win, and so he just left her all burned up. He told me about it, but I was in this cage, see, and couldn't do anything to help her." Nom blew his nose loudly. "Animal Tamer told me our folks went mad with grief and died. All that time I was still in the cage."

Jessica still stood with her hand on his arm, and it was all she could do to keep from crying, too. "But there was nothing you could do."

He straightened up. "No, there's no excusing me. I was in that cage till your friend Timothy came riding in on the wolf and let me out. While I was in the cage, I was trapped in the body of a rat. But as soon as he released me, the spell was broke; I was meself again. I could hardly walk, hardly knew my own name. But I went to look for Brigit. For my mother, too. Seems she didn't really die; the Animal Tamer had lied about that as well. But she was very old. As for Brigit, it was the most amazing thing. She had been changed, you see. Said this man who looked like a tree had come and carried her away and healed her of her burns until she was even more powerful with the *draíocht* than before."

"That must have been the Greenman," Jessica said.

Nom nodded. "It was him. Thought Brigit would kill me, I did. But she's good, you know, and she only laughed and said I was gone a very long time. Then she kissed me, and took me to see the man who looked like a tree. The Greenman helped me get my strength back, but more than that, he forgave me. Since then I been trying to repay my debts."

Unexpectedly, Jessica found herself hugging the grimy, rodentlike little man, her eyes blurred with tears. "It was very good of her to forgive you," she said.

"Said she had no choice but to forgive me, but I don't believe it. 'Course she had a choice. People always do. So I help her out when I can. I've never had the powers that she does. But that don't matter." He shrugged. "I knows a bit about the Animal Tamer and how he works. Knows he can kill folks with a look of that eye. Knows that Tristan's not the true Master of the Market. Tristan's thick as thieves with the Animal Tamer, but he's afraid of 'im, too. Knows the Greenman is the most powerful of them all, but he's good, all the way through."

"So what are we going to do?" Jessica asked.

Nom shrugged again. "We'll see if we can take the necklace from 'em, I 'spect." Giving his dribbly nose one last swipe with his shirtsleeve, Nom got on his feet and began moving silently toward the Animal Tamer's stall.

Jessica felt as if her legs wouldn't move. She didn't want to be anywhere near the Animal Tamer's eye. She huddled by the caravan, wishing with all her might that Cerridwyn or the Greenman were with her, and not just Nom, even if he did claim to know a thing or two.

Nom had only gone a few yards when Tristan emerged from the Animal Tamer's stall, his normally ruddy face drained of color and his hands balled to fists in his leather gloves.

"You've gone too far, Animal Tamer!" he shouted over his shoulder. "This is still my Market!" His voice was high and strained, and a short sword flashed at his side. Jessica's necklace gleamed at his throat.

"Master of the Market!" Nom cried out. He stepped forward, blocking Tristan's path.

Tristan stopped and stared. "What do you want?"

Jessica trembled. This would be the end of Nom. And how close was the Animal Tamer?

Nom's voice was surprisingly firm. "Stop letting the Animal Tamer push you around. He's nothing but stirring up trouble, he is. Drives away all our customers. Wants to run the Market, he does."

"What do you know of it?" Some color had crept back into Tristan's face, and he rested his balled fists on his hips.

"Just what I sees and hears, Master, and what I sees and hears is him tellin' folks that you're getting too much power and he wants the Market back. That's why he put the charm on you."

Nom spoke with such conviction that Jessica almost believed him herself.

"Eh, what charm?" Tristan considered Nom with suspicion.

"That *draíocht* necklace he tricked you into wearing."

Tristan looked down and fingered the ruby pendant hanging from the chain around his throat.

"It's bad magic, it is. Cursed. Things been bad since he gave it to you. First the birds came, then the boy Peter with his poison."

"He wasn't trying to poison *me*, you fool. He was after the Animal Tamer!"

"Wanted to make you think that, he did. And what about the Evil Eye and everyone leaving the Market?" Nom gestured at the empty stalls around them. "And now there's that one." Nom pointed toward Jessica. "Step out here!"

Her heart froze. Cautiously, Jessica straightened and stepped into view.

"She's a *draíocht* girl, too. Got fairy blood, she has. He brought her here with the necklace 'cause he knew you'd want it. Charmed, it is. Me, I don't want no trouble. My sis and me makes a nice profit with our geese, we do, and that's how I'd like it to stay."

Tristan ran his thick fingers over the necklace again. "I'm hearing what you're saying, old man, and it may or may not be true. But one thing for sure, the Master of the Market doesn't hold with fairy folk. I know who does and who doesn't have *draíocht* in my Market!" And Tristan turned his glower on Jessica.

"Oh, my sister turned her into a mute," Nom continued breezily. "She can't cast spells that way. Come here, girlie."

Jessica did not want to move; she had no idea what Nom was planning, but she shuffled forward, remembering not to say a word. When she got quite close, Nom gave Jessica an unexpected shove, and she stumbled to her knees.

Tristan smiled in appreciation at Jessica's rough treatment. "She's interfered with me and my Market already, and I'm wanting her gone, spit-spat." Tristan pointed one meaty finger at Jessica and with the other suddenly ripped the necklace from his throat, breaking the chain. "And I won't be wearing anything from fairy folk." He tossed the ruby on its broken chain into the dirt at her feet. "Now, get rid of her, goose-man, or I'll get rid of you next!"

"Oh, I'll get rid of her meself, yessir, I'll do that. Trouble will stop, you'll see. You're the Master, you is." And Nom gave several subservient bobs of his head.

His red eyebrows knotted into a frown, Tristan puffed out his chest and hurried off, eager to put some distance between himself and the necklace of the fairy girl.

Nom scurried forward and snatched up the necklace in his bony fingers. The ruby dangled, deep as a drop of blood, from the broken chain.

"How did you know what to say?" Jessica whispered.

"Understand him, I do. Pride's the great enemy. Here, take yer pretty thing, and let's be gone."

And Jessica slipped the necklace into a pocket close to her heart, wondering why she would need it for the battle.

✝ ✝ ✝

Electra had come to the Travelers' Market because of the impending battle. She was needed to bear witness, to observe the facts impartially and tell of them accurately. And she had arrived because a new Filidh had come of age. She did not know who would win the battle or what would happen to the boy Filidh. Her job, her calling, was merely to witness events and not interfere, just as her sisters had done at turning points throughout history. They were those who could provide testimony of all that happened. But Electra found not interfering more difficult by the minute. Everything the small man said rang true. It was obvious, she thought, as she watched Jessica put the red necklace into a pocket, that Balor and Tristan never did as they promised. Even she could see this, and she had known humans for only a short time. And there was something more, a rawness she didn't understand gnawing at her from the inside when she heard the word *battle.*

# GATHERING

ESSICA AND NOM made their way toward the caravan of
Julian the Storyteller. Jessica's steps were lighter now that the ruby
necklace from Cerridwyn was curled safely in her pocket. She'd
have to find some way to mend the chain, but first she must find
Sarah. But even Nom had no clever ideas about tracking down the
missing ermine.

"We'll go see the Storyteller. He may know sumthin' that can help
us. He's clever, him and that great wolf of his."

Jessica nodded in agreement and thought of Julian, who, in her own
world back home, was a reference librarian. She remembered how surprised she and Timothy had been to discover him here, between worlds,
at the Travelers' Market. In the Market he was revered as a Storyteller,
living in a small, brightly painted caravan with the wolf Gwydon. Perhaps Nom was right; if anyone knew what to do, it just might be the
mysterious Julian. If only Timothy was here now to help her puzzle it
all out. Why hadn't Cerridwyn told her exactly what to do?

At the very time Jessica and Nom were making their way through the nearly deserted Market toward Julian's caravan, a rumor was spreading through the forest. It was carried on the slightest breeze and traveled with the woodland birds and animals. Birds of every kind, along with deer, badgers, rabbits, foxes, squirrels, and other forest dwellers, were preparing for battle. Some tucked away food and secured their shelters, while others made their way into dank places where agents of the Dark congregated.

Rumors said that the trees were waking and would soon be called into battle; the Greenman had spoken their true names. It had been many years since the trees surrounding the Market awoke and many more since trees in Timothy's world had. Stories held that the trees awoke only at the great intersections of history. And rumors rustled that now was such a time. A true Filidh had once again arisen. He would arrive wearing the crown. The Greenman walked among the trees. His skin was as rough and gray as sycamore bark, his fingers knotted and stiff. Vines sprang from his nose, and tendrils curled from his eyebrows. A covey of quail had taken shelter in his leaves and bobbed in low branches as he strode along the old forest trails. In a voice both deep and raspy, he conversed with the ash and linden, calling them by name. And as he spoke, with a great groaning the trees awoke. Limbs flexed and bark rippled. There was no wind, but the leaves of the forest shook as if a storm brewed. Young saplings bent to the earth and straightened again. Ancient oaks and elms moaned as they shook off years of sleep.

✢ ✣ ✢

Arkell, the eagle, landed heavily in the topmost branches of a sycamore, where Andor waited. The ferret was a nasty burden, and it didn't even offer the promise of a meal. The animal was to be spared; it was once one of the human folk. Now that it was safely out of the open field and away from battle, Arkell could be rid of it. He swooped down and, near the base of a tree, opened his talons and let the animal go.

⊹ ⊹ ⊹

Julian waited outside his caravan. They should be coming soon. He had done what he could, but he would not be able to prevent the coming battle. The outcome of the struggle would affect far more than the Travelers' Market. It would tip the balance of power in Timothy's world as well. For whatever happened in this Market between worlds was connected to all worlds. If the Dark triumphed here, its hold would grow stronger everywhere. If the Dark was held at bay, Timothy would be given a chance to prove his birthright. And Timothy still had no clear understanding of that inheritance and of the perils that would be involved. Maybe it was better that way.

Julian's sigh was deep. The shadow of evil in the Market was growing stronger, but there was beauty, too, and for that he grieved. He loved the people who jostled every day among the stalls—the men, women, and children who listened to his stories, who ate and drank and applauded for the jugglers and musicians. He loved the honest merchants who struggled to make a living. He had warned those who would listen and even those who wouldn't. Many believed his words, and a few caravans were already bumping their way along the forest trail. Merchants who remained closed up shop, and shuttered the windows of their caravans. But others shook off Julian's words as they would a pesky fly. They continued bartering goods, eating, and drinking as the shadows grew around them.

There was one part of the Market he did not visit: the Animal Tamer's section. He knew he was no match for the tricks of Balor. His one hope was that Gwydon had accomplished his task and brought the crown to Timothy. Julian leaned against the painted wood of the caravan, crossed his arms, and scanned the distance.

When he finally spotted them, they were trudging through the thinning crowd, Nom in front, the bedraggled girl behind. He noticed how small they both looked, how tired and disheveled. This night would be a long one, he feared, but he stepped forward to greet them with a welcoming smile. And when he did, he saw that they were being followed. The star girl walked a few yards behind them with a curious expression on her face.

✦ ✦ ✦

The ermine was gone! The Animal Tamer's gaze swept the crowd but caught no sign of it, and a small fire ignited in his heart. He fanned his anger with thoughts of the wolf stealing the crown, the crown that should be his, and the fire became a blaze of hatred. It had all been within his grasp—the crown; the boy, Timothy; and his sister. He had waited so long, and soon the narrow window of his opportunity would close. He'd taken the boy's sister as bait, turned her into an ermine, and still the boy had not returned. He needed Timothy as much as he needed the crown. What he had not been able to win by guile he would now take by force.

He ran his hands through his hair, and when he could bear it no more, he cried out in rage—a long, inhuman howl. The Master of the Market had outlived his usefulness. The Market itself must be destroyed before the boy returned with the crown to claim it!

✢ ✢ ✢

Jessica heard the unearthly cry, and her heart stuttered a beat. A clammy sweat broke out on her palms. Throughout the Market, people paused, the hair rising on the backs of their necks, their skin growing cold. They had all heard the Storyteller's warning, and now his words came back to them. Those who had not already made preparations to leave began to close up shop. Mothers called for children; men and women trundled baskets of goods into their caravans and bolted the doors.

The Animal Tamer's howl was answered by creatures that served the Dark. With a great wrenching sound that shook the Market, a fissure appeared in the earth. The thin crack widened until it looked like a hideous, gap-toothed smile as broad as a wagon wheel. And from this mouth in the earth, a head slithered. A huge emerald-green, crested snake slid its way up and out, its monstrous head swiveling, its forked tongue flicking the air—ten feet, thirty feet, sixty feet of winding green.

Locked inside their caravans, people crouched low, covering their ears as the Animal Tamer's cry wailed on. The earth shook. A curious few ran toward the Animal Tamer's stall. Tristan led the pack. Something terrible was happening in his Market, something that had to do with *draíocht*. When he saw the widening fissure, Tristan stopped, his eyes fixed in horror on the long green serpent that now rose, a slithering barrier, between the Animal Tamer's stall and the rest of the Market. A small group of merchants stood behind him, muttering and crossing themselves, and a few, like Tristan, were spitting and touching their foreheads with the ancient sign of protection from evil.

Julian, Nom, and Jessica had arrived at their destination. They watched from the back of the group as the fissure began to widen yet again. It was no longer the width of a wagon wheel but of an entire wagon. This time, with a gurgling slurp, as if the ground below was filled with something wet and mucky, the earth expelled a large and hideous toad. Out it sprang, black and sprawling, with many muscled legs and a hundred claws, clods of dirt shedding from its flesh.

Jessica covered her eyes, gasping.

"They have gathered," Julian said in a voice flat with grief. His words, bleak and heavy, filled Jessica with hopelessness. She felt Nom tugging at her arm, to pull her away, but her legs refused to move.

And then, quicker than a blink, the great toad jumped sideways, and his tongue, longer than any toad's tongue should be, unrolled like a black ribbon. In one flick it wound around a merchant's broad chest and pulled him, shouting and cursing, into its enormous black mouth.

Jessica could hear the man's muffled cries as the toad's mouth closed around him. Never in her worst nightmares had she imagined anything as awful as the fleshy lips of the toad closing over the man's shrieking head.

The small group gasped; people ran blindly, pushing and shoving, trampling their weaker neighbors to get away. But Jessica's eyes were fastened on the Animal Tamer, who had appeared in front of his stall. Gone were the handsome features, the golden hair, the bronze skin. He was Balor the One-Eyed.

His single eye remained hooded, but Jessica could see the loose flesh of his face sagging over sharp bone, and his twisted lips drew back in a thin smirk as he clambered onto the great snake's back. The serpent reared its ugly head, bright eyes looking to both sides at once. Jessica drew the necklace from her pocket. With shaking fingers, she knotted the two ends together and prayed that it would hold. The ruby gleamed in the late-afternoon light. She felt as if something within her was growing. She stood up taller.

No one could predict where the toad would strike next. Its many legs allowed it to change direction instantly, and in the chaos of shoving bodies, the amphibian seemed to be everywhere, sucking in victims, slashing others with its claws. The snake, too, was hungry. It unhinged its jaw and swallowed a woman whole. The last Jessica saw of her was a pair of stout arms flailing like a windmill as she shrieked like a teapot come to boil.

The snake's great tail splintered one of the potbellied caravans. A couple and their three children within, suddenly exposed, dropped to hands and knees and crawled to hide behind the wheels and splintered boards. Then into the midst of the chaos a shot exploded. Tristan stood, legs spread, gripping his pistol in his gloved hands. He fired directly at the toad, but the bullets glanced off its thick skin.

"Too late for that, my friend!" Balor called out in a triumphant voice. "Before dawn the Market will be destroyed, and you will no longer be necessary. But you won't have the luxury of death, either!"

Tristan's face bloomed purple with rage. "I am the Master of the Market!" A flap of skin rose on Balor's face, and his single eye found Tristan. Instantly, Tristan fell to the ground, writhing in agony like a beetle stuck through with a pin and fastened to a board.

Balor's face was white, and he bent forward, his arms resting on his knees, as if using his Evil Eye had stolen his strength. "I won't kill you yet, my friend. I may still have need of you," he growled.

Jessica couldn't bear watching any longer. Still clutching Nom, she turned to Julian, but his gaze was not on the inhuman battle. He was looking up into the sky.

# THE PIPES
# OF WAR

TIMOTHY CLUTCHED GWYDON'S fur in one hand. In the other he grasped the Uilleann pipes Mr. Twig had left behind in the forest. Timothy's glasses, beaded with moisture, sat crookedly on his nose as he leaned over as far as he dared to look at the ground many yards below. From his seat on Gwydon's back high above the tallest trees, he saw the Travelers' Market spread below him like a tapestry. His heart thrilled with the familiar sight of the bright caravans, their banners snapping in the breeze.

As the wolf flew lower, Timothy's brow furrowed. Something was not right. Many of the caravans were shuttered. People were closing down market stalls, stacking their wares, while others hitched ponies to caravans, preparing for what appeared to be a hasty departure.

Timothy scanned the Market for any sign of Jessica and Peter. They had promised to do everything they could to rescue his sister. A cloud of dust and noise rose from a corner of the Market. As Timothy watched, people fled from the center of the commotion, but Gwydon flew straight toward it. Timothy tried to feel hopeful. He tried to feel brave. He reached up and straightened the small gold crown on his head, and it gave him courage. He had been just in time to save his mother. But would he be able to save Sarah?

Gwydon flew directly into the cloud of dust and noise. A loud crack shook the air, and Timothy gripped the wolf's fur with his one free hand. He leaned out over the great animal's neck, peering through the dust, and his heart sank. Signs of chaos and destruction were everywhere. People were running and screaming. In the midst of the chaos, an enormous black toad with many legs leapt, first in one direction and then in another. Timothy could barely follow the toad's movements as it hopped from leg to leg to leg. He dug his fingers deeper into Gwydon's fur. A huge green snake reared up, Balor seated on its crested back. Timothy almost toppled from the wolf. Once before he'd encountered Balor, and he'd barely escaped with his life. Between the toad and snake, men, women, and children alike were being swallowed like field mice.

"The pipes, Timothy. Play the pipes!" a rough voice called to him as Gwydon dipped low over the chaos. Timothy started. He knew that voice. It was Julian. This hardly seemed the time for playing music.

But Julian shouted again, more fiercely, "Timothy, you must play the pipes!" So Timothy pulled his gaze from the destruction of the Market and slid the bellows under his right arm, steadying himself with his left hand. He pressed his thighs as hard as he could into the wolf's sides, and once he felt secure, he fingered the chanter and pumped his right arm.

Nothing. He tried again, then again and again, until finally he produced a few small squeaks and drones. Perspiration ran down his face. The squeaks began to resemble a melody. Timothy couldn't look down and play at the same time, so he looked straight ahead, toward the lowering sun, playing as the sky melted from blue to rose.

✝ ✝ ✝

Jessica followed Julian's gaze and looked up into the sky. It was difficult to see anything in the swirling dust, but she heard the first few notes. Then, as she craned her neck upward, she saw the most amazing sight: Gwydon was descending through a cloud of dust while a piper wearing a crown rode on his back.

Julian let out a shout of triumph, and Nom cried out, "Knew they'd make it, sure as sure!"

To Jessica's even greater surprise, the piper, who looked so tall and sure as he rode on the wolf's back, was Timothy.

✝ ✝ ✝

When the first notes reached the forest, the newly woken trees became alert. They murmured to one another in voices hoarse with disuse, "The Pipes of War!" Trunks straightened. Limbs stretched. The murmurs strengthened, turning to song. The sound of their voices rose in crashing waves. Soon a terrifying chorus rose from the woods. The trees sang an old marching song that had not been heard for hundreds of years. And with their terrible voices came a great wrenching as the strongest and most able of them pulled their roots from the ground. Trees marched toward the Market.

And the people of the Market who had escaped both the toad and snake cowered once more, thinking an even greater evil was upon them. The great trees fell in behind the Greenman, who urged them forward into battle. The first in line were the alders, followed by the long-haired willows. Thorny wild roses and prickly brambles clung to their trunks like armor. The forest advanced. And on the edge of the crowd, a barefoot girl watched the trees' progress. Even in the swirling dust, she glowed.

✦ ✝ ✦

The music of the pipes disturbed those who had taken refuge in the dark, murky places of the forest and unsettled them like fur rubbed the wrong way. They stirred in their hiding places, unable to keep still. Bats and boars, great spiders and snakes, toads and lizards flew, crept, and crawled to join the crested snake and black toad.

From Timothy's position in the sky on Gwydon's strong back, it looked as if the entire forest was on the move. As the first trees reached the Market, the toad leapt at the front row of alders. The fissure in the earth widened. Giant toads, spiders, and many-legged centipedes, as large or as long as a full-grown man, crawled out. Alders struck out with stout limbs and trampled creatures that crawled and slithered. But the trees' movements were slow. It was easy to escape the powerful limbs by dodging their swings.

The snake, still carrying Balor, wrapped itself around the thick trunk of a willow and sent it crashing to the earth. Balor appeared to have regained his strength. He slashed at the willow's fronds with an axe. He chopped and hacked branches. The mighty elms marched in and stood as shields for the people of the Market who had returned to fight.

Gwydon dipped lower; they were almost to the ground.

✝ ✝ ✝

Jessica tried to make her way to the spot where Timothy and Gwydon were about to land, but her path was blocked by brambles and by toads hopping in every direction. All around her the people of the Market swung axes and swords or even simple boards. They thrust with knives or pitchforks, using whatever they could find to defend the Market. Most humans fought side by side with the trees, but a few joined Balor.

Jessica was blocked on every side, without a weapon, defenseless. Nom had rushed off with a shout, ready to battle with his bare hands if necessary, as if there was nothing he loved more than a good fight. And Julian, well, she had no idea where he had gone.

Her face was scratched by a traveling alder with a berry bush wrapped around its trunk for protection. Something furry rubbed against her skin: a giant brown spider had slid a long furred leg around her ankle. She screamed and shook her leg, but the spider's hairy hold did not loosen as it strove to bite her. Grabbing a sharp rock, Jessica gouged at the hairy leg. A pale orange ooze trickled across her shoe. A hawthorn came to her aid and efficiently severed the spider's leg with a thorny branch. Then, with sturdy limbs, it pummeled the fat, hairy body. Splats of sticky goo spattered Jessica's face and arms, and she felt her stomach rise into her mouth. She kicked the spider's severed limb away from her ankle and was sick on the dry, dusty ground.

✢ ✢ ✢

The landing was difficult. Still wearing his crown and holding the pipes, Timothy jolted from the wolf's back and landed in a heap in the dirt. Just beyond him the battle swirled. He grabbed the pipes with one hand and drew back in surprise as Gwydon, growling and snapping, shoved him with a cold nose toward the battle.

The noise was awful: the groans of dying creatures, the clashing of wood and metal, the shouts and screams—it was nearly impossible to make sense of anything he saw or heard. It was nothing like reading about a battle in a book. Everything was moving so quickly about him that there was no time to decide on a course of action. By his side Gwydon bared his teeth, the fur on his neck rising. His growl started as a low rumble, then crescendoed as he leapt snapping into the fray.

Timothy stuffed the pipes under the limb of a fallen alder tree, making sure they were well hidden by foliage. He had no weapon. How could he defend himself? How could he join the battle? He grabbed a rock. It was heavy in his palm but not too heavy. He had a good throwing arm, his skill honed by years of skipping stones on any body of water he came across. He looked around and saw that a mammoth spider had cornered a young woman against a caravan. She bravely swung a short fence post at the beast, but it advanced, relentlessly. Taking aim, Timothy let the rock fly. Bull's-eye! The creature toppled and lay still. The woman waved her thanks before heading back into the thick of the battle.

Then out of the chaos stepped Julian.

"Impressive shot, but I suggest you arm yourself more effectively," he said simply, handing Timothy a short sword. "I set this sword aside for you. It's smaller than most."

The sword was heavy, but the grip fit Timothy's hand well. He had never swung a real sword before, but he didn't have time to think, and that may have been just as well. Another great spider scuttled toward him. Without pausing to think, he thrust his sword forward and felt flesh give way. The spider toppled sideways, legs twitching, while a substance as thick as yellow custard oozed from its side. Sickened, Timothy used two hands to pull the sword from the body. Sweat ran into his eyes. He saw Julian, a blur of motion, fighting expertly by his side. Wielding a real short sword was different than slashing in virtual reality. His arm throbbed with every blow. An arrow whizzed past him. Timothy dodged to the left, right into the path of a flailing axe. With a thunk, the axe struck the thick limb of an oak that had thrust its way forward to shield him. A wave of relief washed over Timothy. Without pausing, the oak tree lumbered on, the axe still lodged in a muscled limb.

The battle became a blur of hacking, slicing, and dodging. Just when he thought the sword would fall from his weary hands, Timothy heard a child's cry. A large spotted toad had wrapped its tongue around a boy five or six years old. Grasping his sword with both hands, Timothy slashed at the toad's nearest leg in a swift arc. He missed. The sword struck the ground, jarring his aching arms, while the toad struck out with one of its many claws, slicing into Timothy's leg. Timothy swallowed a yelp. Sweat blinded him. He thrust upward as the toad hovered over him, the blade this time meeting flesh. The toad dropped the child, and Timothy yanked back the sword, preparing to strike again. The toad slashed a powerful leg toward Timothy, but the strike fell short. Its thick, fleshy body quivered, its round eyes bulging. Still it did not fall.

At Timothy's feet, the child cowered. Timothy's leg stung bitterly where the toad had slashed it with its claw. The toad again flicked its long black tongue toward the young boy. The tongue was flecked with white foam, and the toad labored to breathe as its fat sides wheezed in and out. Desperate to get the child out of harm's way, Timothy grabbed him by one arm. The boy began to howl.

"I'm not going to hurt you," Timothy cried. With the other hand he kept his sword ready, pointed at the heaving black body of the toad. "You have to get out of here!"

The toad gave a feeble hop, striking out with one leg.

"Run!" Timothy shouted. In frustration, he gave the boy a shove, and that was all it took. The boy ran in the direction of the caravans, crying for his mother.

The long black tongue wound itself around Timothy's ankle, pulling him off balance. He floundered, righted himself, and, reeling with pain, sliced the tongue in two. The toad lurched sideways, the severed tongue still protruding from its fleshy lips, and collapsed in the dirt.

Timothy plunged his sword into the dying toad and withdrew it with shaking hands. He was breathing hard. His pants stuck to his injured leg, and his right arm throbbed. Now, in the thick of the fighting, Julian was nowhere to be seen. Nor was Gwydon. Which side was winning?

A rumbling shook the ground. Oak trees had formed a line, creating an impassable shield. They moved forward as a unit, trampling toads and spiders in their wake. Timothy wanted to cheer, but he was too tired, and his mouth was as dry as old leaves.

Wiping the sweat from his face, he looked for Balor and spotted him many yards away, riding the snake, surrounded by an army of venomous spiders. If there was some way to take down the one-eyed man, the battle might be won! But who could stand up to Balor and his Evil Eye?

*Crack!* Wood splintered on a nearby caravan. Timothy swiveled. Tristan had recovered from Balor's attack and returned with his pistol. This time his target was Balor. Crouching behind a fallen tree, Tristan aimed at the snake Balor rode. But he wasn't close enough to get a good shot at the moving target.

The faintest whiff of something acrid caught Timothy's attention

. . . smoke! A lazy curl of it rose from the far side of the Market. Then, closer, a gorse bush crackled into flame, followed by a young pear tree. Fire blazed from several locations at once. Balor had found a way to turn back the trees! Fire could change the course of the battle.

Timothy turned and saw Julian once again. He battled a spider yards away, oblivious of a wild boar covered with stiff black fur that was charging straight toward him. It was easily three hundred pounds, and sharp tusks curled from above its mouth. Timothy ran into the boar's path. With no time to draw his aching arm back fully, Timothy's defensive blow was shallow, just piercing the boar's flesh. But it was enough to deflect the creature from impaling him.

A tusk grazed his side. Timothy staggered back, a fiery river of pain flowing down his body. His sword protruded, shallowly, from the boar's side. The animal squealed, twisted, and charged again. Defenseless, Timothy tried to run, but his feet wouldn't obey his brain. He staggered. The boar grunted. Timothy collapsed on the ground, something warm and sticky trickling down under his shirt. He covered his head with his arms and buried his face in the dirt. Timothy waited to be trampled. Nothing happened. He raised his head. Julian was facing off with the boar, driving it back with his sword.

Timothy pushed himself upright. The smoke from the burning trees made him wheeze and choke. He staggered from the boar's path. Without a weapon he was useless. He moved his right arm carefully. When it touched his side, his arm came away sticky with blood.

In the madness of battle, it was easy to forget why he had returned to the Market. Where was Sarah? Had she been swallowed or trampled? How would an ermine survive in the midst of the chaos? Pain made his thoughts fuzzy. His legs felt thick and heavy, too ponderous to move.

Painfully, he inched his way to the large alder where he had stashed the Uilleann pipes. The tree lay fallen outside the ring of battle. He curled between the branches, pressing his back against the trunk, hoping the leaves and branches would protect him from view. If he could just rest for a moment, he would fight again. His thoughts whirled. The fire would have to be stopped before it decimated the trees. But how? There was a word for putting out fires, but he was too tired to think. As his eyes closed, the word danced just beyond reach. As usual, when searching for just the right word, he pictured Scrabble tiles, the smooth wood and black letters. *Quench*, Timothy thought, twenty points. He must find a way to quench the flames. He could do that without a sword. He would move in just a minute, but in the branches of the alder, the world began to swirl. How much blood had he lost? Not enough to feel this bad, Timothy thought. His thoughts were confused; they flickered like an old black-and-white movie and then went out.

# THE HEALER

IN HER SLEEP, curled in the roots of the oak tree, Sarah smelled the acrid scent of smoke and heard the sound of thunder. It woke her, nose twitching, and filled her with an overpowering need to flee. The thunder wasn't coming from the sky; it shook the forest floor. As she wormed her way out of her dry den, her tree began to sway. With a tremendous groan, the oak pulled its roots from deep in the earth and took a mighty step forward. Sarah scampered out of its way while sniffing the air. Which way should she run?

Two squirrels scampered past, chittering in high voices. Keeping low to the ground, she ran after them. Noise and smoke billowed from every direction. Trees and bushes were awake and moving. A lone deer fled past in the opposite direction. Sarah hesitated, caught in confusion.

She began to run faster now but blindly, a flash of white among the browns and greens of the forest. Her heart beat fast with fear. Bushes burst into flame as she passed, nearly singeing her coat.

Dusk was falling, but that would be no help to a small white ermine. Even in the darkness she was an easy target.

✛ ✛ ✛

Jessica longed to be part of the battle. She caught brief glimpses of Timothy or Gwydon, and once she saw Nom riding in the branches of a giant oak. What good was the ruby necklace or its magical powers, she wondered bitterly, if she didn't know what they were?

She grabbed a large flat stone and searched for a target. It took all her might to throw the stone, but it found its mark. A large spider flew backward, flattened by the blow. Heartened, Jessica looked around for another weapon and saw instead a gaggle of white waddling into the midst of the battle. It was the geese, honking and hissing, pinching and pulling. The goose woman trudged behind, clucking like one of her own geese and brandishing her herding stick. There was a peculiar gleam in her eye and a quiver of arrows on her back.

"Ah, just who I was looking for. We'd better get busy." The goose woman hummed as she pulled out an arrow and fitted it to the bow at her side. Jessica's heart surged. She was ready to fight, and here was Cerridwyn to show her how.

"You'll need that necklace now." Cerridwyn nodded toward the filigreed chain with the single red stone that Jessica wore.

Jessica eagerly eyed the arrow in Cerridwyn's hands. She remembered how Cerridwyn had taught Sarah to shoot an arrow into the midst of battle. Jessica was ready to learn.

"The necklace is the sign of a Healer, and the Healer's job isn't to fight," Cerridwyn said. "Only a Healer can truly own the necklace.

That's why it never would have done Tristan any good at all. But when a Healer wears it . . . ah, well, that's a different matter. It helps the process."

"But I thought I was supposed to learn from you! And you have a bow and arrows!" Jessica exclaimed, looking longingly at the bow. "I thought I inherited *your* power and skill!"

The goose woman, who was looking more like Cerridwyn with every passing minute, replied, "You have inherited power and skill, but it will not look the same in you as it does in me. The Light only makes you more of who you truly are. You have your own gifts. We're both working toward the same ends, in our own ways."

"What do you mean?" Jessica gazed out longingly over the battlefield, thinking that fighting looked glorious and that healing was always left to the girls.

"If you are going to do useful work, you have to recognize your own gifts," Cerridwyn insisted. "We don't choose gifts, Jessica. They are given. Healing can be the most difficult work of all."

"But I don't know how to heal!" Jessica cried, the knot of disappointment nearly choking her.

The transformation was complete now. Where the goose woman had been, Cerridwyn now stood tall with flaming hair framing a stern face. "Give me your hands."

Reluctantly, Jessica stretched out her cold hands. Cerridwyn clasped them in her large palms. A warm current flowed from them.

"The work will not be easy. It may even exhaust you. Each time you heal, you will lose a little of your own strength. But you will never be emptied." Then Cerridwyn bent down and kissed the top of Jessica's head. "Try it now, child."

Jessica bent over a broken birch sapling that lay a few feet away. Her hands closed hesitantly around the smooth white bark. Although her hands felt warm against the cool bark, nothing happened. She looked up at Cerridwyn, but the woman's eyes were on the birch tree. With a shiver, the broken trunk straightened. A chill ran down Jessica's arms as if all the warmth had left her body through her hands. Her breath caught. She looked at her hands, opening and closing them. They looked no different than they ever had.

The geese had stopped their clamoring and waddled in a white gaggle into the dusk. Cerridwyn spoke as she raised her bow. "You have found one of your gifts, and that's no small thing." She frowned across the battlefield as if searching for the best target. "But even healing and arrows are of little use against fire. If something isn't done soon, the battle will be lost. What we really need now is a *storm*."

With that, Cerridwyn let fly an arrow into the sky. A small puff of wind lifted the hair off Jessica's neck.

✦✦✦

Sarah was surrounded by fire. No matter which way she ran, she faced a wall of flames. Instinctively, she began to dig with sharp claws, making a burrow in the soil to protect herself from the encroaching heat. Not all of the forest was aflame yet, but it wouldn't be long before the fire spread.

The hole was almost deep enough. She would be able to hide in the cool soil while the fire passed over. Hunger was again stabbing at her belly, but there was no time for food, only for digging and finding shelter.

When the burrow was deep enough, she curled into a tight white ball. The tip of her tail stood out like a small black eye. Then another noise penetrated her burrow: not the dreadful noise of the trees marching into battle, but something that resembled human singing. It came closer and paused nearby. Stiff fingers pried into the soft dirt. It didn't take long for the fingers to find her. She drew her head back and bit as hard as she could. Her teeth cut into stiff bark fingers. The fingers scooped her wriggling body up and dropped her into a dark hole.

The hole was a dry space, lined with leaves. It smelled of the forest, not the dangerous scent of humans. And then her new hiding hole began to rock with a steady rhythm. Her exhausted body quieted. She felt safe, and that was enough for now.

# THE BIRDS

DARKNESS ARRIVED WITH the eagles, as if they pulled night in with a flap of their great wings. Below them, flames were bright exclamation points in that darkness, and behind them was the rain.

Fat drops sputtered from the sky. When the first drop landed on her forehead, Jessica glanced up from tending a deer that had been wounded by an enemy's claw. Humans, animals, and trees, injured and dead, surrounded her on every side. Despite the carnage, Jessica wanted to cheer. The rain had come and would extinguish the fire.

"It's raining!" she called out to Cerridwyn, who only nodded and smiled once in response before again taking aim, this time at a target in the battlefield.

Soon the raindrops were falling faster, splattering on the ground and sizzling in the flames. And amid the sound of the rain was another noise: Jessica looked up at the beating of hundreds—no, thousands—of wings.

Birdcall pierced the night. Andor and Arkell were in the front line of the advancing birds, followed by others of their kind: bald eagles from the north, golden eagles from the west. Hawks, kestrels, owls, and sweet-tongued blackbirds flew in a great, sweeping band just behind. Unruly crows and magpies were the rear guard, while sparrows and other small birds darted in and out of the ranks. Only the yellow-eyed starlings had refused to come.

The birds swooped down in formation, pecking and clawing at snakes, toads, and boars. Darkness hid their descent, and as the rain fell harder, its patter covered the noise of their wings.

But Andor and Arkell had another mission in mind now that they had left the ferret-boy behind in the nest guarded by crows. They searched for the one-eyed man who rode the serpent, and for any sign of the boy wearing the crown, the boy they had watched for so long.

The man on the crested snake was not difficult to spot. With his long-handled axe, he hacked wildly at a great stand of oaks. Andor dropped swiftly, as if he were targeting a fish in a river, but the one-eyed man was fast with the axe. It was arcing toward the eagle before the mighty bird could reach the man's face. Arkell saw his chance and followed quickly, talons extended. He managed to grab the axe with one talon, but the man held on with two hands, and, try as he might, Arkell could not part the axe from the one-eyed man's grip.

With both hands occupied, the one-eyed man was unable to protect his face. Andor swooped in, raking with his talons.

Boars, spiders, and toads that battled for the Dark retreated to the forest with the onslaught of the birds. They fled in confusion, looking for places to hide. Some burrowed into the ground; others dispersed into the wilds of the forest. The fires were smoldering now, thanks to the rain. Jessica hurried among the wounded. She was bitterly cold, and weariness hung on her like a heavy cloak.

As she stumbled over bodies—animal, tree, and human—there was one Jessica recognized: a woman with fair hair and a ragged scar on her neck.

It was Peter's mother, Fiona, the baker. Her breathing was labored, and her leg was twisted at a strange angle, but at least she was able to speak.

"Have you seen my son?" she whispered frantically. "Do you know if Peter's alive?"

Motioning her to be calm, Jessica carefully placed her hands on the twisted leg and felt an icy numbness travel up her arm. She kept her hands wrapped around Fiona's leg as she considered how to answer.

"The last time I saw him, he was alive," she said finally. "I think he's escaped the worst of the battle." She thought it better not to mention that the last time she had seen him, he was also in the form of a ferret—and a prisoner of Balor.

The answer and her touch served its purpose. Fiona smiled and stretched the twisted leg. With Jessica's help she was soon able to stand and even walk, though with a limp. "To die in the service of the Light is not a bad thing," she said, "but I'd rather have my boy back."

Jessica dragged herself onward. Now birdcall eclipsed the sound of sluicing rain. Their noise was deafening, and she flinched when a hawk dove too close to her head. The rain had long since soaked through her thin cotton clothing. The number of wounded seemed endless. Many were beyond Jessica's ability to help. She mourned for a large alder, fallen on the edge of the battle. It had been a magnificent tree, tall and broad. Now its leafy branches lay splayed on the ground, blocking her path. A rustling in the leaves caught her eye, but it was only a small rabbit startled by her presence. She stepped carefully among the branches. Her foot thumped against something solid. It was the body of a boy curled in the vee of two limbs, his face hidden in his arms. Jessica bent over to feel for a pulse. A gleam of gold was caught in his curly hair. Her fingers rested on his pale neck. She bent closer. What was that . . . a *crown?*

"Timothy!" Jessica cried out.

The tousled head barely moved. The boy gave a soft groan.

Quickly she ran her hands over his body. Something sticky coated his right side. Blood. The blood wasn't fresh; the wound had closed, and the blood had stopped flowing. He was breathing deep, regular breaths, like someone asleep. Again she called his name, but this time he made no response. The sticky puddle by his side was large.

Jessica bit her lip, praying he hadn't lost too much blood. She called to Cerridwyn, who was tending to the wounded just a few yards away. "I found Timothy, and he's hurt!" Then, very gently, she began to press her hands over his wounded side. Cerridwyn picked her way over severed tree limbs and toppled trunks.

"The wound's closed." Jessica sat back on her heels, hugging herself for warmth. "But he won't wake up!"

Cerridwyn bent her head low and sniffed Timothy's breath. "The animal that attacked him carries a poison of the spirit," she said finally, straightening. "It works as a depressant. While the body may recover, often the spirit remains wounded." Her expression was serious, and Jessica felt her throat tighten.

"But he has to recover!"

"Timothy is sleeping safely for the time being, and there is little else we can do for him now except keep him warm." Cerridwyn removed her shawl and wrapped it around him. "Meanwhile, there are others who still need our help."

"We can't just leave him!" Jessica glared at Cerridwyn. Anger and fear warred within her. She was exhausted, and she had expected more than this from the older woman.

Cerridwyn laid her hand on Jessica's neck. Warmth spread across her back and into her clenched shoulders, and when Cerriwyn spoke, her voice was gentler. "Sometimes waiting is all we can do. It can be harder than doing battle. Timothy's spirit is strong, and there are others who need me." And with those words Cerridwyn turned and walked away.

Jessica crouched by Timothy's side a few moments longer. He looked peaceful. She thought about the time he had taken her place when she was the prey of the Wild Hunt. She could still hear the hounds' excited cries, their snapping jaws, feel their warm breath. And Timothy had let the hounds hunt him instead. Now it was her turn to help him, and she didn't know how.

When she had imagined adventures, she hadn't foreseen all this sadness. Adventures were supposed to be about intrigue and mystery, excitement and danger. Now, as she removed Timothy's glasses and tried to clean them on her crumpled skirt, what she wanted most in the world was to see them all safely home! She gently replaced Timothy's glasses and swiped at her own eyes.

As she stood, she felt as if eyes bore between her shoulder blades. Jessica rotated slowly, and only then did she see the girl just a few yards away, watching her. "Star Girl!" Jessica called out. The girl didn't move, but her eyes locked with Jessica's. Before Jessica could go to her, she heard a groan. Just a few feet away, a merchant lay wounded in the mud. Jessica bent to tend to him.

✛ ✛ ✛

Arkell and Andor would not give up easily. They had come to turn the battle, to lead the charge of the birds. Arkell had managed a few ragged scores on Balor's hideous face, but no more than that. After one last failed attempt to gouge Balor's Evil Eye, without becoming a victim of its deadly glance himself, he changed tactics. He dove at the head of the crested snake that Balor rode. This time his talons drove home, blinding the creature in one eye.

Andor, too, was having a difficult time finding a target while avoiding the Evil Eye. A poisoned arrow, shot by forces of the Dark, whistled by, and Andor swept sideways as it grazed the edge of his feathers. Again and again he flew at the one-eyed man but could do no real damage.

As animals of the Dark retreated, and the birds continued their attack, no one noticed a small ferret who dodged the smoldering fires and ran toward the great serpent that carried Balor. Peter reached the snake as a group of crows circled in to attack. They dove like arrows aimed at a single target. Sitting on the back of the great crested snake, Balor twisted this way and that but still managed to cling to the serpent's back.

Peter leapt onto the snake's tail and ran along the crest of the twisting body, digging his claws into its flesh to keep from falling off. The crows were relentless. Balor's cloak hung inches above the reptile's back. The ferret leapt and dug its claws into the fabric. In seconds Peter had scrambled to Balor's shoulder. As Balor swiveled his head to see what clung there, the ferret bit into his neck and hung on. Balor roared with pain. The axe fell from his grasp as he slipped, arms flailing, from the snake's back. He fell in a heap, the ferret still attached to his neck. The flap of skin covering his solitary eye folded back in fury, and the eye's light struck Andor in mid-flight as he wheeled to dive.

The eagle fell to the ground with a heavy thud, his great wings still outstretched. From behind, Arkell swooped down. Balor rolled to his side, protecting his face with his arms. With all his strength, Arkell struck Balor squarely at the base of his skull, opening a deep gouge where neck and skull joined. A long and harsh cry reverberated into the night, and the earth trembled. The ferret let go and ran.

The serpent slunk away to the open fissure. It disappeared into the ground like a long green tongue drawn in by lips of earth. Only the end of its tail protruded and twitched across the packed earth until it bumped against Balor's body. Wrapping itself tightly around Balor's waist, it dragged him down into the ground.

The many-clawed toad leapt into the fissure. The crack closed over the group, mending like a ragged scar, sealing away snake, toad, and man.

As suddenly as it had come, the rain stopped. But the birds still wheeled, cawing and calling.

Except for Andor, who lay motionless on the ground, Arkell by his side.

It was the mournful cawing of the birds that startled Sarah awake.

# PETER'S RETURN

I N  T H E  S A N C T U A R Y of the tree, voices pulled Sarah from her sleep. They were not the voices of humans, which made little sense to her now, but the speech of birds that brought images into her mind—images of battle, of attack and victory. She also sensed the wind blowing, for her hiding place rocked as if a storm had begun.

The ermine poked her head out of the hole in the tree, where the hard fingers had placed her, and sniffed. The scent of fire, animals, man, and, above all, danger still hung heavy in the air. But there was no storm. Night was approaching. The world was darkening.

One voice stood out among the cacophony:

*"Andor, watchman and noble friend of the Light, I send your spirit skyward, beyond the mountains of the north, beyond the sun and moon."*

An eagle lay prostrate on the ground, and beside it mourned another of the giant birds. The words and image rumbled like a dirge through

Sarah's mind. She crept farther out from her hiding place until only her back legs and tail remained in the hole in the tree. The tree swayed.

And again the tree began to walk.

Sarah dug her claws into the rough bark as the tree moved across the battlefield.

⊹ ⊹ ⊹

The Greenman strode on in the dusk through what was left of the Travelers' Market. What had been a busy, colorful pageant of people and goods was now a ruined battlefield. The snake and toad had fled back into the depths of the earth, Balor the One-Eyed with them. They were not destroyed, he knew, but they would be held back for a time. Now he must find Timothy.

When he came to the fallen alder, he stopped. Curled in the middle of its branches, like a large and sloppy bird, Timothy slept, covered by a shawl. He looked peaceful in his sleep, but the Greenman sensed that poison had worked its way deep into his system. It would require something more than ordinary medicine to rouse the boy, something more than Jessica's or even Cerridwyn's healing touch. Not far off, Star Girl watched as Timothy slept.

The small ermine still clung to the Greenman's side, half in and half out of the knothole. Her curious nose twitched, and her bright eyes shone. Stiffly and slowly, the Greenman bent his twiggy arms. His fingers, now thick and knobby, had difficulty gripping small things. He closed them as carefully as he could around the lithe body of the ermine. She immediately tensed, and he could feel the rapid heartbeat, the taut muscles. Gently he lifted the ermine between his rough fingers and placed her in a crook of his own branches that formed a vee. She clung there, trembling.

Then the Greenman reached up through twigs and leaves until his fingers closed around one of the slender branches above his head. It was, like all his branches, full of new growth and sap. His strong fingers circled, then snapped the limb. A hot flame of pain sent a shudder through his trunk to his roots. Sticky amber sap welled up at the rough wound and then dripped slowly onto the fur of the white ermine.

✟ ✟ ✟

Sarah found herself sitting in the veed branches of a tree. She had no idea why she was there, or how she had gotten there. Dusk had turned to night. And something had dropped into her hair. Her fingers explored the thick, sticky substance on the crown of her head. Why couldn't she figure out where she was? Her memory was confused, as if she were waking from a sound sleep, while fleeting images of dreams still clung to her. The last thing she remembered clearly was being with the Animal Tamer and a crow held by a chain.

She looked down. The ground wasn't so very far away. Before she could jump, however, a familiar, raspy voice stopped her.

"Child"—the voice was deep and unmistakable once you'd heard it before—"your brother needs something only you can give him."

"Greenman!" Sarah cried, looking around in the darkness. "Where are you?" And then she looked up at the tree in which she sat and began to laugh.

Her laughter was joined by a deep, rolling laugh from the tree. Sarah wrapped her arms around the scratchy trunk. Only then did she think about the Greenman's words.

"I don't know where Timothy is," she exclaimed. "And my mother's very sick, and—"

"Peace, child. Your mother is well, and your brother is at your feet."

Sarah climbed down. The moonlight revealed Timothy curled at her feet, and Sarah dropped to her knees. He was breathing regularly, his lips slightly parted; a golden crown perched askew in his curly hair. He clutched a sword in one hand. By his side, pipes protruded from a canvas bag.

Gently she shook her brother's shoulder. "Timothy, it's me . . . wake up!"

But Timothy slept on. She shook him more roughly now. "Timothy! Get up!" When he still didn't stir, she looked up into the face of the Greenman, her heart beating faster. "What's wrong with him?"

"He was injured in battle. The wound is healed, but his spirit is weakened."

Sarah pressed her hand against Timothy's cheek. His flesh was cool to her touch.

"Do you have the gift I gave you?"

Sarah knew right away what the Greenman meant. The last time they parted, he had given her a slender core of wood from his side. She now wore it in a vial attached to a leather string around her neck. Nom had used a sliver of that wood to trap the rat that had bitten their mother. She drew the vial out from under her blouse and held it up toward the Greenman.

"Take the wood, break off a small piece, and put it to Timothy's lips."

Carefully, she broke off a small portion of the wood and bent toward her brother.

But when she touched the wood to Timothy's lips, nothing happened. At least nothing that she could see. She looked up at the Greenman, who loomed over the pair in the dark.

Sarah anxiously, silently counted to thirty.

Still nothing happened. The night all around them was quiet, as if it, too, was watching and listening.

"Can't you heal him?" Sarah asked, looking up at the Greenman again. After all, the core of wood had come from his side.

"Yes, but this is your part of the story. Your task. It's always a gift to be part of healing someone else's hurt. It changes you, too, not just Timothy. Even when things don't work out the way you expect."

Sarah was not sure she understood what the Greenman meant. It would be so much easier if he would just heal Timothy. She thought about the time they had sat together on the roof of their house, outside her bedroom window, talking about wishes. Timothy had wished to be brave, to be wolfproof.

"Timothy, you got your wish. You *are* brave. You're wolfproof now." Still nothing changed. She brushed the hair out of his face. Then Sarah noticed the briefest flicker of Timothy's lashes.

She held her breath.

His eyes opened wide.

"Timothy!" Sarah buried her face in her brother's shoulder.

"Sarah?" Looking puzzled, Timothy pulled himself to a sitting position. "You're a girl again!"

"Of course I'm a girl. What else would I be? Tell me quickly, what's happened to Mom?"

Timothy winced at a stabbing pain in his side and felt for a wound. The boar's tusk had slashed through his shirt. He ran his fingers along a ridge of raised skin; it felt like a scar. "Mom's all better," he said.

"Really?"

"Yes. The infection's gone. I brought her some salve from Peter's mother, and—"

"Where is Peter?" Sarah cut in. She stood looking from side to side as if she expected him to step out of the shadows.

Of course she wouldn't know, Timothy thought. He didn't answer Sarah but grabbed firmly on to her arm and pulled himself to a standing position. He felt very weak, his leg still throbbed from his encounter with the toad, and he had to steady himself on one of the larger limbs of the fallen alder. All around him, in the darkness, lay the debris of battle.

Silhouetted above him in the moonlight was the Greenman. Timothy looked up into his merry eyes and asked the question whose answer he was dreading. "Did we—"

"You fought well, Timothy. Our enemies are gone. Not destroyed, but gone."

"Will someone please tell me what is going *on*?" Sarah's gaze flew from one to the other. It seemed that something tremendous had happened about which she knew nothing. "Ew, what's that?" She jumped back as a sinewy, dark creature ran across her foot.

"A ferret, I believe," said the Greenman, smiling.

"Peter?" Timothy questioned anxiously, looking down.

"Who are you talking to?" Sarah demanded. At the sound of Sarah's voice, the ferret wound itself around her ankle. She cringed, remembering the ferret-legging display.

"I think," Timothy said, gesturing at the dark shape on Sarah's foot, "that's Peter."

"What do you mean?" Bending down, she gently lifted the creature to her face. It stilled in her hands. "How can this be Peter?"

"Remember the Animal Tamer? He did this to Peter just like he changed you into an ermine," Timothy said.

"A *what*?" Sarah almost dropped the ferret in her surprise. But somewhere in the back of her mind were strange images of burrows and mice and eggs. She shuddered.

The Greenman was laughing loudly now. He lifted the ferret from Sarah's grasp.

"Timothy, I want you to cut my branch with your sword. Here, where the sap has dried."

Timothy looked at the Greenman in horror. "I can't do that!" he said. "It would be like cutting a finger or arm on a human!"

"I have already bled once from this wound, and your sister was restored. Peter also needs my restoration."

Timothy took the short sword and carefully nicked the old wound. But the cut was not deep enough. He had to cut again, much harder—Sarah saw him squeezing his eyes shut and sweat breaking out on his forehead—until a shudder rumbled through the Greenman's trunk, and sap welled to the surface.

"That will do," the Greenman said. "Now hold the ferret under the wound."

Sarah lifted the animal until he was right under the thick drip of sap. It trickled onto the ferret's brown coat, and in an instant Sarah's arms collapsed under a tremendous weight. Peter, human once more, dropped to the ground with a thud and a whoosh as the air escaped from his lungs.

He looked up at the faces staring down at him. Then he gingerly got to his feet, rubbing his backside.

"It's good to see you, Sarah" was all he said.

Sarah shook her head from side to side, as if trying to clear her thoughts. "How did—how did you get turned into a ferret?"

"Didn't know I was one, but I guess the same way you got turned into an ermine—by the Animal Tamer. How did you get rescued?" Peter looked from Timothy to the Greenman. And then his face fell. "Looks like I missed the entire battle."

The Greenman smiled a creaky, wooden smile. "I wouldn't say that, not at all. You were more significant than you know. There's much to tell both of you, but it must wait. There are two others who have worked valiantly and need our help." He looked out across the quiet Market.

They could see the silhouettes of people shuffling about, helping the wounded as best they could. Sarah followed the Greenman's gaze. She had always expected victory to be a glorious thing, but this didn't look glorious at all. Even though they had won the battle, humans and trees lay sprawled on the earth, some moaning in pain, many dead. Books about knights and battles always seemed to glance over this part.

"Jessica has spent long hours tending the wounded," the Greenman added a little sadly, "and Cerridwyn has fought well."

"Jessica?" Sarah peered through the darkness, trying to distinguish their friend from the other slow-moving shadows of the night. "And Cerridwyn? But I thought she died."

"Time out of time," replied the Greenman, who was busy retrieving something from beneath the leaves of the fallen alder and handing it to Timothy. "Perhaps these will help."

Timothy accepted the Uilleann pipes. He put the bag under his arm and began to pump his elbow up and down, while with his other hand he fingered the chanter. At first only a few unpleasant squeaks emerged, but then, finally, a simple melody climbed into the sky.

Sarah stared at her brother, a small crease forming between her eyebrows. When had Timothy learned to play that strange instrument? It seemed that there were all kinds of things about her brother that she didn't know. She noticed, too, that Peter was standing very close, and that something else was happening. Across the battlefield the silhouettes of people and animals were beginning to stand a little straighter, moving with more ease. And two of the people were coming closer.

"Jessica! Cerridwyn!" Sarah ran and threw her arms around them.

Jessica looked very tired but also very happy to see Sarah. "You're not an ermine anymore!"

Sarah shuddered. "So I heard."

And then Jessica caught sight of Timothy. "You're awake!"

Timothy dropped the pipes when Jessica grabbed him by the arms. She swung him around in a silly little dance, something the Jessica he knew at school would never do. And for the first time Timothy felt that there might be some victory to celebrate, after all.

But the Greenman stopped the gaiety, saying, "There's still some work to be done, and here is one more member of our party."

Electra, glowing in the moonlight, stepped toward them from behind a fallen tree.

"Star Girl!" Sarah cried, and stopped just short of giving her a hug.

Timothy thought he saw, for the first time, a look of pleasure cross

Electra's face. He put down the pipes, and the group followed the Greenman to where a large eagle lay dead on the ground, the white cap of its head visible in the dark. Timothy saw another eagle perched in a tree not far away, and he thought of the two he had seen in his own yard—the watchmen, Sarah had called them.

The Greenman stooped over the body of the fallen eagle.

"Andor's work in this time is done. But when a noble creature dies, it is good to mourn its passing."

Cerridwyn, meanwhile, had picked up the Uilleann pipes, and now she began to play. She played much more skillfully than Timothy had. The tune, Timothy thought, was liquid sadness, the paralyzing loneliness he felt at times even in a crowd. But there was more than sadness to the music. Something in it also made Timothy feel as if Andor's death didn't end just with sadness, but with significance. *Triumphant,* he thought. Seventeen points.

# THE ROAD HOME

THE LAST NOTES of the Uilleann pipes still hovered in the air when a disheveled Julian appeared, with Gwydon padding silently by his side. The Storyteller's expression was somber as he gazed down at the body of Andor and bowed his head.

Gwydon lifted his face to the moon, and a mournful howl rose into the darkness, a howl that made Timothy feel lonelier still. Blood had soaked through the sleeve of Julian's shirt, and Timothy noticed he kept the arm pressed to his side.

Cerridwyn looked at Jessica. "Tend to his wound, dear." Jessica stepped forward and placed both hands on the injury. In moments, the strain on Julian's face eased, and he was able to move the arm, though a little stiffly.

"How did you do that, Jess?" Sarah asked.

"Cerridwyn taught me. My necklace is the sign of a Healer." One hand fingered the ruby stone. "At first it wasn't what I wanted to do. I wanted to be able to shoot arrows like you or fight with a sword. But now it's okay. When I place my hands on a wound, it begins to heal. It's not like there was never a wound at all. It's just as if healing has begun. And something happens to me, too. I get cold and tired, as if I've given a bit of myself away."

Timothy again ran his fingers along the raised scar on his own side and winced where it was tender. He looked curiously at Jessica. She was the last person he would have imagined in that role.

"You can heal. Timothy has the crown and does battle and plays the pipes. But I don't do anything special," Sarah said.

"Not all gifts are evident right away," the Greenman answered. "Sometimes you have to wait for a gift to develop or be revealed."

Sarah looked at the ground, and Timothy could tell that wasn't the answer she was hoping for.

"And what about Mom?" she asked. "Is she really well?"

"As your brother told you, the poison from the bite is gone, and she's in no danger from it now. But she will be weak for some time and will need your help. That is why I'm sending you home soon."

In his mind's eye, Timothy could see his mother just as he had left her, cheerfully propped on pillows, better but still very weak. He wanted to be home with her, but he also longed for something else he couldn't quite name. He lifted his fingers to his head and found that the golden crown was still in place, even after all that he had been through. "What will happen to the Market?" he wondered aloud.

No one spoke for a moment, and Timothy knew they were all, as he was, imagining the wreckage they would see in the daylight. What about the animals that had been captive in the Animal Tamer's stall? Had they managed to escape? What would they do?

Finally, Peter spoke up, a small catch in his voice. "And what's happened to my mother?"

"Fiona's fine, Peter." Jessica was glad to be able to offer him some hope. "She was hurt, but I helped heal her. Trust me, the first thing she asked about was you. It's just . . . Where will you live now?"

Peter's face broke into a smile, as if a great weight had been lifted off him. "We'll manage. It's not like we haven't had trouble before. The Market always survives!"

"But isn't there one of your company still missing?" the Greenman asked.

Timothy looked from side to side. "The ratcatcher!" he cried. "Where's Nom?"

And just as the words left his lips, a terrible booming shook the ground. It came toward the little group like a cresting wave, and Timothy suddenly wondered what had happened to his short sword. He wondered, too, if Cerridwyn had her bow and arrows with her. But Julian and the Greenman didn't appear alarmed, and Gwydon continued to sit peacefully by Julian's side.

A large oak tree lumbered into view, and there, high up in its branches, rode Nom, waving his spindly arms and shouting.

"Looks like we beat 'em, we did!" Nom cried. "Crawled back into the dirt, they did, back where they's came from! And how do you like that, trees fighting and all?" Then he paused. "Smells like stoats and ferrets been here." His sharp nose twitched wildly. "Sneaky animals, just like rats. Can't abide 'em!"

Timothy poked Sarah in the ribs. She scowled and hissed into his ear, "Timothy James, you have a lot of explaining to do!"

"Brother," Cerridwyn said, addressing Nom, "we have work to do if we are to turn this Market to rights."

Timothy noticed that Cerridwyn's hair was growing shorter and grayer, her back a little more rounded. Soon she was no taller than Timothy—the goose woman once more.

"Come down out of that tree, and help me get to work!" she commanded.

In response, the oak bent its branches as close to the ground as it could, and Nom jumped down.

But something was still bothering Timothy. "Greenman, what's happened to Tristan?" The children looked at one another.

"The Master of the Market?" the Greenman asked solemnly. "I think he will find that *his* master was not kind."

"His master?" Sarah asked.

"He means the Animal Tamer, I expect," Peter volunteered. "Tristan always did everything the Tamer told him to."

"Is Tristan gone?"

"Just changed, I'm afraid," said the goose woman, twirling her stick as if at one of her geese. "It will take all I've got to keep him in line."

"He's a goose now?" Timothy asked.

"A gander," the goose woman corrected with a shake of her head. "And he'll be the terror of the gaggle."

Peter began to laugh, and soon the others joined in. "It fits him, somehow. Now he can puff out his chest all he wants! But the Market still needs a Master," he added more seriously.

"Don't you remember your legends?" Julian said, ruffling Gwydon's fur. "A true Master of the Market is a Filidh. There is one being prepared even now. But it's late. Dawn is coming."

The darkness was beginning to lighten just the tiniest bit. The Greenman looked from Sarah to Jessica to Timothy. "Yes, and it's time for you three to be leaving. Arkell will see you safely home." He gestured for the goose woman to give Timothy the pipes. "Timothy, see that these are returned to their owner. He has more to tell you. And you two"—he indicated Timothy and Jessica—"don't trade your gifts again! You'll be needing them."

Timothy took the Uilleann pipes from the woman's weathered hands, feeling a terrible sense of loss welling up inside him. *Desolate*, he thought, a word that sounded as bleak as its meaning and worth only nine points. He looked at the Greenman and wondered how long it would be until he saw him again.

"And I have things to discuss with these other fine fellows. Come." The Greenman and the oak strode off side by side toward the forest, where the other trees waited.

"Wait," Timothy called, but his voice came out small and choked.

The sky was pale pink and the clouds were touched with silver. In contrast, the Travelers' Market was a dark wound in the forest. Timothy looked at the charred earth, the splintered caravans. Already vultures were circling over the dead.

"Peter, I know your mother's looking for you. Best come with me." The goose woman nodded toward the boy.

An expression of anguish crossed Peter's face. He looked at Sarah.

Sarah met his gaze, and Timothy could tell that his sister was trying not to show how she was feeling. "Go, Peter," she finally said. "I'm sure Fiona misses you terribly."

"But you're coming back, right?" Peter asked.

"I hope so. I want to . . ." Sarah didn't say anything else.

Peter nodded. Jessica gave him a quick hug, and Timothy did the same.

"The Old Ways are awake again tonight. Timothy, you've traveled that road before," Julian said. "Arkell will lead you three to it. Follow him. Gwydon and the star girl will travel with me."

Timothy looked up at the clear sky, which was now tinged with blue, and saw the morning star shining in the vast distance. If this was a book, he thought, the story should end now. But it wasn't a book. It was his life, and apparently he still had normal things to do: his parents to see, school, chores . . . Timothy sighed and ran his fingers over the crown on his head, just to see if it was still there.

For now, it seemed, he would have to content himself with showing Jessica and his sister his skill at balancing on the back of a moving road.

# SHADOWS
# IN THE NIGHT

**A**RKELL LED THE CHILDREN to the same stand of birches and the same path Timothy had traveled once before.

"It just looks like a trail in the woods." Sarah was frowning.

"It is. But it's not just any trail; it's an Old Way, one of the ancient roads." Timothy looked at Sarah and Jessica's puzzled faces. "It's another type of portway that helps you travel through time, like when we first came here to the Travelers' Market. But it's even more amazing." Timothy could feel his excitement growing. "When the Old Ways wake up and carry you, it takes a little getting used to. You just have to try to ride with it." When he'd traveled this portway, it had taken him a while to find and keep his balance, much like the first time he had ridden a skateboard. He hoped he could do it again, especially in front of the girls.

"Watch me, and you'll get the hang of it." He stepped onto the trail. Underneath his feet, the road shifted. It flexed like a muscle. He looked over his shoulder. Sarah and Jessica stepped cautiously onto the path.

The ride on the road was not as glorious as Timothy had hoped. For one thing, Sarah caught on very quickly—it must have been from all her years of dance—and for another, Jessica didn't seem to be nearly as impressed by his skill as he had hoped she might. Glancing behind him, Timothy could see Jessica and Sarah both balancing upright on the moving road, better than he had done his first time. Like him, they must have known it was quite impossible for a road to wake up, or to travel by a portway at all. But, Timothy decided, it was better not to dwell on the impossible too much these days.

⊹ ⊹ ⊹

Later that night, long after Timothy should have been asleep, he crept into Sarah's room.

Sarah sat up, her long hair in tangles around her face, and pulled the covers close around her shoulders. "The portways haven't failed us yet. It's always as if hardly any time has passed here at home. And Mom looks better."

"Yeah, she does."

"Much better. Timothy, you did a good job. She never would have survived if you hadn't come back."

"Maybe. Or maybe it was just the new antibiotic." He burrowed under Sarah's comforter with her to ward off the chill in the room. The November nights were growing colder now.

"How can you say that after everything we've seen?" she protested with a broad yawn.

"Because now that we're back, it all seems like something I imagined."

But Timothy was too tired to puzzle anything out; he was hardly even aware of Sarah still talking. He was asleep when the first gust of wind rattled the windowpanes, and he was already dreaming when two cats leapt onto the roof outside Sarah's room.

They hissed at the branch wedged in the window casement. "It will take a storm to move that wood," said one cat to the other.

"We can wait. Perhaps the old professor sleeps without protection."

"Then he will soon enjoy our company."

The larger of the two cats padded to the edge of the roof. On the front porch, Prank, Timothy and Sarah's orange tabby, arched her back, the fur rising in pumpkin spikes. Above her, the two cats slipped like shadows off the edge of the roof and back into the night.

# AT MR. TWIG'S HOUSE

TIMOTHY HAD ARRANGED to meet Jessica after school on Wednesday to return the Uilleann pipes to Mr. Twig. That meant he would have to miss chess-club practice and, as a result, the tournament the following week, but somehow that didn't seem as important as his errand.

Sarah would meet them there after ballet practice. She had been very quiet that morning as they got ready for school. At first Timothy thought it was just because she was so tired. But when he'd wondered out loud what Peter was doing, she told him, in a very un-Sarah-like way, to shut up. Then she'd slammed the front door on her way out to catch the high school bus.

Timothy had shrugged his backpack over one shoulder and checked his pocket to make sure the Greenman's leaf was there. He'd taken the pipes from the closet and buried them in the bottom of his oversized pack before taking a brief glimpse at the assigned chapter in his geometry book. Then, after helping his father bring his mother breakfast in bed, he'd headed out into the frosty morning.

All in all, it was a *very* unsatisfactory day.

The school day plodded along more slowly than any other Timothy had ever known. He caught sight of Jessica's curls in the hallway once, and the fact that she was laughing with one of her old friends annoyed him for some inexplicable reason. He snapped at his friends at lunch, couldn't answer the question when called on in history, and found his locker door jammed in PE, which made him lose points for arriving late on the basketball court.

Jessica was waiting by the city bus stop just as she had promised. She wore a short white jacket with some type of fake fur trimming the hood and cuffs. It was already growing dark, and they'd have only a short time at Mr. Twig's before Timothy would be expected home.

"So, how was your day?" he asked in a conversational tone, once again repressing that inexplicable feeling of irritation.

Jessica smiled and pulled up the hood of her jacket. "Jordan invited me to a Christmas party, and my poem was selected for the lit mag. All in all, not too bad."

The bus groaned to a stop, and Timothy followed her up the steps, now feeling thoroughly out of sorts. Jessica slid off her hood, and Timothy noticed that if he looked carefully, he could see strands of red in her brown hair. Then he thought it was odd that he should be noticing at all.

He scooted as far away from her as he could on the seat. "The pipes are in my bag," he said glumly.

"Do you think there's a reason we're supposed to go to Mr. Twig's, other than just returning the pipes?" she asked.

"Don't you remember? When we were at the Market, the Greenman said he'd have more to tell us," Timothy said. "I didn't really want to come home, you know."

Jessica looked straight at him. "I didn't, either. It doesn't seem real now, does it?"

Timothy thought for a minute. "No, it's being here that doesn't seem real. There, wherever *there* is, seems more than real."

☩ ☩ ☩

Mr. Twig, professor of mythology—emeritus, as he liked to point out—lived in an old, tree-lined neighborhood across town. The first time Timothy met him, he was dressed all in blue from his sweater to his socks. He favored consistency. He was also prone to asking disturbing questions. A light glowed in the front window, and Timothy could see the silhouette of a man sitting in a chair, reading.

"Good, he's home." Timothy shifted nervously as he waited for Mr. Twig to answer the front door. The only other time he had been at Mr. Twig's house, the professor had asked him if he believed in evil. The memory still sent shivers down Timothy's arms.

"Do you think he left you the pipes on purpose?" Jessica asked. "He might have intentionally left them behind in the woods, so that you'd have them when you came back to the Market."

"You never know with Mr. Twig. You'll see. The last time I saw him, we talked about parallel universes."

☩ ☩ ☩

The door swung inward, and Mr. Twig, dressed all in shades of brown, greeted them in stockinged feet, reminding Timothy of a woodland elf.

"Well, well, what a pleasure, Timothy James Maxwell and a friend. Come in, come in." Mr. Twig waved them into his warm living room. A book lay facedown on a chair by the window, and a fire warmed the hearth.

"This is Jessica. We've come to return your pipes." Timothy slid the backpack off his shoulder and pulled out the instrument.

Mr. Twig raised his generous eyebrows. "I expected you'd be returning them someday. Now, young lady, have a seat." He gestured toward the red couch where Timothy and Sarah had sat a month ago on their last visit. It was there, Timothy thought, that they had first heard the name *Balor*, and he shuddered.

There was a knock at the front door.

"Ah, more visitors." Mr. Twig swung the door open to Sarah. She stood on the porch, rosy-cheeked, her ballet bag over her shoulder. "Come in, Sarah. We've quite a party here. I don't often get this many visitors in a week!" Mr. Twig seemed delighted to see them all. "Have a seat. Let me make some tea."

Timothy held out the pipes. "We probably don't have time for tea. We need to be home before dark."

Mr. Twig looked disappointed. He took the pipes in one hand. "Very wise for many reasons. Well, have a seat for a moment, anyway, and tell me what you've been up to. The last time I saw you, Timothy, you were trying to put my eye out and asking me questions about parallel universes." He laid the Uilleann pipes tenderly on the table next to his chair.

Timothy flushed and then said, "It would take a long time to explain everything . . ."

"I see at least that you have your sister back safe and sound. I suspect the pipes were a help to you there."

"Did you leave them there on purpose?" The question that had been rattling in Timothy's brain popped out.

"I thought they might be of some use, to you in particular, Timothy. Were they?"

Timothy sat down on the couch in between the girls. "They were. But how did you know they would be, and why were they?"

"Ah, more questions! I suspect the girls can help me answer that."

The girls glanced at each other, Jessica frowning and Sarah looking puzzled. "When Timothy blew the pipes," Jessica said, "the battle changed in our favor."

"Of course it did. It always does when a Filidh arrives." Mr. Twig sat back in his chair, looking very satisfied with himself.

*Filidh.* There was that title again, Timothy thought.

"Your mother is an O'Daly, isn't she?" Mr. Twig steepled his fingers. "Yes, but . . ."

"Remember that the Filidh is a hereditary title handed down for generations through the family O'Daly. And that the last true Filidh turned his back on his calling for promises of power. So why do you think you have the crown, Timothy James Maxwell? No one chooses the crown; the crown chooses him. A Filidh is a keeper of the word, of memories, tasked with reminding people of the true stories, and in that way the Filidh is a guardian. And with that title comes another." Mr. Twig paused. "The Master of the Market."

"I knew it!" Jessica pounded the sofa arm. "It's just what Julian and Cerridwyn told us. And Timothy must find a special stone to prove his birthright."

"Correct. The Telling Stone, most often referred to as the Stone of Destiny," said Mr. Twig.

"Wait a minute!" Sarah's face puckered with confusion. "When did you hear all this?"

She looked at Timothy.

Timothy hesitated. He found that things went better when he didn't mention her time as an ermine.

"When you were eating mice!" Jessica grinned, both dimples flashing. Sarah glared.

Mr. Twig held up a bony hand. "Not just the Telling Stone, although it is the most famous piece of the legend, but the three other treasures, as well: the Dagda's Cauldron, the Spear of Lugh, and Nuada's Sword, the Claíomh Solais. These are the things Balor needs to control the Light. But he can't find them without a Filidh to lead him to them."

At the name of Balor a stillness entered the room. Timothy felt as if all the air had been sucked from his lungs. Then Mr. Twig continued. "Until you recover these items, the Dark will be searching for you. There are not many places where you will be completely safe." He stared into the distance and cleared his throat, then glanced once more at Timothy.

Timothy's heart had begun to pound so loudly that he was afraid everyone would hear it. "Not safe? What do you mean?"

"Unfortunately, just what I said. You're very desirable to the Dark, Timothy."

Sarah's eyes widened, and Jessica shifted on the couch.

"What can he do?" Sarah said.

"The servants of the Dark have their own agenda. The three of you can keep them from realizing it, but Timothy is the most at risk. As for what to do . . . first find and step upon the Stone of Destiny before any real harm can be done. But be cautious. And let your friends help you." Mr. Twig sighed. "And of course, you will have the help of the Stewards of the Stone: Julian, Gwydon, and me."

"Stewards?" Timothy asked. "You?"

"Yes, me. There are many of us throughout history, some of whom you have yet to meet. Steward is an ancient title, one that binds us together to ensure the Stone of Destiny can fulfill its mission and to help anyone who is a true Filidh claim his place upon it. That means we aid the Filidh in the quest and block anyone or anything that might interfere."

"Do you know where the stone is?"

"I do not. Being a Steward doesn't mean we each know the stone's current location. It means we know the stone's purpose. We each have a particular skill to offer the Light. I wish I could tell you more about your risk, but I don't know how the assault will come. Only that it will."

"But that's not fair!" Jessica's voice was shrill. "You can't tell someone that something awful is going to happen, when they can't do anything about it!"

"No, I suppose it isn't fair. But it is true. And I speak truth to the three of you because I believe you can bear it."

Timothy's face had turned very pale. "It's okay, Jessica. Mr. Twig's right. It's better to be on guard, isn't it? Even if I don't know what is coming or what, exactly, I'm supposed to do." He turned to Mr. Twig. "Where do we start?"

All three children looked at Mr. Twig expectantly.

"Keep in mind that I am one who studies myths. I can tell you what I know from the past, but whether it will work in the present or not"— he shook his head—"I do not know. What I know is that, according to legend, the stone, the Lia Fáil, roars with joy when a rightful king puts his foot upon it. Many kings of Ireland were crowned on the stone, and the stone always tells the truth. Any true Filidh will also induce a cry from the Telling Stone. But the stone was stolen many years ago. and ever since . . . well, there has been no way to prove rightful succession, as you yourselves have seen at the Market with Balor's pawn Tristan."

"Who stole the stone?" Sarah was leaning forward in her chair, her eyes sparkling. She always loved a mystery, Timothy thought.

"We don't know who took the stone, but I suppose it must have been the work of the Dark, though I don't know even that with certainty. What I do know is that the stone failed to cry out when the Dark tried to place a false king on the throne. Then the stone was taken by force from Ireland to Scotland. There are rumors it was taken to England, and others say it is still hidden in Scotland. Either way, you can see that the Dark would not be eager to have a true Filidh arise and reclaim the Stone of Destiny. The Dark would stop at nothing to prevent that."

Timothy's mind was whirling. "If nobody else has been able to find this stone and the rest of the treasures, how can we?"

Instead of answering, Mr. Twig stood and walked to a tall cabinet. He removed a key from around his neck and unlocked a small drawer.

"Rowan wood," he said, laying his hand on the ancient piece of furniture. "Protection against any uninvited guests." Then he withdrew a leather pouch from the drawer. "I have debated long and hard about whether or not to give this to you," he said quietly. "Once it is in your possession, your risk increases. However, without it you will have little hope of getting further in your quest." Finally, Mr. Twig smiled. "But now that I've seen how the pipes respond to you, Timothy, I think it is time. I believe the three of you may be able to see something here that I have missed."

Gesturing for the children to follow him, Mr. Twig went to a small round table near the fireplace, where the three gathered close around him. His fingers trembled as he tenderly worked open the pouch, and Timothy saw that the leather was old and worn, as if it had been handled often over many centuries. Slowly, Mr. Twig drew out a small roll of paper. It was the color of old leaves, brown and stiff. He had to hold both ends down to keep the paper from springing back into a roll.

An unusual pattern of lines and dashes that Timothy recognized immediately filled the corners of the paper. They were runes from the Ogham alphabet he had seen in Julian's caravan. Blooming between the lines, like flowers on a vine, was an intricate border of animals and birds in deep reds, blues, and greens. In the center of the paper there was a drawing that resembled a map, except that it wasn't like any map Timothy had ever seen. You couldn't tell north from south, east from west, and instead of roads there were only lakes, mountains, and trees. A tall-masted ship sailed in a corner.

"It's beautiful!" Sarah gasped, looking as if she would like to reach out and trace the drawings with her finger. "Is it very old?"

"Very. It came into my possession many years ago, but its secrets are locked to me."

"Is it a map?" Jessica asked, as if reading Timothy's thoughts. She bent low over the paper. "It doesn't look like a normal one."

"It very well may be, but I believe it is also more than a map. Maps aid navigation; map *ciphers*, however, though they look normal, have a code hidden within them. As a navigation tool alone, this map is flawed. However, I believe this map can lead you to the Stone of Destiny. As a Steward, I've protected it for the Filidh."

"Are you sure this stone is here in our world?" Sarah asked.

"The kings crowned on this stone ruled in your world. So, yes. The stone is needed here."

A tapping sound on the window made Timothy jump. The tapping grew to a patter, louder and louder, as a sleety rain began to fall.

"This document is not something that should be kept open for long," Mr. Twig added hurriedly, and with a deft movement rolled it back up and slid it into the pouch. "There are many who would like to find it." He handed the pouch to Timothy. "Above all, it must be kept safe."

Timothy's eyes widened in alarm. The day had dimmed with the sluice of sleet against the windows. The shadows in the room lengthened. Sarah checked her watch. "I think we need to head home, or our parents will be worried about us."

"Again, a wise idea," Mr. Twig agreed, escorting them to the door. "I expect that I will be hearing from you again sooner rather than later."

Timothy tucked the pouch inside his backpack. The three children walked silently out into a gray late afternoon, each wrapped in thought and quickly chilled by the stinging rain. A *Filidh.* He whispered the word, trying out the sound of it. And a quest! He looked at Jessica and Sarah trudging by his side. Wherever their adventures took them from here, they would go together.

"Do you think we can figure out the cipher?" Jessica asked. "I don't like the sound of an assault coming." She looked at him from under her hood, the cold rain plastering stray curls to her cheeks.

Sarah looked at him, too.

The word *assault* rattled in Timothy's mind. Seven Scrabble points. Did it mean a physical attack? It reminded him of *onslaught*, a word that also made him nervous and offered thirteen points. He held the bag tightly against his chest and wondered if being a Filidh meant always feeling afraid and trying not to show it.

# THE MAGICIAN'S TRICK

T HURSDAY.

Timothy's body occupied the third desk in the third row of Mr. Petty's health class, but his mind was elsewhere, wandering far outside the classroom walls.

He was riding Gwydon, the great wolf, through miles of endless blue sky. Below, the banners of the Travelers' Market snapped in a fresh breeze. Behind him on the wolf, Jessica laughed and tightened her arms around his waist. They could see his sister, Sarah, just below, waving and calling to them. At her side was the Greenman, his stout arms pushing skyward and his deep voice calling—

Timothy's forehead thumped onto the desk. The girl sitting behind him sniggered. Blood rushed to his face. He peered from the corner of his eye, careful not to turn his head, to see if anyone else had noticed. The bored, slack faces were reassuring. How many of them also navigated alternate worlds? For the last week he'd puzzled over the map now safely hidden behind a loose piece of paneling in the back of Sarah's closet along with the crown. He'd gotten nowhere. Every night, with curtains drawn, he and Sarah pulled the map out of its leather pouch and spread it across her bed. Despite being very good with ciphers, he couldn't find a code-breaking technique that worked on this one. There were two kinds of trees in the forests, fat round ones and a few skinny trees with bare branches. There were strange animals in the borders. What was significant?

While Mr. Petty, each of his three chins waggling, droned on about the human circulatory system, Timothy considered Mr. Twig's warning that whoever had the map would never be safe. Every time he unrolled the map, he felt exposed, as if he were being watched. Just thinking about it made him shiver. The map had become a presence that beckoned him, even in his sleep.

"Remember to take notes. There will be a quiz on this documentary next week." Mr. Petty stalked the room. Timothy rested his chin on his hand and tried to pay attention to the film. But instead of taking notes, he sketched a coastline on his paper. It echoed the coastline of the map where the ship sailed. But, try as he might, he couldn't remember all the details.

Outside, the rain was relentless. Christmas was coming. During winter break he'd have more time with Sarah and Jessica to solve the map's riddle. His eyelids drooped as the film drew to a conclusion, when suddenly the PA system squawked to life. His head snapped to attention just inches before smacking the desktop again.

"The winter assembly will begin in five minutes in the gym. Please arrive quietly and sit with your sixth-period class," the principal announced.

With a sigh of relief, Timothy stood and stretched. All around him, students noisily scraped chairs across the worn linoleum, jostling their way to the door. Mr. Petty called to them in his high, petulant voice, "Remember to walk, not run, in the hallway, and stay with me!" But no one listened. They pushed through the door, flooded into the hall, and, like a rushing river, tumbled their way toward the gym. Timothy let himself be swept along and dumped through the gymnasium doors. Friends shouted to one another, students in the bleachers pounded their feet on the risers just for the sound of it, and the band squeaked out "Winter Wonderland." He climbed to one of the highest benches, finding a seat next to Gillian. She was lost in her latest anime book, her tongue peeking out of her mouth in concentration. She barely looked up.

"Hey, Timothy," she mumbled. She pulled her tongue back in and flipped a page.

Far below, he could see Jessica, wearing her student-body-VP shirt. Student council members and cheerleaders lined the floor in front of the bleachers. They were bouncing with practiced enthusiasm, encouraging each grade level to cheer louder than the others. Misery. Timothy hunched down to wait the assembly out.

The special guest—every assembly had a special guest, Timothy had noticed—was nobody very special at all, just Morley the Magician. He made his living attending school assemblies and birthday parties, repeating the same magic tricks Timothy had learned years ago. Timothy thought he would rather do just about anything than Morley's job, day after day, facing audiences of sticky-faced toddlers or wisecracking teens.

This time, however, there was a new twist to Morley's act. After drawing flowers from a hat, after making balls disappear and linking rings that then magically separated, he rolled out a cage that housed a sleek black bird. It was larger than any crow Timothy had ever seen. The hum of voices silenced in anticipation.

A warm sensation against his hip made Timothy reach into his pants pocket. The Greenman's leaf grew hotter even as his finger closed around it. He drew it out, clenched in his palm, and looked around the gym. An ordinary day in an ordinary place. There must be something wrong with the leaf. Or perhaps it was warning him to be careful when he left school? He wished he could talk to Sarah or Jessica. In the meantime, he zipped the leaf into the front pocket of his backpack.

"Let me introduce my assistant, Rankin the raven. Ravens are among the most intelligent animals known to man." As he spoke, Morley opened the cage door and drew the bird out on his arm. "Their intelligence is far superior to that of their closest relative, the common crow." The raven cocked its head as if in agreement.

"I will now need a volunteer from the audience."

Dozens of hands fanned the air. Morley leaned close and whispered into Rankin's ear. He straightened. "My assistant will choose the volunteer."

Timothy leaned forward on the bleachers.

Morley held his arm aloft, and with one thrust of its wings, Rankin flew into the audience. The students howled with laughter. Some covered their heads with their arms. Timothy made himself as small as possible and pulled his backpack tightly against his shoulders. Rankin was flying straight toward him, he was sure. But the bird detoured to snatch a sparkling earring that dangled from a girl's ear. Several students applauded. The bird dropped the earring and was back on course. Timothy ducked too late. The bird landed on his head.

On the gym floor Mrs. Robinson, the principal, blew a whistle. "Enough!" She turned to Morley. "Call back your bird; this is getting out of hand!"

The raven's sharp feet dug into Timothy's scalp. Timothy tried to shake the bird off. Rankin clung to his hair. Timothy threw up his arms; the bird hopped to his shoulder. The students roared their approval. Climbing halfway down Timothy's back, the raven pried at the zipper of his pack. It began to poke its pointed beak into every pocket. Morley smiled a long, thin smile, intently watching Timothy and Rankin.

"Get off me!" Timothy stood and tried to knock the bird from his backpack. Then the gym's lights went out. The crowd hooted and hollered. They stomped their feet. A few teachers tried ineffectively to calm things down. Nobody listened. The only light filtered in through the small windows above the top risers.

Timothy remained standing, his heart thudding. Shadows moved around him. The raven made clicking sounds as it clung to his backpack. Then, in the dark and chaos, the bird shrilled. An icy finger of fear worked its way down Timothy's spine. The students' voices crescendoed in triumph. There was no longer any rule or order. If he tried to escape in the dark, he risked tumbling down the bleachers.

Timothy remembered the crows at the Market, unruly, raucous birds, but they were nothing like this raven. They had fought against Balor in the battle. Mr. Twig's voice played in his head: "I can't tell you when it will come, only that it will come." His thoughts flew to the map hidden in its leather pouch in Sarah's closet, and just as quickly he tried to conceal his thoughts, to make his mind go blank.

The emergency generator kicked in, and the gym filled with light. Teachers blew whistles, the band began to play "Frosty the Snowman," and the general pandemonium subsided.

Mrs. Robinson took Morley's arm to guide him off the gym floor. He whistled for Rankin. Immediately, the bird flew from Timothy's bag to alight on the man's outstretched arm. Timothy scanned the gym floor for Jessica. She was staring straight up at him.

"Are you okay?" she mouthed.

Timothy's heart contracted. The leaf! No wonder it had been hot! What an idiot he had been to ignore its warning! He reached for the zipper on the bag's pocket. The zipper was open, the pocket empty! Here, in the middle of an ordinary day, in the most ordinary place he could imagine, he had been found, and the leaf was gone.

# SCOTLAND!

**D**ARK CAME EARLY NOW. Headlights shone in the dusk as Timothy made his way home from the bus Thursday evening. Why would the magician's bird steal his leaf? That was easy: Without it he would never know if danger was present. Who had it? Now, that was a more difficult question. And if they, whoever *they* were, had found the leaf, had they found the map, too? Timothy was sure they were searching for it. He looked over his shoulder. Three birds hunched like black knots on a telephone line. Were they ravens or crows? Could they read his mind? Timothy's heart beat wildly. Cawing, the knots unraveled, and the birds swept down. Timothy ran, his backpack thumping against his side.

In his yard, blackbirds chortled in the branches of the poplars. Were there always so many birds? Timothy sprinted across the yard, half expecting Rankin to swoop down and attack. Once inside, he ran straight upstairs to Sarah's room. His breathing was loud and shaky. He drew the blinds before turning on the bedside lamp. Even behind the closed blinds, the overhead light felt too revealing. Then he pushed his way through the forest of skirts and pants to the very back of Sarah's closet. He needed to touch the map. To know it was safe. He ran his finger under the loose paneling in the back of her closet. With a deep exhale of breath, he closed his hand around the leather pouch. The map was still there.

Timothy sat on Sarah's bed to think. Without the leaf, how would he know whom to trust? He held the pouch close to his chest, arms crossed over the stiff leather, and waited for his heart to slow. Mr. Twig had told him, had told all three of them, that the Dark would be searching for this map. School had always seemed mundane, not the sort of place for adventures. Now the memory of the raven's prying beak made Timothy sweat.

How long would the map be safe? He needed to find a more secure hiding place. He loosened the end of the leather pouch and inserted one finger. He could feel the map coiled within. It was urgent that he solve the cipher.

"Timothy! Are you up there?"

His father was calling from the base of the stairs. It was early for him to be home. Timothy checked his watch: just before five. His mother should return soon with Sarah from ballet practice.

"Be right there!" he called in response. He slid the map back behind the closet paneling, hurrying so his dad wouldn't ask any questions.

As he ran down the stairs, Sarah and his mother swept in the front door. Their cheeks were rosy with the cold, and the tips of Sarah's ears were red. Her hair was pulled back in the tight chignon of a dancer, and she carried her shoes and workout clothes in a backpack along with her books.

"Sorry we're late." His mother pecked his father on the cheek and winked at Timothy. "I know you've got good news for us," she said to her husband while unbuttoning her coat.

Sarah raised her eyebrows at Timothy, and he shrugged and then furrowed his eyebrows, signaling to her that something was wrong.

"Well, come in and get warm." Timothy's father threw an arm over Sarah's shoulders and led them into the kitchen. "Timothy, Sarah, I've been thinking about this all day and figured I'd better just get home and tell you. We're spending Christmas in Edinburgh!"

Time froze. Timothy could see his father, mouth slightly open, eyes shining, expectant with delight. His mother was beaming. His own heart plummeted like a stone in water.

Sarah shot a quick glance at Timothy. He tried to force a smile to his face. "Scotland?" The word came out like a squeak, as if all the air had been knocked from his lungs.

"I've been asked to speak at a conference in Edinburgh on climate change. The conference is actually between Christmas and New Year's, so I thought we might as well spend the whole vacation there."

Timothy's mother took a tray of lasagna from the refrigerator and stuck it into the microwave. "Isn't that exciting? Edinburgh! I can bring my paints, and we can do some sightseeing during your father's meetings."

Timothy thought fast. He had to decipher the map. It was the only way he was ever going to find the Telling Stone. That meant he'd have to take the map with him. And what if the solution was here at home? He had planned to use the entire vacation to work on the map problem. "Ah . . ." He stalled.

Sarah cut in. "Are you sure you two wouldn't rather have some time alone together?" She looked from her mother to her father.

*She's good,* Timothy thought, *very good.*

A small line appeared between their mother's eyebrows. "We thought you two would be delighted—"

"Oh, we are," Sarah cut in again. "It's just that you say you never get away."

"This will be a family trip. An opportunity to see a part of the world you've never seen. We can get away alone some other time." Mr. Maxwell's voice was firm.

"Great!" said Sarah.

"Yeah, that sounds great," Timothy echoed, hoping they couldn't hear the disappointment in his voice.

"This is going to be a Christmas to remember!" His father grabbed a yogurt from the refrigerator, and his mother playfully swatted his hand.

*It sure is,* Timothy thought. At any other time, he would have jumped at the chance to go, but now . . . He followed Sarah out of the kitchen and grabbed her arm as soon as they were in the hallway. "Today, at school, during the assembly, a raven stole the Greenman's leaf."

"What are you talking about?" Sarah looked at him as if he were crazy.

He explained about Morley and Rankin.

"How could you let that happen?"

"I didn't *let* it!"

She motioned him up the stairs. "What about the you-know?"

"It's safe. I checked. But the raven tried to open my bag, poked around in all the pockets. I'm sure it was looking for the map." Timothy followed her to her room. Even in his own house, he found himself looking over his shoulder, listening for noises from the other rooms. "We can't go to Scotland. We have to stay here and solve the cipher. We might not have much time before something else happens."

Sarah was already in her closet. Timothy could hear her burrowing behind the clothes.

"It's still here!"

"I already told you that."

She reemerged with a scarf tangled in her hair.

"We'll have to take the map with us. Didn't Mr. Twig say something about Scotland and rumors that the special stone might be hidden there?" A furrow of concentration pleated her brow. "This doesn't sound like a coincidence to me."

"What am I going to do about the leaf? How will we know when things are dangerous?" Timothy did a backflop onto her bed.

✚ ✚ ✚

Timothy loved lasagna, but tonight the food was a heavy lump in his stomach. Sarah ate with concentration, staring only at her plate. His father was so busy telling them about the highlights of Edinburgh that all Timothy needed to do was nod occasionally while trying to devise a plan. First, he must find a safer place for the map. Then he had better tell Mr. Twig that they were going to Scotland. If he and Sarah and Jessica could just get a little time alone with the map before they left, to try to work out its solution—

"Timothy, did you hear what your father just said?" His mother looked at him with a puzzled frown. "There's a torchlight procession a few days after Christmas in Edinburgh. There are pipers and drummers and—"

"Fireworks," added his father. "And, best of all, they have a full-size replica of a longship that they burn at the end."

"A longship?" He'd read about longships, many-oared Viking boats. A life-size model would be amazing to see.

But Sarah cut across his thoughts. "Would we be able to take a friend with us?"

"For Christmas? I don't think many families would want to have their children somewhere else at Christmas." Their mother shook her head.

"But what about Christmas Eve services and our Christmas stockings and—" Timothy improvised.

"I didn't know my children were such traditionalists," Mr. Maxwell interrupted. "We can celebrate Christmas in a different country for once, you know. After all, we'll still be together." He wiped his mouth contentedly on a napkin.

Timothy didn't say anything else for the rest of the meal. Sarah must have been referring to Jessica when she suggested bringing a friend; he could tell by the way she'd tried to catch his eye. Perhaps he could pretend to be sick. In his heart, though, he knew it was hopeless. Once his father got an idea in his head, it was impossible to change his mind; he'd guard it as fiercely as a dog with a prize bone.

After dinner Timothy and Sarah sat on her bed, the map carefully unrolled between them. Timothy told Sarah again about everything that had happened at school. But the retelling couldn't conjure the sense of sheer dread Timothy had felt when the magician stared straight at him and the lights went out.

"Mr. Twig said something would happen. I just didn't expect it to be at school and so soon!" Timothy burrowed his feet under the comforter. "We're not safe until we find the special stone."

"Are the rowan branches still at the windows?" Sarah didn't look up as she spoke. Her head was bent low over the old map, her hair fringing her face.

"Yeah, I checked when I got home."

"Timothy, you're good at codes. Why haven't you been able to crack this one?"

"Mr. Twig couldn't figure it out, and he had the map forever!

Besides, maps aren't codes. I don't know how to figure out a map of someplace I've never seen." Timothy pictured the word *stymied* spread out before him in gleaming Scrabble tiles, thirteen points. It was a funny, old-fashioned word, but it expressed exactly how he felt.

"But it can't be impossible. After all, you're the one who's supposed to find the Stone of Destiny. You're the Filidh."

He stared harder at the map, but no matter how hard he stared, the map wasn't giving its secrets away. The dominant features were forests, two groups of mountains, and what appeared to be a coastline. But the forest could be anywhere. Nothing was labeled. Codes followed patterns. Once you found the pattern, the solution was possible, even if it took a lot of work. But maps, as far as Timothy knew, had to have a starting point. A *You are here* arrow would have been helpful. This map had no legend to guide them. "We have to go back to Mr. Twig's. We have to tell him we're going to Scotland and that I have a few more questions about the map." Timothy checked the date on his watch. "We leave in less than a week. The question is, how are we going to protect the map until then?"

Sarah walked to the window and wiggled the sash, making sure it was locked. "How are we going to protect ourselves?"

# SILVER DUST

**T**HAT NIGHT TIMOTHY didn't sleep well. When he did manage to drift off, his dreams were a troubling collage of ravens and magicians. He'd put the map under his pillow, and now in the early-morning light he slipped his hand under his head just to reassure himself; it was still there. The thought of leaving it and his crown in the back of Sarah's closet all day while he was at school was intolerable. No, it was more than intolerable; it was excruciating—an interesting word he had never been able to use in Scrabble but one he kept in reserve just in case.

Timothy wrapped the comforter tightly around himself, reluctant to rise from the warm cocoon of his bed. The room was cold, and the light coming through the window was a milky white. Snow light, Timothy thought. He shuffled to the window. The sky was gray flannel, heavy with the expectation of snow. Last year there had been no snow for the holidays, only a thin and disappointing dusting late in January. Maybe this year there would be proper snow for Christmas. Then

Timothy remembered: They wouldn't be home for Christmas this year. He wondered if it snowed in Edinburgh.

It was Friday. Tomorrow they'd be able to visit Mr. Twig again. Timothy had decided deep in the middle of the night that he would have to return the map to Mr. Twig; it would be safest there. He would leave the crown with him as well. He couldn't take the map and crown to Scotland with his family and put them all in danger. But what could he do with them in the meantime? He pulled on his clothes, adding an extra sweater. He ran his fingers through his hair while worry continued to nip at his stomach. School wasn't safe, and he had the feeling his own house wasn't, either. He remembered the rowan branches on his windowsill keeping the one-eyed cat out. Jessica had given them enough from her tree for every windowsill in the house. A few extra branches were piled in the garage. It might help to put some right inside Sarah's closet.

Timothy mumbled to his mother's back as he passed her in the kitchen and hurried to the garage with Prank at his heels. The cold waited for him. He shoved his hands into his pockets and sniffed the air, hoping to catch the scent of snow. The garage was not much warmer than outside. Timothy gathered the last three slender branches and sped back to his sister's room. He placed the limbs inside her closet, against the false back to their secret space. Grabbing a banana from the fruit bowl and his backpack, he ran for the bus stop.

&#10010; &#10010; &#10010;

All that morning Timothy waited for snow and for a chance to talk to Jessica. By lunchtime, it looked as if neither was likely to happen. The problem with someone like Jessica, he thought grumpily, was that she was never alone. Finally, in desperation, he stopped by her table at lunch. She sat surrounded by three of the most popular girls in school. A large boy, who had recently taken to shadowing her every move, hunkered at a table nearby. Timothy paused and leaned in toward Jessica. "We're going to Scotland for Christmas." He hoped he had spoken quietly enough that only Jessica had heard.

"So?" Tina Salcedo stared up at him, her brown eyes ringed in dark shadow. Timothy thought she looked like a skinny raccoon.

Jessica raised her eyebrows and flipped her hair. "Is Sarah going, too?"

"The whole family," Timothy muttered. Tina snorted. Timothy didn't stick around to hear Jessica's response. He'd imparted the information. He'd talk to her later.

That afternoon the bus was a war zone. Outside, a freak windstorm tore the limbs from trees and sent garbage cans careering down the sidewalks. On the bus, spitballs pelted like rain. The bus driver pulled over twice and told everyone to quiet down. Even then, the noise subsided only until the bus moved once more. The energy in the air was palpable.

But Timothy was distracted; the map absorbed his thoughts. He would just tell the old professor that he'd failed. That he had no idea about the solution to the map. That he wasn't worthy of being a Filidh.

His heart beat heavily in his chest, and he wondered for the millionth time who in his family had been the Filidh before him. Who had turned to the Dark? Timothy tried to cheer himself up by remembering the fireworks and the longship promised in Edinburgh, but a sense of failure whipped through him like the wind, weighing as heavily as the leaden sky.

By the time the bus reached Timothy's stop, the wind had slowed. Clouds skimmed the tops of the tallest trees. Drivers flashed on their headlights. Timothy picked his way over stray branches and debris, thinking of his warm kitchen and the muffins he hadn't had time to eat at breakfast. He nervously checked the treetops for birds.

When he rounded the corner to his street, red and blue lights almost blinded him. A flashing police car was parked in his driveway. Timothy ran.

He pushed his way through the front door. In the living room, his mother sat bewildered among the litter of a ransacked house. A police officer was talking into a cell phone. Cabinet drawers were tossed onto the floor, their contents spilled, sofa cushions overturned and torn open. Mrs. Maxwell ran one finger back and forth across her eyebrows the way she did whenever she was distressed.

"Mom?" Timothy's voice caught in his throat.

"Timothy." She looked up. "We've had a break-in. Your dad's on his way home. I was out at the grocery store." She gestured vaguely toward two paper bags.

Timothy dropped his backpack on the floor. "Are you okay?" He had a sudden vision of Sarah's closet, the door open and the map and crown gone. It took all his will to keep from dashing upstairs to see if they had been discovered.

"She's fine, son." The officer clicked shut his phone and cracked his neck. He reached into his shirt pocket and drew out a small notebook. "We just need to determine if anything's been stolen. Why don't you take a look around and see if you notice anything missing?"

Timothy quickly scanned the living room. It was a shambles, but as far as he could tell, everything was still there, including a new camera sitting in plain view on the coffee table.

"Strangest thing." The officer shook his head. "They left that nice camera. Something must've frightened 'em off." He looked at Mrs. Maxwell. "Don't you worry, ma'am. Crime in the middle of the day like this—neighbors must have seen something."

"Usually drug-related." A female officer walked into the room, clicking off several shots with a digital camera.

Timothy inched toward the stairs. "I want to check our bedrooms." He took the stairs two at a time and burst into Sarah's room. Just as he had imagined, everything was overturned. Books and clothes were tossed indiscriminately across the floor. The closet door was open! But the three rowan branches still lay inside as he had left them. Heart racing, he removed them, then loosened the panel on the back wall. It was too dark to see anything. He thrust his hand into the opening. The map in its leather pouch and the crown were still there!

Timothy grabbed the pouch and crown and pressed them against his chest. He could feel his heart still beating wildly. He should keep them with him until he went to Mr. Twig's tomorrow. He could sleep with them by his side. At least he'd know that they were safe. He looked around Sarah's room and shuddered. No place felt safe. Better to leave them back in the closet with the rowan wood as protection. Reluctantly, he placed the items behind the panel in the closet again.

Nothing in Sarah's room or his own room, as far as he could tell in the chaos, was gone. His computer still hummed on his desk, and his mineral collection still lined the windowsill. His bed was just as rumpled as he'd left it, but along one side was a long, ominous gash.

Sarah and his father were standing in stunned silence in the living room when Timothy returned downstairs.

"Sarah, go check your room," Mr. Maxwell ordered. "Timothy, anything missing?"

"It's a mess, but everything's there."

His father nodded, and Timothy followed Sarah up the stairs.

✠ ✠ ✠

"Timothy, the map? Tell me it's safe!" Sarah, still bundled in her ballet sweats and parka, waited for him on the landing.

"The map and crown are fine. I put rowan branches inside your closet before I left this morning." He followed her into her bedroom. "But if rowan branches work, and we have them on the windowsills, how did the Dark get into the house?"

Clothes and books were tumbled across the floor. Sarah's favorite collage hung in tatters from the wall. She collapsed on the bed, head in hands. "It's worse than I thought!"

Timothy sat down next to her. "It wasn't a robbery. Someone was looking for the map."

"How do you know?"

"I just know. It was the Dark, looking for the map. Think about what happened at my school."

Sarah was quiet for a moment, staring at the ceiling. "I've got something to tell you, too. I came in the back door when I got home. There's silver dust on the back deck."

Timothy gaped at his sister. "Star Girl wouldn't do this. Show me."

Timothy grabbed his flashlight, and Sarah followed him out the back door. It was murky dusk now, the lights of the city reflecting off the low clouds. As the flashlight beam played across the deck, Timothy saw a faint glitter.

Sarah bent down and ran her fingers through the dust. "She was here." Then she scraped the dust into the cracks between the boards with the toe of her shoe. "I don't want anyone else to see this."

"I'm giving the map and crown to Mr. Twig tomorrow. I haven't solved the cipher, and we can't take them with us to Scotland. It will only put everyone in danger."

"How do you know that taking them to Edinburgh isn't exactly what we're supposed to do, especially if there's a chance the stone is in Scotland? And how did the Dark get into the house?" Sarah echoed Timothy's question.

A lone crow cawed overhead and landed in the bare branches of the sycamore. Timothy shrugged deeper into his jacket. He looked up at the windows of their house. "I don't know what we're supposed to do. But, look, the rowan branches are gone from the windows. Even the wind is against us." He felt a cold deeper than the bite of late afternoon, as if eyes followed him from the shadows, but except for the lone crow, the yard was deserted.

# ELEGTRA

TAR GIRL WATCHED the night deepen. As the sky darkened from blue to black, a screech owl hooted softly above her head, its feathered horns dark silhouettes against the sky. From her perch in a locust tree across town from the Maxwells, she could identify six stars of the Pleiades glowing just above the horizon. Tonight the astronomers would again wonder about the missing seventh star, the lost Pleiade. Few would know which star was missing, and fewer still would be able to give the name of the missing sister, Electra.

The Pleiade sisters had been called many things over hundreds of years: doves, maidens, flames. Each description captured a part of the truth, but none could describe them entirely. Now scientists peered through ever-evolving telescopes and defined them as an open star cluster and pinpointed their distance as four hundred light-years from Earth. But many astronomers still used the old names from Greek myth when referring to them individually: Alcyone, guardian of the winds; Merope, the youngest and most eloquent sister; swarthy Celaeno; Maia, the eldest; twinkling Sterope; Taygeta of the long neck; and Star Girl's own name, Electra, the bright and shining. There had been names before these, given when the world was new. On any particular night of winter in the northern hemisphere, six or all seven of the sisters were visible from Earth. And that variability had led to speculations, legends, and stories of a missing sister.

Electra had heard the call when November darkened to December, when she and her sisters became visible in the sky soon after dusk. The call meant it was time for her to watch, to bear witness. Each time one of the sisters was summoned, it was to a crossroads of history. Sometimes it had been a momentous event, such as the crowning of King Hugh O'Neill of Ireland, when the coronation stone cried out in joy. Sometimes it was a moment of sadness so great that all creation was called as witness, as when fires of the death camps burned day and night. Often the events were increments as small as finches, events unnoticed by most, such as when the boy Timothy stood against the Dark and received a crown. Each time, something greater than the event itself hung in the balance. Electra knew that all the happenings of thousands of years were mere prelude to a story that was still unfolding. And it was her task now to witness and not intervene in the affairs of humans.

From her tree, she witnessed two figures enter the professor's house. It was in the quietest hours of night, right before dawn. One wore the shape of a werewolf and the other a hunched hag, but she had seen them before in other guises. They entered stealthily, turning the knob of the locked door, though they needed no doors to enter. Methodically at first, they began a search. As their frustration grew, the search became frenzied. Drawers gaped like open mouths, books flew to the floor, and in the middle of the racket, the old professor in striped pajamas staggered in from his bed on knobby bare feet, a baseball bat clutched in his hands. Before he saw their shadowy shapes, he hesitated, as if he could feel their presence, a coldness in the air.

The wolf thing reared onto its back legs, towered as tall as a man, and snarled, but the hag was swifter. She struck a blow from behind that sent the old man sprawling.

Electra watched as the two shadowed figures left without finding whatever they had come for. She watched still when the professor pulled himself to his feet and, with a trembling hand, dialed the phone.

Later she watched the dark shapes visit the house of Timothy and his sister, Sarah. The sky was flanneled with clouds, and the scent of snow lingered around the edges of the afternoon when the dark ones moved toward the empty house.

This time they looked like two young women out for a winter walk, bundled against the cold and wind that tore at their clothes. Electra noticed how they rang the doorbell and waited on the front porch. Anyone passing by would assume visitors had come to call. Then, when no one responded, they wandered toward the side yard. Where the rowan branches were set in the windowsills, they could not enter the house. Electra followed silently, her long silver hair brushing the backs of her knees, her bare feet quite comfortable on the freezing ground. Once they were out of view from the road, the outlines of the two young women blurred to shadows. The shadows grew thick and took the shape of large cats, easily leaping the fence and disappearing into the backyard. The winds grew stronger. They roared through town and swept about the house. Outside an upstairs window, a branch came loose and fell.

Electra watched the cats enter the house through that window and transform once again into dark shapes. While they searched, she hummed. It would not snow yet, she thought, looking at the sky. The leaves had fallen from the red twig dogwood growing near the bare garden plot. Its branches stood out among the browns and grays like stiff red arms. Soon it would be time for her to move on. The cats re-appeared on the roof. They carried nothing with them. One leapt deftly to the top of the fence. The other opened its mouth as if to yowl. She could see the pointed teeth, the pink throat. But no sound emerged, just a ribbon of inky black, as dense and cold as despair.

# PROFESSOR TWIG

I N THE EARLY HOURS of Saturday morning, long before the rest of his family was up, Timothy was awake. He took the map and crown from under his pillow. He spread the map across his comforter and tried, once again, to puzzle out its secrets. But nothing came to him.

Timothy, with the map and crown inside his backpack, was only too glad to escape the house with Sarah after lunch. His parents were busy putting the house back together and seemed relieved to have them go. Timothy and Sarah had arranged to meet Jessica at the city bus stop and return the map to Mr. Twig. Sarah had tried calling the professor several times that morning, but the phone rang unanswered.

"Tell me about the break-in," Jessica said, rubbing her mittened hands together.

"It was awful. Everything's a mess! Nothing was stolen, and nothing really important was broken, except my mom's latest painting was slashed. She was pretty upset about that." Sarah stomped her feet to keep them warm.

"They had to be looking for *it*." Even though there was no one else waiting at the bus stop, Timothy couldn't bring himself to say *map* out loud.

"Did Timothy tell you about the silver dust?" Sarah asked.

Jessica nodded. "It had to be Star Girl. Do you think she scared off whoever it was?"

"I don't know." Sarah exhaled, and her breath hovered like a white phantom in the air. "But after what happened at your school, nowhere seems safe."

"I can't believe your family is going to Scotland before we've figured anything out." Jessica's voice was muffled behind her scarf, and Timothy noticed that she didn't look at either of them.

He was consumed by his own gloomy thoughts. It irked him to return the map to Mr. Twig without having made any progress on it. If he, Timothy, truly was a Filidh, he wasn't a very good one. A puff of warm air hit his face as the doors of the bus swung open.

The sky was still low and brooding. The weatherman had predicted snow before nightfall. Houses were festive with Christmas lights, and Timothy, his face turned toward the gray world, could see decorated trees in windows. They had decided not to get a Christmas tree this year, since they would be leaving before the holidays. Timothy loved the ritual of getting up early on a weekend, going into the forest, arguing over just the right tree, and returning home to cinnamon rolls.

As if she could read his thoughts, Jessica tried to cheer him up.

"Don't feel so bad, Timothy. Mr. Twig doesn't know what any of it means, either, and he's a professor. You'll probably have a great time in Scotland. Better than I will with my cousin Riley." Jessica's three-year-old cousin was the terror of the family.

The porch light shone at Mr. Twig's house, and all three children considered it a promising sign. A wreath of holly festooned the shiny black door. Jessica impatiently pushed the doorbell. Timothy, still brooding, kept his hand wrapped around the strap of his backpack, where the map lay hidden with its secrets.

"Hurry! I'm freezing to death," Sarah moaned. She leaned her ear against the door to listen for footsteps. "Try ringing again."

Jessica pushed the bell a second time. No one came.

"He's got to be here! We're leaving in four days!" Timothy knocked just in case the bell wasn't working.

"He's not home, you know." A thin woman in red fuzzy slippers and bright blue earmuffs stood on the walk. "Ambulance took him this morning."

"What happened?" Sarah asked in alarm.

"I told you. The ambulance took him. All kinds of strange people always going in and out." She shook her head. "My husband says—"

"Do you know what hospital he went to?" Jessica interrupted the flow of words.

"Can't expect me to know everything that goes on." The woman gave them a sour look and shuffled back toward her house.

"Wait!" Sarah called after her. But the woman crossed into her yard without turning back. "Now what do we do?"

"We find him," Timothy said. The three children huddled around a table at a nearby coffee shop while Jessica used her cell phone. There were three hospitals in town. On the second call, she got lucky. "There was a Mr. Robert Augustus Twig admitted at O'Conner this morning. The receptionist wouldn't say why, just that he's there."

"How far away is it?" Timothy blew on his cup of tea.

"It's right on the bus route. We pass it every time we come here." Sarah looked at Timothy as if he were half-witted.

"Well, I guess I never noticed. Let's go."

✠ ✠ ✠

The air changed the minute you walked through hospital doors, Timothy thought. It became medicinal and sterile. *Hygienic*, he thought. Seventeen Scrabble points and a very useful word, even if he didn't much care for the sound of it. A confusion of signs and elevators filled the main lobby. People waited on vinyl couches and plastic chairs, their necks craned to watch the news on an overhead TV monitor. Was there any place more forlorn than a hospital waiting room, Timothy wondered. A woman wheeled her son toward the elevator, his casted leg propped on a cushion. People spoke in hushed voices; they fidgeted and checked their watches. The quiet and discomfort were contagious. The threesome walked silently to the information desk.

"We're here to visit Mr. Twig." Jessica bit her lower lip. "He was admitted this morning."

"Just one moment." The woman pushed her glasses up on her head and picked up the jangling phone. "O'Conner Hospital."

Sarah turned her back on the receptionist. "They might not let us in to see him," she worried in a hushed voice. "Sometimes only family can visit."

"That's easy—we can just say we're his grandkids." Jessica unzipped her coat. "Why are hospitals always so hot?"

"What if they ask for proof or something?" Timothy eased the backpack off his shoulders. His shirt stuck to his skin, and he longed to be back out in the cold air.

"Now, how can I help you?" The woman peered at them over the top of red glasses that had slid to the tip of her nose.

"Mr. Twig. We're here to see Mr. Robert Twig."

"Right." The phone began to ring again. She entered his name into her computer and frowned at the screen while reaching for the phone with her other hand. "Third floor, room 312. Hello, O'Conner Hospital."

Before the receptionist could ask any questions, the three hurried to the elevators and rode up to the third floor. Getting into Mr. Twig's room proved easier than Timothy had thought. A nurse asked who they were visiting and only nodded when Jessica mentioned they were grandchildren. "I didn't say whose grandchildren," she muttered under her breath.

"He's resting comfortably, but I wouldn't stay too long, or you'll tire him out," the nurse said.

Timothy paused in the wide hospital doorway. The room held two beds separated by a blue curtain. Mr. Twig reclined in the bed nearest the door. Timothy had never thought of Mr. Twig as feeble before. If anything, he would have described him as *spry*. A good Scrabble word, he noted. Nine points. But *spry* was a word used only to describe old people. No one ever called kids spry. Now Mr. Twig looked anything but spry. The bed seemed to have shrunk him. He was a bushy-eyebrowed skeleton propped on white pillows. Beneath the wild brows, his eyes were closed.

"Is he sleeping?"

"Certainly not!" The old man's eyelids fluttered. His eyes snapped open wide. Timothy jumped. Mr. Twig struggled to sit up.

"Can I help you?" Jessica plumped a pillow behind his back. And Timothy remembered her on the battlefield at the Travelers' Market, tending to the wounded, the ruby necklace gleaming at her throat. That Jessica seemed a lifetime away from the Jessica anxiously hovering in the hospital room. Timothy wondered if she was wearing her necklace now and if she could do anything at all to help Mr. Twig.

"Thank you." His rattling cough didn't sound healthy to Timothy. "It seems I've had an 'episode.' At least that's what they're calling it. Funny how they use euphemisms to describe things. Not a heart attack exactly, but something close." He closed his eyes again. "The old heart couldn't take the shock of confronting *them* in the night."

They crowded around his bed. "Them? Intruders? Did they hurt you? Are you going to be okay?" Timothy asked, and then felt stupid for asking it so bluntly.

"Not just any intruders. As for my heart, they want to put a stent in, something to keep the arteries open, and I should be good as new." His eyes again popped wide and fastened on Timothy. "You still have it, don't you?"

"Yes, but I haven't figured anything out, and our house was burglar—"

"And there's another problem," Sarah cut in. "Our parents are taking us to Scotland for Christmas vacation."

"We thought it would be better, safer, if we left the map with you."

Mr. Twig put one bony finger to his thin lips. "Hush. Don't even think it. I'm in no shape, after what happened."

"What did happen?" Jessica asked, sitting on the foot of his bed.

Mr. Twig motioned for them all to draw closer. "I was attacked." He pointed to his cheek and turned his full face to them.

For the first time, Timothy noticed a large purpling bruise.

"They'd finally come for the map." The professor's hands trembled. "I knew they would at some point."

"Who came?" Timothy found that he was whispering.

"Just like I told you, none of us are safe until you find the coronation stone."

"Mr. Twig, who came looking for it? Because someone broke into our house, too." Sarah's face knotted with concern.

"*His* people. The Bent. Servants of the Dark. I heard a thumping in my house late at night, and when I got out of bed"— here his voice dropped so low that Timothy could barely hear the next words, even though he was leaning in as close as he dared—"there was this creature in my living room, going through my personal things. No doubt in my mind at all what it was after. Hit me with something, and I went down. Told them here that I got the bruise when I fell, of course."

"Mr. Twig, I don't know if this will help, but I'd like to try," said Jessica as she gently placed her hands on his bruised cheek.

As Timothy watched Jessica grow pale, he remembered what she'd said about giving a bit of herself away when she healed others. The bruise began to fade.

"You've taken away all the pain!" Mr. Twig grasped Jessica's hand in thanks.

"I know I can't heal everything. I'm never sure what will heal and what won't, but I'm glad I could help you," Jessica said.

The same nurse reappeared, clipboard in hand.

"Time to let your grandfather have some peace. He has surgery scheduled for Monday morning, and we want him rested up for it."

Mr. Twig's other hand clamped on to Timothy like steel. "You've got a job to do. Keep it safe."

"But what about taking it to Scotland?" Sarah asked.

"Alba," Mr. Twig murmured. "That's what Scotland was once called. A very interesting choice. Dangerous, perhaps. After all, it's the land of the sídhe, the fairy folk, the Good Folk. I told you that there are rumors of the coronation stone associated with Scotland, rumors that the stone may be hidden there."

"Then it's exactly where we should be going!" Sarah's whisper was just a little too loud.

"I did tell you it's time to leave." The nurse frowned at them.

"We'll be back to check on you," Jessica said. As soon as the nurse was out of earshot, she added, "What are the sídhe?"

But Mr. Twig had already closed his eyes once more, the bruise fading further from his cheek.

# THE SÍDHE

**T**HEY ARGUED ON THE BUS.

"We have to take the map with us. Mr. Twig said the Telling Stone might be connected to Scotland. Then Dad ends up with a business trip to Edinburgh?" Sarah's voice was an urgent whisper. "Too much coincidence. I think it's a sign."

"But all he said in the hospital was, 'an interesting choice.' He didn't say anything at all about the map." Timothy looked over his shoulder. Just the regular type of commuters you'd expect to see on a bus. But what was regular anymore? "It puts us all in danger."

"So, who broke into his house?" Sarah tucked the ends of her red scarf into the neck of her wool coat. "It isn't a coincidence that both of our homes were searched."

"He called it a creature. It had to be something pretty horrible!" Timothy shuddered. He remembered how the professor's hands shook when he told the story.

"He's having surgery on Monday. He won't be in any position to keep the map safe." Jessica frowned at Timothy. "Besides, I think Sarah is right. You'll need it to hunt for the coronation stone." Timothy noticed that Jessica wasn't looking at either of them. She was fiddling with a tissue in her lap, tearing it into tiny pieces.

"We don't even know what geography the map shows. There aren't any labels. The forest and hills could be anywhere! Even if it is somewhere in Scotland, how do we find out where?" Timothy clutched the backpack firmly in his lap.

"At least you both get to go." Jessica's lap was covered in a little mound of tissue now. "When I get home, I'm going to look up the sídhe. If you don't want to take the map to Scotland, you can leave it with me."

Timothy and Sarah were silent for a moment. Timothy realized he hadn't thought about how Jessica felt about being left behind. "When he gave me the map, Mr. Twig said my friends should help me. If Scotland is where we search for the Stone of Destiny, then somehow we need to end up there together. My parents would be happy to have you come with us."

Jessica shook her head. "There's no way my parents will let me miss Christmas with cousin Riley."

She looked up from the mound of torn tissue in her lap, and Timothy noticed that her eyes were wet. He said the first thing he could think of to distract her. "And what about the silver dust? What does Star Girl have to do with stealing the map?"

Neither girl answered.

Timothy sat silently, listening to the hum of wheels on the pavement, the shifting murmurs of the other passengers, his own breath, the whir of questions inside his head.

"I hope Mr. Twig will be all right," Sarah ventured.

"Don't worry; I'll visit him while you're gone. It will give me an excuse to escape the three-year-old terror."

✛ ✛ ✛

When Timothy and Sarah returned to the warmth of their house, their mother was sitting at the dining room table, a map and two guidebooks for Scotland spread out next to her laptop. Everything looked almost normal, as if there had been no break-in. "I'm making a list of sites we won't want to miss. You'll want to think about packing soon."

"Mom, it's still four days away. No one packs that soon." Sarah peered over her mother's shoulder at the map.

"Suit yourself. I've already started. Make sure you pack warm clothes; it'll be cold and wet this time of year." She pointed to a city on the map. "This is Edinburgh, where we'll be staying."

Sarah looked where her mother's finger rested. "Scotland looks like a funny hat on the top of England," she said with a laugh. Then she looked closer. "Oh, there's Loch Ness. That's the only thing I know about Scotland, the Loch Ness Monster."

"Scotland's full of myths and fairy tales. Nessie's just the most famous one. I remember my grandmother telling me about selkies and the sídhe."

"The sídhe?" Sarah stared curiously at her mother. "But we're not Scots, are we?"

"Well, the O'Daly side is Irish, but there's a little bit of Scots in our background, too. There was a fair amount of back-and-forthing between Scotland and Ireland. Anyway, my grandmother O'Daly always loved fairy tales. She used to tell stories about the sídhe all the time to your Aunt Ellen and me."

"You never mentioned the sídhe before. What are they?" Sarah tried to sound casual, but she could hear Mr. Twig's words ringing in her ears.

Her mother took off her reading glasses and rubbed her eyes. "They're the fairy folk, descendants of the Tuatha Dé Danann, ancient kings and queens of Ireland with supernatural gifts. According to legend, they live in a world parallel to ours. I saw a painting of them once." Her eyes took on that dreamy expression she got whenever she began talking about art. Sarah needed to keep her on track.

"What are they like?"

"They're tall and handsome and rather fierce. Not little people with wings. The sídhe go their own way, Grandmother O'Daly used to say. They don't have much to do with the lives of men except to use them for their own purposes. I remember her saying that you never want to get on their bad side. When she was growing up, she always set a bowl of milk out for them on special nights. She said her brother Edward made fun of her but that she thought he believed in them more than she did. Great-uncle Edward left home as soon as he could. Supposedly he made a vast fortune but ended up dying as a penniless recluse. I don't really know. He never kept in touch with the family." Mrs. Maxwell stretched and got up from the table.

Sarah stared at her mother's back as she walked into the kitchen. Her mother always managed to surprise her. Now that she had a nugget of information to share with Timothy, she realized that her brother had disappeared as soon as they came home.

Timothy sat cross-legged on his bed in the semidarkness. The only light was his bedside lamp. On his head he wore the delicate golden crown, the crown of a true Filidh. The antique map was unrolled and spread across his knees, and in the soft light from the lamp, its jewel tones glowed.

"The crown! Why are you wearing it?" Sarah asked.

He started at her voice, and his fingers ran along the rim of the crown self-consciously. "I thought it might help me with the map." He shrugged. "But it hasn't."

"When you wear it, I can remember the Travelers' Market, the Greenman, everything. It's so easy to forget."

"I know. Sometimes it seems like none of this ever happened."

"Timothy, I found out something about the sídhe."

Timothy raised his eyebrows. "You did?"

"Yeah. Mom brought them up. Our great-grandmother O'Daly believed in the sídhe. Mom said that they're a kind of fairy that has little to do with the affairs of men and that you never want to cross them."

"A fairy?"

"I don't think she meant the Disney kind. She said they're descendants of the Irish gods, and they're tall and handsome and fierce. Her grandma used to tell her and Aunt Ellen stories about them." Sarah sat down on the bed and tucked her legs up under her chin. "But Mr. Twig wouldn't have mentioned them unless they have something to do with finding the Telling Stone."

"Maybe they're dangerous, and he was trying to warn us." Timothy stared intently at the map. "Look here, maybe I've found something." He pointed to hatch marks in the corners. "That's Ogham; at least I think it is. It's a really ancient language. And these marks, over here, look like Ogham, too."

Sarah studied the series of hatch marks. "It just looks like lines to me."

"When I was in Julian's caravan at the Market, he had a book. The entire book was written in this script, Ogham. At first it didn't look like anything to me, either, but the more I stared at it, the more it began to make sense." He looked up at Sarah. "I can't explain it any other way except to say it was as if I could gradually read a language I had never seen or heard before. Like when you could understand what the birds were saying at the Market. I can't understand the script anymore. Now the words look like they did to me at first, hatch marks."

Timothy adjusted the crown on his head. "The words feel like they are just beyond reach." He traced the Ogham symbols with his finger. "There are four words here. They must label the pictures."

"There are the pictures," Sarah pointed out. "A cauldron, a spear, a sword, a stone. Aren't those the things Mr. Twig said Balor needs to control the Light? And then all these animals and flowers. It's like a treasure hunt." She chewed her lip. "There's a coastline here." She pointed to the lower right-hand corner of the map. "Ships like that sailed the ocean." She ran her finger across the old paper. "It's so beautiful."

"I thought we were supposed to all work together to find the stone. That's what Mr. Twig said when he gave me the map—'rely on your friends' or something like that. We'll be leaving Jessica out if we go to Scotland without her."

The sadness in Timothy's voice surprised Sarah. He rarely showed his feelings. "I felt that way—sad—when we left the Market. As if we were leaving all our friends behind," she mused, thinking about Peter. She walked to the window. Why did feelings have to be so complicated? "Look, Timothy. It's started to snow!"

Timothy sprinted to the window.

Tiny white-corn snow sputtered from the sky. The sprinkling left a tattered cover on the ground. It would take a long time to transform the gray landscape. But Sarah felt her heart lighten.

+++

The light snow continued through most of the night, leaving a world coated with a fine white crust as if the ground, bushes, and trees had all been dusted with powdered sugar.

Jessica sighed and returned her gaze to the kitchen counter where she was working. Her mother had been busy most of the day preparing the house for Christmas. Not that they had ever made much fuss about holiday preparations before. Christmas was usually a simple celebration, just another day off but with presents. When she was younger, her father had hauled out the artificial Christmas tree every December. But in the last few years it had stayed in its dust-covered box in the basement.

Now that her aunt and uncle had decided to come for the holidays with Riley the Terrible, however, everything had changed. A squat tree from the grocery-store lot sat proudly by the grand piano. Her father was putting up strings of lights. Their threadbare old stockings had been replaced with bright, quilted ones.

Jessica sighed again. She was not in the mood for Christmas. She was not in the mood to entertain a demanding and undisciplined three-year-old cousin. More than anything she wanted to be part of Timothy and Sarah's trip to Scotland. She gave one last vicious stir to the bowl of molasses-cookie dough. Somehow, Christmas cookies had become her assignment. She dropped large spoonfuls onto the greased cookie sheets and licked the sticky brown dough from her fingers.

Every adventure from the very first time she had found the mysterious note in the mail had involved all three of them. Together they had met the Greenman in the woods, had been given special gifts by Cerridwyn. Together they had visited the Travelers' Market and fought against Balor and the evil powers of the Dark. Together they had been charged with finding the Lia Fáil, the missing Stone of Destiny, along with three other treasures. They had been a team. And now they weren't. Jessica slipped the tray of cookies into the warm oven and brushed the curls from her eyes with a sticky hand. One more taste of the sweet dough. She twirled her index finger in the soft mess sticking to the bowl and licked it thoughtfully.

"The cookies smell fantastic! Come take a look at the tree." Her mother bustled into the kitchen, a strand of tinsel glinting in her hair.

"Riley's only three. I don't think he'll even notice how the tree looks," Jessica muttered as she followed her mother into the family room.

"Oh, don't be such a Scrooge." Mrs. Church ruffled Jessica's curls. "They should be here by suppertime, and I don't want any long faces. It's a long flight from Saint Louis. What's eating you, anyway?"

Jessica looked at the fat little tree festooned with red and gold balls, twinkly lights, and tinsel. "It looks great, Mom. They'll love it." She gave her mother a hug. "I mean it, it really does."

Mrs. Church beamed. "And I just know your cookies will be delicious."

By the time her aunt, uncle, and Riley the Terrible arrived, Jessica felt almost cheerful. Cookies were piled high on bright red plates, carols from a new CD rang through the house, and her father had started a fire in the fireplace. Even though Christmas was still a week away, the Churches were ready.

✝ ✝ ✝

But by Monday morning, Jessica had been more than ready to escape to school. Riley was worse than she'd remembered. He was so cute, with his wispy blond hair and round brown eyes, that he could get away with anything. He had been up much of last night fussing inconsolably. Now she rubbed her eyes. Her own head felt thick, filled with cotton from lack of sleep. Only two and a half days of school left before the break. Usually she couldn't wait for the holidays, but now she wasn't so sure she wanted to be home. She imagined the Maxwells had spent the weekend packing, getting ready to leave on Wednesday. She'd had no time to check in with Timothy and Sarah since Riley arrived. And there had only been time for a hasty conversation with Timothy in science class that morning. He'd assured her the map was safe.

Jessica hunched into her coat and pulled the hood tight. The walk home from the bus stop was long and lonely. The sky was gray and thick. No more snow fell, but a white crust still covered the frigid earth. Her father had said it was too cold to snow, and Jessica, watching her breath puff into small white clouds, believed him. She shivered in through the front door, unprepared for the sight that greeted her. Riley sat in Mrs. Church's lap, covered from head to toe with small red spots. His face was flushed and his eyes glazed.

"Riley has the chicken pox, and now his father's feeling poorly. We can't send them back home. I'm not sure what to do," her mother fretted, holding a cold washcloth to the child's forehead. "You've never had them, you know. And you've never been vaccinated. It would be best if there was somewhere else you could stay for a week or so. But at Christmastime!" Jessica thought her mother was about to cry. "The doctor said it's extremely contagious."

"Never mind, Mom. I've got an idea." She dropped her backpack to the floor and told her mother about the Maxwells' invitation.

"We can't impose on anyone over the holidays," her mother continued as if Jessica hadn't said anything at all.

"Seriously, Mom. Listen, I have an invitation. I just didn't think it would be good to be gone at Christmas. I suspect I could stay with the Maxwells starting today."

# PART 2

# WHEN MYTHS WALK

# EDINBURGH

**O**F COURSE SHE'S welcome. Have her come over tonight. We've got a big place to stay in Edinburgh. Let me know about the ticket." Mrs. Maxwell hung up the phone.

"Who was that?" Timothy asked.

His mother smiled across the dinner table. "It looks like Jessica Church will be traveling with us to Scotland if her mother can get a ticket. She'll stay with us tonight."

"What?" Timothy swiveled his head between his mother and his sister.

"Her cousin just arrived and came down with chicken pox, and now it looks like his father isn't feeling well, either. They think it's best if Jessica has somewhere else to be for a week or so. What do you think?"

"That's great!" Sarah sent Timothy a swift kick under the table.

"Timothy?" His mother raised her eyebrows.

"Great!" This was better than he could have hoped for. He took a bite of corn bread. Things were definitely beginning to look up. Perhaps Sarah was right—they were all meant to go together.

✛ ✛ ✛

Timothy awoke in a sweat, covers tangled around his legs as if he'd battled Balor in his sleep. Something right on the edge of consciousness was pulling at him, making his heart pound. In a few hours they would be leaving. The map and crown were safely stowed in his backpack. Everything was packed. So what bothered him?

He sat up in bed and tried to sort out his worries. They were like the crumpled homework papers that ended up in the bottom of his backpack. He pictured removing each one and smoothing it flat for inspection.

Mr. Twig had come through his operation just fine. They'd talked to him on the phone yesterday. He had a new stent in his heart and would be going to celebrate Christmas with his sister on the coast. Jessica was really coming with them to Scotland. She was already sharing Sarah's bedroom. So far, so good.

But two worries remained, the two he had tried to ignore all along by stuffing them under everything else that was going on in his life. No matter how carefully he smoothed them out, they still looked very bad. What if the creature that had searched their houses pursued them to Scotland? And the second worry was even worse. What if he, Timothy James Maxwell, future Filidh, failed at his very first task and was never able to decipher the map?

Carefully stepping over his binder and the previous night's bowl of popcorn, Timothy padded to the window. Outside, a white world glowed. Snow lay in thick and peaceful drifts over the sleeping town. A full moon shone like a bright new coin. If only he felt as peaceful. His worries crouched beside him, a lion ready to pounce. He was sure that if he had the Greenman's leaf, it would be hot to the touch and glowing an angry red.

┿ ┿ ┿

Brian McMorn, Mr. Maxwell's colleague, was a tall man with thick black hair, prominent cheekbones, and a nose as sharp as an eagle's beak. As promised, he met them at the airport, stepping forward briskly to shake hands with Timothy's father, exclaiming as if he had just found a long-lost friend, "Finally, face-to-face—not just e-mail anymore. And this is your family! I've been waiting years to meet all of you." His dark eyes darted to Timothy's mother and then lingered over each of the three children. "Mrs. Maxwell." He extended his hand and nodded. Then he looked at the children once again. "I've been mistaken. I thought you had only two children, Arthur."

Mr. Maxwell chuckled. "Just Timothy and Sarah are mine. This is their friend, Jessica Church."

Mr. McMorn made a stiff little bow from his waist, but not before Timothy noticed him look pensively at Jessica and raise one eyebrow. He also noticed that McMorn had almost no accent.

"Let's be on the road, shall we? Night comes early this time of year." Mr. McMorn took Timothy's father by the arm and talked about arrangements for the climate conference while they wheeled their baggage behind them.

Timothy yawned. It had been no use trying to sleep on the plane. No matter which way he turned, it had been impossible to get comfortable. And they had left the house so impossibly early, 4:00 A.M., changed planes once, and been in flight ever since. He had no idea what time it was, here or at home. He reached into his pocket and, after peeling off a residue of lint, popped his last piece of gum into his mouth.

People hurried toward departure gates, strolled through airport shops, or sat slumped in plastic chairs, reading while waiting for their flights. Anyone here could be after the map. He tightened his hold on his backpack. Without the Greenman's leaf, he felt completely vulnerable.

Jessica rubbed the sleep from her eyes. She hadn't had any trouble sleeping at all, Timothy noticed with envy. In fact, she looked as if she had just awoken from a refreshing nap while the rest of them slogged along behind his father and Mr. McMorn.

"I'm starving. Do you suppose this airport's food is as bad as ours at home?" Jessica looked hungrily at the shops they passed offering scones and pasties.

"I just want to get some sleep." Sarah yawned. "I read they eat haggis here. It's a sheep stomach stuffed with . . ."

Timothy felt his stomach roil. To distract himself he checked the crowds for signs of Scottishness. It was a theory he had seen on public television: People from a particular country would develop facial traits based on their language. The way they spoke would move the muscles of their face in ways that produced national characteristics. He really wasn't sure what he expected a Scots facial type to be, but he was sure he'd know it when he saw it. But the people in the Edinburgh airport looked just as diverse as the people at home. It was going to be more difficult to identify a true Scotsman than he'd thought. There wasn't even a kilt among them, and Timothy felt vaguely disappointed. What little he knew of Scotland came from *Braveheart* and seeing a performance of *Macbeth* with his family. Kilts had figured prominently in both.

Despite his tiredness, despite the worry that they might not be safe, even here in Scotland, a smile spread across Timothy's face. It would take more than a night without sleep to dampen the start of this new adventure. They were nearer to the Telling Stone; he could feel it.

✚ ✚ ✚

For such a tall man, Mr. McMorn's car was surprisingly small. Timothy wondered how they would all manage to fit. They were just able to jigsaw the luggage into the trunk, or *boot*, as McMorn called it.

"This may be a bit tricky. I was only expecting four. But we'll manage by cozying up. Arthur, you're up front with me, and maybe"— he looked at the three children thoughtfully—"your son will squeeze between us. That will allow the girls in the back some comfort."

Timothy eyed the front seats. They were designed to hold two comfortably. Perhaps he and his father were meant to share one seat, but that was optimistic, and he resigned himself to straddling the parking brake with his backpack in his lap.

Even though he knew people in Scotland drove on the left side of the road, it was startling to see the steering wheel on the opposite side of the car. He slid in, and McMorn folded his tall body into the driver's seat, while his father, who was a bit heavier, squished in on Timothy's other side. There was something about Mr. McMorn that made Timothy uncomfortable, although he seemed pleasant enough. He caught a whiff of aftershave or hair tonic, sweet and sharp. It made him want to sneeze.

The road from the airport wound through fields and farmland under a leaden sky. Timothy's eyelids drooped, but he forced them back open, not willing to miss a single sight. "How close to the coast are we?" his mother asked from the backseat.

"Just ten kilometers to the Firth of Forth. Six miles, that would be. We get a stiff breeze from the sea in the winter months. I'm afraid you haven't come at the pleasantest time of year for sightseeing." He veered sharply left, and Timothy gazed over a deep green field flecked with white sheep. "Unless you're interested in myths, that is. Then December's a fine time to come. We're full of traditions like Hogmanay— New Year's Eve—and First-Footing. And Edinburgh's magical at Christmastime, especially the Old Town."

When Mr. McMorn mentioned myths, Timothy felt his skin prickle. He wanted to exchange a look with Sarah and Jessica, but he was crammed too tightly between the two men. The parking brake was wearing a hole in his hip.

"What's First-Footing?" he asked.

"An ancient tradition." McMorn flicked on the wipers as rain began to splatter the windshield. "On New Year's Day the first person across the threshold should be a tall, dark-haired man to bring good luck to the household. Makes me a popular fellow." His laugh was dry. "Of course, there are folks no one wants as a First-Footer: a man whose eyebrows meet in the middle; women, especially redheaded ones; grave diggers; or thieves. Even ministers bring ill luck."

"So what happens if one of them comes first?" Sarah leaned forward, her blond hair brushing Timothy's neck.

"Well, you can't turn them away—it wouldn't be hospitable. So, to prevent twelve months of bad luck, old-timers throw salt into the fire. Others put up crosses made of rowan wood."

Sarah flicked Timothy on the back of the head.

"Sounds like the Scots are a superstitious people," Timothy's father said.

"Aye, we are, but most superstition is grounded in truth. Norman invaders were fair-haired, so a black-haired man was safe. Did I mention, First-Footers should always bring a gift—a bottle of good whisky, a lump of coal, and shortbread or buns."

"Why a lump of coal?" Jessica's voice was muffled from somewhere in the backseat. "That doesn't sound like much of a gift to me."

"To keep the house warm all year."

The rain became a torrent. The wipers fanned furiously.

"We've ordered up some true Scottish weather to welcome you."

Through the flooded windshield, Timothy watched fields give way to tall stone buildings on narrow streets. Sarah sank back into her seat, and Timothy shifted his sore hip, trying to get comfortable.

"We're almost there now. You've a flat on Frederick Street. One of my colleagues is off for the holidays and offered to lend you her place. We thought it would be better than a B and B for a family. You can cook meals."

"That's so kind." Then Mrs. Maxwell gasped. The gray flood was pierced by thousands of lights.

"Fairyland," Sarah breathed.

Buildings and trees twinkled with tiny white lights that reflected in the rain. In the center of it all, a brightly lit Ferris wheel towered over the surrounding city. Beyond the wheel blazed an enormous Christmas tree.

"I said it was magical. The tree was a gift from the people of Norway. It's on the castle mound. There's a German Christmas Market and an outdoor skating rink. Not a bad place to spend the holidays."

Perhaps Mr. McMorn would be able to help them, thought Timothy. He knew the local traditions. They sped through narrow streets, and he began to drift into sleep. He must have dozed, for the next thing he knew, the car had pulled to a stop, and Mr. McMorn was opening the passenger door, holding an umbrella for his mother and the girls.

Timothy inched his way out of the car, feeling as if the parking brake had worn a permanent groove in his hip. Rain pelted his face, and the stinging cold shocked him fully awake.

Rain poured down his neck and squished in his sneakers as he looked up at a wall of gray and red buildings. Edinburgh seemed to be a city carved out of stone.

"Hurry up, Tim, and grab your stuff." His father, a suitcase under each arm, hustled up the stairs, following McMorn and the women. Timothy grabbed his duffel along with his backpack and sloshed toward the flat.

It was a tall, narrow house with steep stairs running right up from the front door. Timothy stood dripping in the entryway, unsure where to go.

"Up here," his mother called out, and Timothy followed her voice up the polished wood staircase and into a small sitting room.

"Since it's up a flight of stairs," his mother said, beaming, "we'll have good views of the city."

Timothy looked out the three tall windows that faced the street and saw nothing but sheets of rain.

Mr. McMorn had turned on the gas fireplace, and Sarah dried in front of it while Jessica unlaced her soggy shoes.

"This way's the kitchen and a small eating space. The next two doors are the bedrooms and bath." Mr. McMorn led them into one room with a queen-size bed and a second room so small that the two twin beds and a tiny dresser filled it wall to wall. "The couch folds out in the main room."

"Perfect for Tim," his father said. Timothy thought of sofa beds with their metal bars and thin mattresses and sighed.

"Now I'll leave you to get settled and be back around seven to take you to dinner. There's a grocery down the street and a pharmacy."

"You've been so kind." Timothy's mother extended her hand.

"Not at all." And he gave the same stiff little bow. "I'll be happy to show you around a bit, whatever you'd like to see." His dark eyes lighted on Timothy. And Timothy flinched as if an insect had crawled across his skin.

✝ ✝ ✝

The Dog and Parrot was overflowing with customers. It was the first time Timothy had felt completely warm since arriving in Scotland. The damp, as his father said, seemed to settle into your bones. They pushed into a tall-ceilinged room with dark wood paneling and a polished bar that ran its length. A chalkboard displayed the daily specials: lentil sausage soup and fish and chips.

"Same special most days, but the food's reliably good," McMorn said. "Follow me; I think I see a table in the back."

"It's just like all those old jokes. A man came into a bar with a parrot . . ." quipped Mr. Maxwell.

Timothy followed his father's stare. There at the end of the bar was a man with bushy red sideburns and a bright green bird perched on his shoulder. It was busily grooming the man's facial hair and nibbling at his ear.

"Hamish McInturff. He's a bit of local color and half owner of this establishment." McMorn nodded.

"Why doesn't the bird just fly away?" Sarah asked.

"Hamish keeps his wings clipped. He's the pub's mascot, Wally, a green-cheeked Amazon. Named after William Wallace, a great hero of Scotland who helped drive the English out."

"Can the bird talk?" Jessica stood on tiptoe to see over the crowd.

"Sure. The bird's useful for bets on what he might say. And his wolf whistle's the terror of the ladies. But we'd best grab that table while it's still empty."

Timothy shouldered his way through the noisy crowd with Sarah and Jessica following. McMorn led them to a table in a far corner where nearby a rowdy group enjoyed a game of darts. The tables were picnic style with benches, and Jessica slid in on one side of Timothy, Sarah on the other.

"Well, this is wonderful! We're in a Scottish pub with a talking parrot." Mrs. Maxwell's eyes sparkled as she shrugged off her dripping raincoat. Timothy noticed she'd brought her travel guide with her and sighed. "I was hoping to take you up on your offer, Mr. McMorn—"

"Brian, please."

"Brian, then. I've been reading about Edinburgh Castle."

"Yes, the castle, our crown jewel. Every trip should begin with a visit to Edinburgh Castle. I can't accompany you, but I'd recommend you start there tomorrow. It's only a short walk through the gardens, and there are plenty of guides." A waitress came and took their orders for drinks. "Do you have any interest in any other particular locations?"

Again Timothy felt McMorn's gaze settle on his face, and it was as if a spiderweb brushed against his skin. He ran his fingers across his cheek to flick it off. Mr. McMorn smiled. Under the table, Jessica gave him a sharp little kick. Timothy shot her a glance from the corner of his eye. He wondered if she felt it, too.

"Perhaps the children have something special in mind?"

"I'd like to go on the Ferris wheel," Jessica said decisively.

"And ice-skating would be fun," Sarah added.

The girls, Timothy noticed, looked completely untroubled as they sipped their spiced cider.

"What about the German Market? What, exactly, is it?" Mrs. Maxwell asked.

McMorn nodded. "It's a collection of stalls set up on the Royal Mile—the streets of Old Town Edinburgh between the castle and Holyrood Palace—at Christmastime. Quite traditional, charming, and popular. We've a large German community here. And for another excursion I can recommend Wynde Alley, a lane filled with curious shops."

"I'm afraid I won't have that much time for sightseeing," Mr. Maxwell said. "We've got meetings tomorrow and—"

"That's all right, Arthur." Mrs. Maxwell patted his hand. "We know it's mostly work for you. I'd like to spend a little time painting, myself."

"Don't worry. Edinburgh's a safe enough city for the kids to wander, and I've a car if you decide to travel any distance," Mr. McMorn supplied.

Timothy thought of the map. He needed time alone with Sarah and Jessica. "We don't mind poking around on our own."

Mr. McMorn looked at Timothy down the length of his long nose. "No, I don't suppose you do. Now, who's brave enough for a taste of eel?"

✝ ✝ ✝

By 10:00 P.M., Timothy could hardly hold his eyes open. His parents had slipped off to bed, and from the other bedroom he could hear the girls chattering. As soon as the light clicked out in his parents' room, he gave a soft knock and staggered sleepily into the girls' room.

"I'm too tired to think about the map tonight." Sarah was already lying down, and he could see her wiggling her toes under the covers.

But Jessica sat up, pulling the blue blanket up to her chin. "There's something strange about Mr. McMorn. Didn't you feel it? When he looks at you, it's as if he's about to swallow you whole."

Timothy shuddered, picturing the serpent at the Travelers' Market unhinging its jaw. "Yeah, there's something off. When he looks at me, I can feel him on my skin like an insect."

"He seems perfectly nice to me," Sarah said. "Are you sure you're not just tired? I know I am." She yawned broadly. "Besides, Dad's known him for years. If we had the Greenman's leaf, we'd know for sure if we could trust him."

Timothy looked at the floor. The boards were worn. He wondered how many feet had walked across them over the years. Why did he feel so guilty whenever the girls mentioned the leaf? How could he have known what the magician's raven would do? Maybe he should have protected it better.

"We'll just have to rely on our instincts about who to trust, like everyone else. I'm sure we'll all make plenty of mistakes before this adventure's through." And Jessica slid down under the covers, but not before she caught Timothy's grateful smile.

# THE CASTLE

URING THE NIGHT, a stiff breeze swept the rain away, and long before Timothy was ready, the sun blazed into the small sitting room, waking him from a sound sleep. He propped himself up on one elbow and looked out the tall windows. Before him was a rain-washed city of old stone buildings with chimney pots balanced on every roof like top hats.

No one else in the flat was awake when Timothy reached into his backpack and pulled out the map. He half expected that unrolling it here in Scotland would change the map somehow, make the cipher clearer, but it was the same beautiful old map that he had unrolled in his bedroom with the same puzzling configuration of forest, fields, and coastline. He let his eyes roam over the Ogham symbols. They were still indecipherable. Before he could give the puzzle more thought, he heard stirring in his parents' bedroom. He quickly rerolled the map and slid it into its pouch in his pack.

"What a morning!" His mother stretched in her terry-cloth robe. "I think I found a little cereal in the cupboard for breakfast. We'll have to do some shopping today, but after we see the castle!" Humming, she padded into the kitchen and set a kettle of water to boil.

His father emerged already dressed in a button-down shirt and tie. "Sleep well, Tim? I'm off to the conference while you go exploring. McMorn's picking me up at eight." Timothy thought he looked a bit wistful.

"We'll find the good spots and take you back later. That way you won't have to waste your time on touristy stuff," Timothy said as he tied the laces on his sneakers. Sarah and Jessica were still locked in the bedroom they shared. He could hear them laughing and talking as they dressed. Outside, the sun was shining. If there were clues to be found, he wanted to get started. Why did girls always take so long to get ready?

✢ ✢ ✢

Timothy, Sarah, Jessica, and Mrs. Maxwell stopped at the end of Frederick Street and stared. There, like a crown set on a precipitous cliff, was Edinburgh Castle.

"It looks like it grew right out of the rock," Sarah exclaimed through the red scarf that wound over her chin and mouth.

"It's beautiful!" Jessica clicked her new digital camera, an early Christmas gift from her parents.

But Timothy said nothing. There were no words to explain what he felt. The castle set against a brilliant sky did look as if it had risen from the rocks beneath it. It was ancient yet alive right here in the middle of a bustling city. An icy gust blew up Frederick Street, and he plunged his hands deep into the pockets of his thick coat.

A breeze to snap banners, Timothy thought. In his mind's eye he saw them flying from the turrets, imagined guards shivering in the winter sun as they paced the rock walls. It was a fortress offering protection on all sides. Any enemy would be an easy target as they attempted to scale the rocky face. Timothy thought back to all the stories of knights and castles he had read when he was younger. This was so much better. It was a true *stronghold.* He mentally added up fifteen Scrabble points.

"Timothy!"

He hadn't noticed that the rest of them had crossed Princes Street, the crowded thoroughfare in the New Town of Edinburgh, where they were staying, while he was lost in his own imaginings. They were clustered around the statue of a soldier on a horse, a soldier with a tall, pompous-looking hat.

"The German Christmas Market's down at that end of the street. For the castle it seems we just have to cut through the gardens and then up the paths." Mrs. Maxwell hesitated. "Mr. McMorn didn't say quite how steep the paths were."

"Oh, come on, Mom. Just think of the views you can paint later." And, leading the way, Sarah struck out across the gardens toward Edinburgh Castle.

✛ ✛ ✛

By the time they reached the main gate, they were all winded. The paths wound steeply up the hill, eventually changing to a narrow, cobbled road.

"We enter by the portcullis gate," Mrs. Maxwell gasped as she tried to catch her breath and read from the guidebook at the same time.

The gate was narrow, and the path that led to it was flanked by tall stone walls. Timothy had expected a wider entrance, like he saw in movie castles, but this made much more sense. A narrow gate would be easier to defend. Two heavy outer doors, the portcullis itself, and a latticed gate that dropped down to sharp points added to the security of the castle. Timothy nodded with satisfaction. This was how a castle should be.

"Imagine riding up here on a horse," Jessica said. "The guards would probably watch you from the two little windows."

"Embrasures," Timothy said. "They're narrow slits to defend the castle. You can shoot arrows out through them, but it's difficult for an arrow to be shot back."

At the mention of arrows, Sarah squinted up at the windows. "You'd have a nice, clear shot" was all she said. Timothy smiled, remembering her wild shot that had sent him tumbling from Gwydon's back when the Wild Hunt rode.

The gates led to an open area that held an array of cannons. Black and shiny, they pointed north toward the sea. Directly ahead, a steep and winding stone staircase led to the upper parts of the castle.

"I think we need a tour guide to explain everything." Mrs. Maxwell was already walking to the information booth.

Inwardly Timothy groaned. There were few tourists in the chilly December wind, and it would be so much better to be alone and imagine the castle the way it used to be.

"Look over here! You can see the whole city!" Sarah, her red scarf flapping behind her, leaned over the worn stone wall.

"I think I can see our street!" Jessica snapped another photo.

Timothy sidled away from the girls. He didn't want to see the city as it was today; he wanted to imagine a fifteenth-century Edinburgh with rolling fields in the distance, small farms and forests marching toward the town.

"Luck is with us today—a tour starts in ten minutes, and it's free!" Mrs. Maxwell joined the girls looking out over the city. "Just imagine what this view would be like at sunset. We have to go up to the next level to meet our tour." She pointed at the narrow stone staircase winding up to the castle heights.

Timothy sprang ahead. The stairs, with no tourists in his view, looked just as they would have hundreds of years ago, the center of each step worn to a cradle by thousands of feet over the centuries.

At the summit were more cannons and a large cobbled square surrounded by buildings. There were tourists, too, but Timothy did his best to ignore them.

"A guide meets groups in the middle of the square. I suppose we just wait here." His mother read from the brochure in her hand, but Timothy wasn't listening. He was staring at the approaching figure of a tall man with floppy hair. The man was dressed in a blue plaid kilt and wore a dark blue beret. And in that moment, Timothy knew that they had come to the right place.

"If you'll gather around, ladies and gentlemen, I'm pleased to begin our tour here in Crown Square."

A few tourists began to wander in the direction of the tour guide's voice. Timothy opened his mouth, but before any words came out, the guide arched an eyebrow at him and gave a deliberate wink. Julian! Julian the reference librarian from home was here in Edinburgh as a tour guide?

Mrs. Maxwell and the girls, still chattering about the view from the castle, crowded next to Timothy.

"I don't believe it! Isn't that—"

Timothy gave Jessica a swift poke in the ribs, and she cut off her words in mid-sentence.

"I don't think he wants us to say anything," Timothy whispered into her ear. Her curls tickled his nose, and he couldn't help noticing that she smelled spicy, like cinnamon. He pulled back quickly and looked at his sister instead. Sarah, her cheeks red from the wind and eyes shining, beamed with excitement but managed to not say a word.

Julian began, "Crown Square served as the main courtyard for the castle. It dates from the fifteenth century and was built on the south-facing slopes of Castle Rock. The square is built on an artificial platform above a series of great stone vaults. It was originally known as Palace Yard but was renamed after the discovery of the Scottish Crown Jewels in 1818."

Then he walked to a large basket set on top of the wall. He lifted it with both hands, holding it up for the small group of tourists. "A basket on top of the wall was used to signal that the enemy was coming. Four baskets set together on the wall meant *the enemy was coming in force.*" And with those words he again looked right at Timothy. There was no mistaking his meaning, and he heard Jessica catch her breath by his side.

Timothy remembered the feeling of being sought out by the magician's raven in the school gym, and once again he felt exposed, as if the chill wind could strip away any sense of security. He realized he had missed the rest of what Julian had said, and he willed himself to focus.

"We are surrounded by the Scottish National War Memorial, the Great Hall, and the Royal Palace." Julian gestured toward each building as he spoke. "The Royal Palace is where the royal family would stay when they were in danger. They didn't like to stay there all the time, because the castle was extremely cold, so they usually stayed in Holyrood Palace, at the other end of the Royal Mile. The Royal Palace also contains the Honors of Scotland, which are the Scottish Crown Jewels"—and here he paused—"and *the Stone of Destiny.* It's also called the Telling Stone, because it identifies a true king."

Now he had Timothy's complete attention. Sarah's hand gripped his arm.

"The Scottish kings placed their feet on it during their coronation." Julian smiled benignly at the group. "But there's some controversy surrounding the stone, as you will see today." He turned sharply and led the group toward the Royal Palace.

Jessica clutched Timothy's other arm. "The Telling Stone. That must be your stone, the one you're supposed to find. But would we have to steal it from the palace to keep it from Balor?"

"If the stone's right there in the palace, why do we need a map?" Timothy wanted to hurry forward and perhaps get a word with Julian.

"It's too easy. I mean, if the stone has always been here, in plain view, then why didn't Balor and his friends take it long ago?" An anxious furrow creased Sarah's brow. "And did you hear what Julian said about the enemy coming in full force? I think he was warning us."

"Look, if we hang back here, we'll miss something. I'm going to try to get close enough to Julian to talk to him. You two distract Mom or do whatever you have to do to let me get a moment with him."

"We'd better hurry; they're going in the door." Jessica watched as the first of their group entered the arched doorway. "It doesn't look like much of a palace to me, at least not like one I'd like to live in."

The palace was symmetrical, made of the same rough stone as the rest of the castle. It had a square, crenellated edge on top like Timothy had made on sand castles when he was small. It looked solid and important, more like a fortress than a palace.

Mrs. Maxwell waited at the top of the steps. "Come on, we don't want to miss anything our guide has to say. He's awfully interesting, don't you think?"

"Yeah, he's interesting, all right," Timothy mumbled as his eyes slowly adjusted from the bright winter day to the dimmer world of the palace.

"It was here that Mary, Queen of Scots gave birth to her only child, James, in June 1566." Timothy listened impatiently as Julian led them through rooms of portraits and fireplaces, into Mary, Queen of Scots' chamber, heavy with dark painted wood carved with thistles. A wooden shield of two unicorns with the red lion hung between the beams. Every time Julian stopped to speak and point out more information, Timothy moved forward, attempting to start a quiet conversation, but it seemed as if Julian deliberately made it impossible to talk. He never again caught Timothy's eye and avoided any attempts at private conversation. Impatience gnawed at Timothy like a hungry animal. He couldn't look at one more room!

"Well, I wouldn't want to live in here; it's too cold and formal." Jessica squinted up at the ceiling. "I do like all the carvings, though."

"I can't believe we're just looking at all this stuff when the Stone of Destiny is somewhere here in the building!" said Timothy.

"It might not be your special stone. But then, why is Julian here?" Jessica puzzled.

"And why doesn't he hurry up?" Timothy strode ahead, peering into the next room.

Julian led them out a side door. Timothy couldn't hold back any longer. "What about the jewels and the coronation stone? When do we see them?"

Julian looked directly at Timothy, but it was as if he didn't now recognize Timothy at all. "If you'll follow me, young man, the Honors of Scotland and the Stone of Destiny are the next things that we'll be viewing."

Mrs. Maxwell looked over at Timothy. "I didn't realize you were so interested in history, Timothy. I knew this tour would be the right thing to do!"

# THE STONE OF DESTINY

**T**HE CROWN, SCEPTER, and sword looked exactly as Timothy imagined they should. *Regal,* he thought, a paltry six points for such an impressive word. Julian referred to them as the Honors of Scotland. Each was kept secure in a glass case. Unlike Timothy's simple gold crown with a single leaf, this crown looked like a true king's crown. It was a circlet of gold set with pearls. Four slender arches bore enameled oak leaves over a red velvet bonnet. The arches met at the top with a large gold and black cross. A white border of ermine edged the crown. He poked Sarah. "Look, it's ermine!"

Jessica compressed her lips, trying not to laugh, but it erupted in a snort.

Sarah narrowed her eyes at them both, and Mrs. Maxwell turned to look pointedly at all three.

Julian had already begun his lecture. "The first time the Honors of Scotland were all used together was for the coronation of Mary, Queen of Scots in 1543 and the last for the coronation of Charles II at Scone in 1651."

"Wasn't that Bloody Mary?" Sarah whispered.

"After the Treaty of Union in 1707, the Honors were no longer required and were locked away in a chest within the castle. There they lay undiscovered for over a hundred years, until Sir Walter Scott found them."

Timothy leaned forward until his nose almost touched the glass and imagined what it would be like to fight with such a magnificent sword. In the battle in the Travelers' Market, he had used a short sword and found that it was much more difficult to wield than it looked in the movies.

"And in this case"—Julian flicked a switch, and a rock the size and shape of a plump pillow sprang to view—"is the famous Stone of Destiny."

Timothy felt his mouth go dry. How could it be exposed like that, his missing stone on view for every tourist?

"It is encased in armored glass so that it is quite safe from any who would attempt to remove it." Julian paused and looked over the entire group, letting his eyes rest briefly on each of the children. "The stone has an intriguing history, which is tied closely to the history of Scotland. Let me tell you a story."

Timothy remembered Julian as he was in the Storyteller's tent, his eyes half closed and Gwydon at his feet. The tourists shuffled into comfortable positions and looked expectantly at the tour guide. At first, Timothy had trouble listening to Julian's words. His thoughts still whirled. If this was his stone, how was he, a twelve-year-old boy, supposed to collect it from its armored place? And why hadn't the Dark come for it long before?

"Timothy, pay attention. This is important," Sarah hissed in his ear.

"The Stone of Destiny is called the Lia Fáil. It came to notice in 503, when Saint Columba brought it to the magical Isle of Iona to be the coronation stone."

Timothy had read of Iona in stories about King Arthur. Some people believed Arthur was buried there, ready to return one day to rule England.

"It's difficult to say where the stone came from before that time. Many believe Ireland, and others say the Holy Land—that it was the stone where Jacob laid his head. It certainly does have the shape of a pillow."

"Or a very large loaf of bread," Jessica whispered into Timothy's ear.

"Legend says that the Stone of Destiny came from Ireland and that it cried out whenever a true king put his foot on it. When the Vikings came in 843, the stone was taken to Scone Abbey here in Scotland for safekeeping. For many years every Scottish king was crowned there.

"But in 1296, King Edward I's men stole the stone and took it to England. It was his way of saying that England ruled over Scotland and that Scotland's destiny would now be in English hands."

Timothy couldn't help himself. "Does the stone still cry out?"

Julian smiled. "A good question, young sir. It is said that the stone lost its voice when it left Scotland. But there are others who believe that *the stone never left Scotland at all.*"

Timothy could feel Julian's eyes burning into him as he continued.

"They say that the stone had no voice because the true Stone of Destiny never went to England. It was hidden by the monks of Scone Abbey as Edward's men approached and that the true stone is still in hiding today."

"Are you saying that this isn't the true coronation stone?" a heavy woman in a plaid coat asked indignantly.

"I'm merely sharing the stories surrounding the stone. Fast-forward to Christmas Day 1950. Before dawn, in the gray hours, while most of the country slept, four young Scots broke into Westminster Abbey and stole the coronation stone, all three hundred and thirty-six pounds of it."

"I've heard about that." A man leaning against the far wall spoke up. His girlfriend lounged next to him, examining her fingernails. "They brought it back to Scotland. Imagine stealing it right out of Westminster Abbey—heroes in my book!"

Again Julian smiled his long, thin smile. "Many Scots feel that way. The four allegedly hid it in the boot of their getaway car and sped toward the Scottish border."

"The boot's the trunk," Mrs. Maxwell leaned over and whispered.

"We know," said Sarah.

"Four months later, the stone was found at Arbroath Abbey, draped in a Scottish flag. It had become a political symbol of Scottish independence. After the patriots had made their point, the stone was returned to England and remained there until November 1996, when it was returned to Scotland. And on Saint Andrew's Day it was placed here, at Edinburgh Castle."

"Is there any evidence that this is a fake stone?" The heavy woman furrowed her brow. "Of course, the crying-out part is all a load of nonsense."

Julian took a moment before answering. "The stone you see here is made of sandstone. There's much sandstone near Scone Abbey. There's no record of what the original stone was made of. As for crying out, the world is full of truths we do not always understand. But now, if you will follow me, we will proceed to Saint Margaret's Chapel, the oldest building in the castle."

The three children fell to the back of the group.

"Did you notice he was looking right at us when he said that monks hid the stone?" Jessica's cheeks were flushed, and her eyes were bright.

"But if it's a story everyone knows," Timothy protested, "why wouldn't it have been found before now?"

"Maybe the stone is waiting for the right person—you know, like the sword in King Arthur's stone." Sarah stuck her hands into her pockets as they left the palace. Outside, the wind scoured the castle mound.

Jessica pulled up her hood. "He's giving us a message, Timothy. I'm sure of it. We just need to get him alone to find out what it is."

✚ ✚ ✚

The chapel was a small irregular stone building that looked nothing like any church Timothy had ever seen. It was only about ten feet wide, the size of a small bedroom. Julian explained it was the oldest building in Edinburgh.

Timothy moved to the very front of the group, hoping to catch Julian's eye, to have a chance to speak with him privately. Behind Julian, a small stained-glass window sparkled in shades of blue. It depicted a young woman with two long blond braids. Timothy stared hard; it was as if his sister, Sarah, had modeled for the window.

"In 1314, thirty men climbed the north face of the cliffs to capture the castle. The castle had never been taken by a direct assault against its gates. It was taken then, by surprise at night, *when an attack was least expected.*" Julian's gaze again rested on Timothy. And again, Timothy felt as if he were being warned. He looked at the other tourists in the group, his heart pounding. But their faces gave away nothing.

Julian led the group back outside. Timothy realized that he had fallen to the back of the crowd. While Julian thanked the tourists, Timothy pushed forward. The lady in the plaid coat grabbed Julian's arm and kept talking as Julian walked back toward the gatehouse.

"Excuse me!" Timothy interrupted.

Julian looked at his watch. "I'm sorry." He moved the woman's arm away from his and nodded toward Timothy. "I've got to meet another tour."

"But—" Timothy's objection was whipped back in the wind.

"He can't just walk away like that!" Jessica stood with her hands on her hips, chin thrust forward.

"Maybe he told us everything we need to know," said Sarah. "Something's going to happen when we least expect it."

Timothy was afraid she was right.

Mrs. Maxwell called to them from the edge of a small walled yard. "Over here."

"It's a dog cemetery!" Sarah cried, reading the sign. "Soldiers can still bury their dogs here. See? Some of the headstones show carvings of the dogs." Stone steps led down to a pocket-size grass lawn surrounded by a horseshoe of headstones. "It says that this is for regimental mascots and officers' dogs." She knelt in front of the headstones, reading off the names of faithful hounds.

But Timothy looked over the stone wall. The little cemetery hung out over the cliff of the castle mound. Two hundred sixty feet down, he thought. At least he had paid attention to something Julian said. How had the army scaled this cliff to take the castle by surprise? How would *they* be taken by surprise?

"It's time for the firing of the cannon," Mrs. Maxwell called. "We'll have lunch, and then this afternoon I'm going into the gardens to paint. I'm not sure I want you going off on your own . . ." She hesitated.

Timothy knew she was torn. "It's the middle of the afternoon. We'll be fine."

He followed her up the steps, hoping his words sounded more convincing than they felt to him.

# THE CARTOGRAPHER'S SHOP

**A**FTER A STOP for shortbread that they munched as they walked, Timothy, Sarah, and Jessica made their way down the Royal Mile, passing shop windows decorated with Christmas garlands and twinkling lights.

"Julian said the real Telling Stone might still be hidden in Scotland," Timothy mused aloud. Every few yards he looked back over his shoulder. Now every face seemed sinister. Every footfall a threat. Jessica matched his stride. "We need to find out about Scone Abbey."

"At least we're all together." Sarah linked arms with Timothy and Jessica. Overhead, two crows cawed from a rooftop.

A group of girls, their faces partially concealed by scarves, walked toward them. Timothy's heart accelerated, but the group passed by without a glance. He took a few deep breaths. He'd go crazy if he suspected everyone.

Sarah pressed her nose against the window of a bookstore. "This is the most Christmassy place I've ever seen. It feels like we're in a Dickens novel, even if we're not in England."

"Especially in the alleys." Jessica disappeared into the narrow gap between two buildings. "It's a city of alleys and stairs." The alley led them to a steep bank of stairs past the back of a butcher's shop, where two men in white aprons sat talking.

Timothy and Sarah followed her up the short flight of steps and paused on a landing that opened into two alleyways, one leading right and the other left. "If we keep the Ferris wheel and the castle mound in view, we can't get lost. Which way?" Jessica pointed to the two alleys. Timothy read aloud, "Milne's Court and Wynde Alley."

"Wynde Alley!" exclaimed Jessica. "McMorn said that was a lane of unusual shops!"

Timothy let his eyes explore the narrow passage as far as he could see. The cobbled lane was deeply shadowed by the stone buildings that stood guard on either side. Shops were announced by old-fashioned swinging wooden signs.

"Okay," Timothy said. "But we can't just shop. We need to go over everything Julian said about the stone."

"It *is* only three days till Christmas. I have to do a little shopping." Jessica offered Timothy a piece of shortbread. "I could live on this."

With the wind as their escort, they started down the alley. The upper stories of buildings leaned so far into the lane that the blue December sky became a narrow river above them.

"Look. It's a milliner." Sarah stopped in front of a wavy window.

"A what?" Timothy, did a mental search but couldn't find a meaning for *milliner.*

"A hatter."

Hats of every shape and size filled the window. A wide-brimmed hat of peacock blue with a green feather balanced next to a yellow hat that looked like a turban with a great red brooch. Cream-colored gloves and a paisley red parasol completed the display. "Maybe we should go in here, just for a minute." Sarah looked hopefully at Jessica and Timothy. Jessica already had her hand on the brass doorknob.

"You can if you want. I'm not going to waste my time. After all, we didn't come to Edinburgh to shop!" Timothy stuffed his hands into his pockets. Was he the only one who registered why they had likely come to Scotland in the first place?

A bold gust of wind almost made him reconsider. Wynde Alley funneled the draft between the buildings. He trudged a few yards farther, keeping close to the sides of the buildings. A striped cat appeared out of nowhere. Timothy started. It hurried past with a prize in its mouth, a limp mouse. There were few people on the street. Everyone, Timothy thought, must be sitting inside some pub near a fire. That would be tons better than a hat shop.

Dry leaves skittered along the cobbles. When he checked over his shoulder for the girls, Timothy saw that the alley was now deserted. He would go around the next bend to see what was ahead and then go back and drag the girls out if he had to.

Light glowed from a lower window. A wooden sign and handsome gold lettering across the window proclaimed SEABORG CARTOGRAPHERS. A map shop! Timothy cupped his hands by his eyes and peered into the tiniest workshop he had ever seen. Every nook and cranny was filled with rolled papers, paints, and inks. Maps papered the walls, draped the tables, and were rolled and stuffed above the heavy timbers at the ceiling. The long worktable was cluttered with ink bottles, brushes, and pens. In one corner a deep green enameled stove squatted like a benign monster with a fire in its belly.

In the middle of the chaos, two people worked. An angular woman with thin silver glasses perched on the tip of her beaked nose sat at the table, painting. Close to the stove, a bald-headed man overflowed a rocking chair as he read. There was something so peaceful about the scene that Timothy hesitated before turning the iron doorknob and walking in.

"May we help you?" The man stood, carefully marking his place in his book. His hands, Timothy noticed, were neat and small, much too small for a man of his size. His bald head was a terrain of veins, just like roads on a map. The man stood looking at Timothy with a quizzical expression.

"I, ah, saw your store, and I love maps." Timothy couldn't think of anything else to say, but the man smiled, and the woman replied without looking up from her work.

"Then you've come to the right place. We illuminate maps, sell maps, trade maps." Her fine silver hair was held back with a tortoise-shell clip. Her face was lined and creased, marked by faded freckles, but her ink-stained fingers worked deftly.

"Enjoy a look round, then. I'm Newton Seaborg, and this is my wife, Maggie. We've owned this shop for thirty years."

"That's Maggie for Magdalene." She centered a magnifying glass on a stand over a section of work. "I'm the illuminator. He's the historian."

Timothy felt as if he had stepped inside the cabin of a boat. Every inch of space was used efficiently, from the wooden shelves that ran to the ceiling to built-in cupboards and benches. Cupboards and doors closed with elaborate iron hinges. Even the polished wood walls were used to display dozens of intricate maps. He moved closer to the warmth of the stove. Mrs. Seaborg continued her work with the finest of brushes.

"These are the historical maps." Mr. Seaborg gestured to one side of the room. "The oldest go back to the 1500s, and, of course, they're kept behind glass."

Timothy looked up at the framed maps, and his heart gave a small excited shuffle. This was the kind of place where he might be able to find out more about *his* map!

"These are the newer maps and the ones clients have asked to have illuminated." Newton pointed out brilliantly colored maps with intricate borders, tall-masted sailing ships, and a variety of sea monsters. "Maggie's workmanship." Bottles of ink, stands of brushes, and fine-nibbed pens lined a wooden shelf below. Not a single space in the tiny shop was unused. Not a single corner was square.

"I didn't know anyone illustrated maps anymore."

"Well, I do. See this brush?" Maggie held it aloft in her speckled hand. "Made from a single mouse whisker."

Timothy gaped. He wanted to ask how they'd gotten the whisker from the mouse. "Some people want to have their maps personalized with a family crest. Or look here." Maggie motioned to Timothy. A tall-masted ship sailed across the bottom of a map bordered with hounds and hunting horns. "The name on the ship is the name of my client's own ship. And these are his hounds. He's an eccentric breeder of hunting dogs. John Ahearn."

Timothy looked closely at the running dogs and gripped the edge of the long table. The memory of the Wild Hunt rushed back. "Did you say *Herne*?"

"*A*hearn," Maggie corrected. "Why, do you know him?" She tucked a silver strand of hair behind her ear.

"I, ah, I know a Herne, and he hunts." Timothy pictured the rider and his great, slavering hounds. He recalled the dogs' red eyes. How they had once chased him as their prey. The hounds on this map were brown and gold, a running pack. When he looked closely, he could see more than a tumble of hounds. There was prey as well: torn rabbits, felled stags. A few of the dogs bared long teeth. Timothy drew back. "It's probably not the same person, Herne and your Mr. Ahearn."

"I'd be happy to bet you on that."

"Excuse me?" Timothy was sure he must have misheard her.

"I said, I'd be happy to make a wager."

"Maggie's a betting woman." Mr. Seaborg beamed. "Why, she'll bet on just about anything. Isn't much I haven't lost to her at one time or another." He chuckled. Timothy noticed that Newton Seaborg's feet in shiny brown loafers were as small and neat as his hands.

"Betting keeps life interesting. This Ahearn fellow, he lives in the Lake District in the north of England. He has a hunting lodge there." Maggie talked around a thin brush held in the corner of her mouth. It wiggled up and down as she spoke.

This time Timothy's shiver had nothing to do with the cold. The conversation was slipping away in directions he hadn't intended.

"How do you read an old map, one without a legend?" Timothy needed to keep the conversation going in the direction of his map, the one that even now was rolled and hidden safely between his shoulder blades, buried deep in his backpack.

"Take a look here." Newton Seaborg directed Timothy to the back wall, where dozens of framed maps patchworked the paneling. He tapped the glass with a manicured finger. "Not all maps have legends. Legends are absent from the oldest maps. When they exist, they generally only state the differences in the size of towns and tell whether they're fortified or not. Later, large abbeys were added, but really complete legends only go back to the beginning of the nineteenth century."

He reached up to one of the low beams and pulled out a roll of paper tied with a blue ribbon. "This is a copy of a very old map." He swept books and papers to one end of a table, making room.

Three large islands, pink, gold, and green, floated in a blue sea. Two sailing ships rode the waves. "A map of the British Isles by Abraham Ortelius. It was made in the late 1500s. Ortelius was a very famous Belgian cartographer, one of the best. Now notice, the directions are not what we'd expect today. North is oriented to the right."

Timothy tilted his head. Now the location of the islands made sense. He'd thought that north was always in the same place on maps.

"Here's another by him, a bit older and an original." He tapped a handsome map in a gilt frame right above Timothy's head. "A beauty. This one is just of Scotland."

Timothy read aloud, "1584, Scotiae Tabula."

"North is oriented to the right on this one also. It's hand-colored, a very valuable map. Maps that are colored close to the time they're made are called 'contemporary color,' and it makes them more rare and valuable." His marble eyes opened wide for emphasis.

Timothy was thinking about how to work in a question about his map. "So, if a map isn't labeled, and there's no legend, how do you know what it shows?"

Mr. Seaborg carefully replaced the map of the British Isles. "Well, now, that's a puzzle, isn't it? It's rare that a map not be labeled or have a legend, but there are other clues you can look for—coastlines, for instance, and geographical features. If you know how old it is, that helps. 'Course, old maps are full of distortion, the scale's usually off, and there's little triangulation." He ran a hand over his bald head. "Is there a particular map you have in mind?"

Timothy wanted to tell Mr. Seaborg about his map, but he remembered Mr. Twig's warning and hesitated. If only he still had the Greenman's leaf. "I saw a map once and I never could figure out what it pictured. It had some odd markings on it, too. And it was illuminated," he added, glancing over at Maggie Seaborg.

She had paused in her work, listening. Light glinted off her glasses, making her eyes invisible.

"Odd markings? Could be another language. I'd have to see it, or some expert would. How old did you say it was?" asked Mr. Seaborg.

"I didn't, but I think it's very old."

"Most maps like that would belong to collectors, extremely valuable. Where did you see it?" One of the veins in Mr. Seaborg's head began to throb.

Timothy looked away. He'd gotten himself stuck. Mr. Seaborg was a map historian. Of course he'd be interested in the location of a rare and valuable map. He could dodge the question, pretend he didn't hear. "A friend in America said he thought the map might have a cipher."

Mr. Seaborg's eyes lost their intensity. He blinked and rested one hip against the long table. "There are a thousand stories of map ciphers, most of them false. Most times people think they've found a treasure map with a hidden code." He giggled. "Not to say there are no map ciphers; it's just that they're very, very rare. Would you like a cup of tea?" He plugged in an electric kettle that seemed out of place in the antiquated shop.

Timothy nodded. "Thank you."

"These strange markings—what do they look like?" Maggie Seaborg was still looking at him, now over the top of her silver-rimmed glasses. "Can you draw them for me?" She handed Timothy one of the fine-tipped pens and a scrap of paper.

Timothy could picture some of the Ogham script. Hesitantly, he drew two of the symbols as best he could remember them.

"I see." Mrs. Seaborg pressed her lips together. "What you have drawn looks very much like an old alphabet called Ogham, young man, but not quite. And you still haven't said where you came across this map."

Timothy squirmed. Mrs. Seaborg wasn't someone who was easily distracted. The teakettle's shrill whistle made him jump. Everything in the room seemed to be waiting, listening.

The silver bell on the inside of the door jangled. A burst of brisk air saved Timothy from answering. Sarah and Jessica, cheeks bright with cold, clattered into the shop.

"We looked everywhere for you! I should have known you'd be in here." Jessica held a very large bag.

"Oh, look at all the maps!" Sarah stood in the middle of the room, turning in every direction.

"I suppose I should get more cups." Mr. Seaborg opened one of the finely milled cupboards and paused with his head still buried inside. "Of course, there was the map of Saint Brendan's Island." His voice was muffled. He straightened, two more teacups in hand. "Now, that was a map cipher." He poured the boiling water over a strainer of loose tea leaves into a large china teapot.

Sarah's eyebrows shot up. "Map cipher?"

"It was believed for a time that the Irish monk Brendan sailed to an island in the North Atlantic. The location of the island was a secret to all but the holiest of men, so the map showing the location of the island was drawn as a cipher. The cartographer used geographical markings as a code. Of course, there was never a real island, which was discovered after another group of monks spent a long time decoding the cipher and setting sail. All this talk of Ogham put me in mind of it."

"What kind of a code?" Timothy looked at Jessica from the corner of his eye. He could see that she was listening carefully.

"Trees. I believe it had something to do with trees."

"Are you sure about that?" Maggie stretched her thin arms over her head. "Are you sure it was trees, Newton? We could make a small bet—my earrings for your last hairs?"

"Now, Maggie." Newton Seaborg ran his hand over the three or four hairs left on his bald head.

Maggie Seaborg swiveled on her stool toward Timothy. "I can read

Ogham. I had an Irish grandmother. Not that you *do* have that map with the funny symbols, I bet."

"Ah, here we go." Newton Seaborg deftly poured the fragrant tea into a cup for each of them.

*She knows Ogham,* Timothy thought, and *Mr. Seaborg knows about old maps. Maybe it's a sign. If only I had my leaf!*

# CODE CRACKING

**B**ACK IN THE apartment, Timothy, Sarah, and Jessica crowded into the smaller bedroom. Timothy had the map unrolled even before hats and gloves were off.

"North isn't always to the north," said Timothy.

"And trees can be important. The one cipher Newton Seaborg mentioned had something to do with trees." Jessica pulled off one mitten with her teeth.

Sarah looked closely at the trees. "The bare trees aren't all the same. Look, some of them have more branches than the others; you almost need a magnifying glass to really tell."

Timothy gazed out the window as he tried to make sense of everything he had heard and seen at the Seaborgs' shop. But Sarah's observation about the trees caught his attention. He'd been so absorbed trying to figure out the general terrain, he hadn't paid much attention to individual features. "How many trees are there?"

"Just a minute." Jessica counted under her breath. "Forty-eight, why?"

Timothy rummaged through his backpack for paper and a pencil. "Let's see how many of each kind."

"Some have lots of branches, and here are two with only two branches on each side."

Sarah began to point out the small differences among the forty-eight trees.

Timothy drew one of each type on his paper and then wrote a number under each tree, signifying how many of each appeared on the map. "We know that *e* is the most common letter in English."

"How do you know this is English?" Jessica frowned.

"We have to start somewhere." Right in the middle between "some" and "where," Timothy's voice did something strange. It sounded as if the word was cut in half by a band saw. One part of the word went up and one part down. Startled, Timothy looked at Sarah and Jessica out of the corner of his eye and wondered if they had noticed.

"What was that? That funny thing your voice just did?" Sarah stared at her brother.

Timothy wanted to shrink into the map. "I don't—"

"Maybe your voice is changing. It happens to boys," Jessica said.

Jessica sounded much too smug, Timothy decided. "I just got something caught in my throat. Can we get back to the map? As I was saying, *e* is the most common letter in English. So, we look for a symbol that's repeated a lot. Next we look for two-letter words. Two trees together. In two-letter words, the second letter in the word is usually *o, s, f,* or *n.*"

"*On, if, we, is, as,*" Jessica muttered. "*We* has an *e* as the second letter."

"And these three trees clustered together are the same three clustered together over here!" Sarah pointed to identical combinations of three trees.

🌲🌲🌲

"Quit talking. I need to think." And once again Timothy's voice betrayed him. What if this was going to happen all the time now?

"Hormones," said Sarah without looking up from the paper where she was scribbling.

Timothy kicked her in the shin. Things might have deteriorated further if Mrs. Maxwell hadn't chosen that minute to come through the door.

"Tonight's the Scottish dance concert, remember?" Mrs. Maxwell was humming as she unzipped her parka and dropped her bag of painting supplies onto the floor. "I haven't had such a good day painting in, well, I don't remember when! But I was worried about the three of you the whole time. What happened to checking in with me?"

"I guess we were distracted," Timothy muttered.

"We went to a hat store." Jessica drew a bright blue beret from her shopping bag and set it on her curls, which gave Timothy time to slide the map under a pillow.

"And some of us ate shortbread until we could hardly walk." Sarah looked pointedly at Timothy and Jessica.

"One reason you have a cell phone is so you can keep it turned on and answer when I call you." Mrs. Maxwell stared at each of them in turn. "Otherwise, you won't be going out on your own. Understood?"

They nodded.

"The concert's at seven. Your father should be home any time now. Should I heat up some soup?"

The last thing Timothy wanted to do that night was go to a concert of Scottish dancing. Now that he suspected the trees might contain a code, all he wanted to do was work on cracking it. He looked at Sarah and Jessica. Jessica looked just as disappointed as he felt.

Sarah followed her mother into the kitchen.

"I don't want to go to the concert. Do you?" Timothy asked Jessica in a hushed voice.

She looked at Timothy from under her blue cap. "I want to ride the Ferris wheel."

"Okay, let me see what I can do, as long as we can work on the map, too."

It took some advanced negotiation techniques. By the time Mr. Maxwell arrived home and the soup was finished, Timothy and Jessica had the promise of an evening at the German Market and riding the Ferris wheel if they texted every half hour.

"But you have to promise that you won't go ice-skating without me." Sarah didn't look completely happy about the arrangement, but she wasn't willing to give up the dance concert, either.

"Okay, no ice-skating until tomorrow when we can all go." Timothy could hardly wait to be off.

"I hope Mr. McMorn won't be disappointed that we're not all going. It was awfully nice of him to offer to take us," Mrs. Maxwell worried.

"He didn't buy the tickets yet. I'm sure he'll understand that dance concerts aren't to everyone's taste." His father looked, Timothy thought, as if he would rather go to the German Market and ride the Ferris wheel, too. "I almost forgot." Mr. Maxwell thumped the side of his head. "We've been invited to the home of a colleague of mine for Christmas Eve supper. Nessa Daring. She's a botanist who studies plant adaptation to climate change."

"Interesting." Mrs. Maxwell cleared the dishes. "Everyone's working so hard to make us feel at home, but I don't know anything about botany."

"Don't worry. Nessa always has something interesting to talk about."

⊹ ⊹ ⊹

Edinburgh's night was strewn with lights. Everything was illuminated, from the giant Christmas tree on the castle mound to the twinkling colored lights strung across busy Princes Street. The sky was clear and the air bitter cold. The fiery wheel dominated the city, making everything festive.

"It's the tallest Ferris wheel I've ever seen! And we're going to ride it," Jessica said smugly. She was still wearing her blue beret, and a wool scarf with silver threads was wound around her neck.

"I've been working on the code. We've got two four-letter repeated words and two two-letter repeated words. So I plugged in some word possibilities." He shifted his shoulders. It would be better if he didn't have to wear his backpack everywhere he went, but it was the only inconspicuous way to keep the map with him.

Jessica wasn't listening. "Look at all the market stalls."

Stalls lined Princes Street Gardens, and people of all ages filled the streets. Normally, Timothy would want to explore, but now it was a distraction from the tree code.

"Christmas ornaments! I should get some new ones for my mother, since we started decorating again this year."

"Are you paying attention to anything I said?"

Jessica looked at Timothy. "How often do you get to be at a German Christmas Market in Scotland with one of the biggest Ferris wheels in the world just down the street?"

Timothy's frustration rose like a balloon. "Don't you remember that someone broke into our house? We have to find the coronation stone, soon. All of us. That's the reason we wanted you to come, too."

"That's the only reason?" Jessica turned to look Timothy straight in the eye.

Her cheeks were red with the cold, and so was the tip of her nose. She was so close that Timothy could see flecks of amber in her hazel eyes and a tiny white scar right above her left eyebrow. And for the first time he noticed that he was looking at her eye to eye. For some strange reason he felt dizzy. Nice, two *z*'s, twenty-seven points, he thought, if only Scrabble had two *z*'s!

"I said, is that the only reason?" Her voice was sharp, like the old Jessica, the one who had tormented Timothy at school.

"Why else?"

"You're an idiot!" Jessica's eyes had narrowed to slits, and Timothy thought of a cat about to pounce.

Things were not going as he had planned. He had imagined they would find a warm place to sit and work out the map puzzle, solve it between the two of them, and then ride the Ferris wheel in celebration. Now Jessica was being completely unreasonable. He wasn't sure what to do. "I didn't mean to be rude. It's just that we've got a chance now to figure this out, and I thought—"

"The problem is you think too much, all the time. Sometimes you need to have fun. Here, let me show you something. But first I want some cider." She grabbed Timothy's arm and dragged him toward one of the stalls selling bratwurst and hot cider. Jessica bought two ciders and a sausage, and then they hunted through the crowd for a bench.

The hot cider burned his tongue, but the sausage was magnificent, juicy and spicy. "Want a bite?"

"No. Give me some paper," Jessica said.

Timothy rummaged through his pack and brought out a piece of very crumpled paper and a mechanical pencil.

"Let's start with the short words, two or three letters. That should make it easier," Jessica said. "I've copied down the trees, so we can work on the code. If it is a code."

Timothy looked at Jessica in surprise. He didn't know that she paid much attention to cracking codes.

"The short words are usually articles like *an* or *the* or prepositions, right?"

Timothy stared at her. "Yeah."

"You're not the only smart one, Timothy James Maxwell. I just may know more about grammar than you do. Look, these two groups of three trees are exactly the same. "So it could be *and* or *the* or *out* or—"

"There are too many three-letter words." Timothy cut her off. "There aren't as many two-letter words, especially ones that are used frequently. Maybe we should start there, with the two two-letter words we found."

Jessica nibbled a strand of hair. "*On, in, an, to, go* . . . Seems like there are lots of two-letter words, too."

"Okay. Look. These three words all start with the same letter." Timothy pointed to two of the three-letter words and one of the two-letter words.

Jessica interrupted. "Did you know that *the* is one of the most common words in English? Let's just pretend the word is *the*, then the two-letter word would—"

"Have to start with *t*, making it *to*!"

"I'm going to write it down, just in case." In a small neat hand Jessica wrote the words on the scrap of paper. "But what about this group of trees? There are nine trees in the group!"

Timothy shook his head. "I don't know. The only letter that matches is the last letter in the word, an *e*. But that's all we know right now."

"I can't take this anymore! Let's try again tonight with Sarah. I'm cold, and I want to ride the Ferris wheel, even if you don't." Jessica folded up the piece of paper and put it in her pocket. She pulled the mittens back on and, without turning around, headed in the direction of the lighted wheel.

Reluctantly, Timothy put the paper with the copy of the tree code in his bag. "Okay, okay. I'm coming."

# COMPASS POINTS

IFTY-FIVE DEGREES, FIFTY-FIVE minutes north; three degrees, ten minutes west. The latitude and longitude placed Electra in Edinburgh. What she would witness here, she did not know, but already forces were gathering in this northern city. As the year turned toward the time of greatest darkness, the struggle between Light and Dark always intensified. Each year the Dark hoped to quell the coming of the Light. Now it was mid-winter's day, the shortest and darkest day of the year. This far north, the sun set very early by human time, four o'clock. But the revelers in Edinburgh's Winter Wonderland seemed not to notice. They shopped and ate, ice-skated and rode the giant blazing wheel.

As she watched the crowds of merrymakers, there were three things that she knew. The first was that the boy and the one-eyed man were both here, somewhere in the crowd of people. The boy was closer—she was sure of it. And the third thing was that she must not intervene. The affairs of humans were only to be witnessed. And there was something else, a restlessness in the air, as if the night itself were stirring.

✢ ✢ ✢

"How long have we been waiting?" Timothy looked at his watch.

"Oh, stop complaining. I bet we'll get on in the next seating." Jessica craned her neck to look up at the descending gondolas. They had been waiting an awfully long time. But the wheel was slowing, and, sure enough, people were being helped out. "Come on, Timothy, it's our turn!"

But Timothy wasn't paying any attention to Jessica or the Ferris wheel. He was standing with his mouth wide open, and he was staring at a girl.

"Come on!" The words had barely slipped from her mouth when Jessica, too, was shocked into silence.

"It's Star Girl. We've got to talk to her!" Timothy said.

The star girl was winding her way down the platform, clad only in a long blue dress; even in the bitter cold her arms and feet were bare. Her long silvery hair reflected the wheel's thousand lights. As if she heard them, she looked right in their direction.

"Star!" Timothy called out.

"Please step into the gondola." The attendant took Timothy by the arm.

"Hurry up!" A little girl behind them gave Timothy a shove.

"There's nothing we can do now. She's seen us, and she'll wait." Jessica grabbed Timothy's other arm and hustled him on board.

They were the only two in their gondola. And as the Ferris wheel lurched into motion, both Timothy and Jessica leaned over to wave at Star Girl.

"Wait for us!" Timothy called out.

Electra solemnly nodded.

"This is so amazing!" Jessica looked out over the German Market into the vast night sky. "What do you think she's doing here?"

"I don't know, but it's another sign that we're in the right place after all."

"Maybe she'll know something about the map." Jessica hugged herself against the cold.

Now that he was sure Star Girl would be waiting for them, Timothy relaxed. It was amazing, riding a giant Ferris wheel in Scotland right before Christmas with Jessica. Timothy stole a look at her. Jessica was leaning out as far she could, looking below and chattering about the people skating on the ice rink. Timothy wasn't really paying attention to anything she said, but he liked the sound of her voice and noticed that when she was very cold, her cheeks flushed red, just like when she was very excited.

The dark silhouette of Edinburgh Castle loomed above them. A copper moon floated above its pointed towers and buttresses, while wisps of cloud passed like a tattered flag.

"It looks like it could be right out of stories of King Arthur and the Knights of the Round Table." Jessica looked at Timothy. "If I look down at the stalls below, I can imagine myself at the Travelers' Market again."

"Me, too." Timothy recalled the bright wagons and stalls of the merchants in the Market between worlds, the friends he had made there, and, with a shiver, the terrible battle fought there. "Sometimes it seems like something that happened to someone else, like the map is something I brought back from a dream." Timothy's words surprised him; he wasn't used to sharing confidences with anyone but Sarah.

"I know. And I was never more frightened than when you left and Sarah was turned into an ermine. I thought everything depended on me and that I would make a mess of it all."

The wheel had reached its apex. Below, the night city glowed, and beyond the city a sprinkling of lights faded into vast darkness. The gondola rocked gently, a small world suspended between earth and sky.

"But you didn't mess up. You found Cerridwyn, and you healed people. Lots of people wouldn't have survived without you."

"I remember you riding in on Gwydon, wearing the crown and playing those pipes and looking absolutely terrified." Jessica laughed, and the fragile connection between them was broken.

"Yeah, well, I guess I did look pretty funny." Timothy's voice squeaked again, but instead of being embarrassed, he laughed with Jessica. "And now I sound just like those crazy pipes I tried to play."

"You didn't look funny at all. In fact, I thought you looked kind of glorious."

Timothy had never been called *glorious* before, and certainly not by a girl. He liked the sound of the word, the way it made him think of battles and honor and knights. At the same time he wasn't quite sure if Jessica was mocking him. He slipped a sideways glance in her direction, but she was looking up into the sky, lips slightly parted, and from her expression he had no way of telling at all.

# A HORN IN THE NIGHT

UST AS SHE HAD PROMISED, Electra was waiting at the base of the Ferris wheel. As quickly as possible, Timothy and Jessica made their way toward the slender girl. Timothy noticed that most people who passed her stared at her in disbelief, and many gave her a wide berth.

She waited until Timothy and Jessica were almost to her side and then moved quickly into the crowd. They followed her closely. She stopped only when they had reached the edge of the carnival rides, where darker alleyways joined with Princes Street and the shadows were thicker.

"Can we go inside somewhere? I'm just about to freeze to death!" Jessica's teeth actually chattered in her head.

"Looks like there's a pub down there." Timothy pointed down a side alley where a rectangle of light spilled onto the dark street. Now he led the way, with both Star Girl and Jessica close behind.

The Lovely Lady was a neighborhood pub, out of the main tourist center but crowded with locals, families, and kids. Timothy and Jessica both ordered hot ciders while Star Girl waited at a small table in a corner.

"Star, why are you here? Is something important about to happen?"

"I have come to witness, and where I am called, I go," she said simply.

"Are any of the others here—Gwydon or Cerridwyn?" Jessica continued.

"*He* is here."

"Do you mean the Greenman?" Timothy asked hopefully.

"Balor of the one eye is here, and others are gathering as the darkness grows."

The warmth of the pub faded as if all the light, chatter, and cheer had been sucked out with the name of Balor. He was like a black hole, Timothy thought, sucking everything good into oblivion. "He's *here*?"

Electra nodded. "During these days, when the darkness prevails, he is bold. There is always a battle as the year dies. I have seen many before, and there will be many more between now and the end of time."

How much could he tell Star Girl? She saw everything, but did she take sides? He didn't know. Telling her about the map would be a risk, but with Balor so close, it was one he was willing to take.

"Mr. Twig gave us a map with a puzzle."

Eyes wide and lips parted, Jessica shot him a look across the table.

"And they came looking for it." Electra's voice was calm and sure.

"Yeah, they did. There's a code in the map, and we have some of the letters, but not enough."

Jessica's face was pinched with worry now. "Timothy, I don't think we should—"

"Every map is a picture of a place in one particular time. Coastlines and boundaries change with time. Only the points of the compass are constant: north, south, east, and west," Electra added.

"But this map doesn't have any compass points. We were just getting a few more letters. Here." Timothy pulled the creased sheet of paper from his backpack, checked to make sure that nobody was seated nearby, and smoothed it on the table. He stared at the rows of trees, the few words he and Jessica had managed to decipher.

Electra was silent.

Wasn't she going to offer anything else? Maybe Jessica was right. He never should have shown her.

"Look!" Jessica's voice was loud with excitement, and people at other tables began to glance in their direction. She dropped her tone to a whisper. "Here are a few more letters we missed!"

She carefully wrote, *a-ainst the* - - - - -

"Against the something!" Timothy's voice cracked again, but this time he didn't pause.

"If there is no compass, something else must be used to show direction." Electra gazed serenely over the crowd.

"And this word must be *stones!*" Timothy filled in the letters they knew.

"But what about stones?" Jessica asked.

Electra stood abruptly. "Listen, do you hear it?"

"What?" Jessica asked.

"A hunting horn. The battle is about to begin."

"I don't hear anything!" Timothy checked his watch. "We have to meet my parents and Sarah in ten minutes!"

Jessica looked toward the door. Timothy followed her glance.

A tall man with golden curls walked in. His clothes were strangely formal: a dark vest and jacket, a silver-tipped cane. On his arm was an elegant woman with auburn hair piled high on her head. People turned to stare.

Timothy's heart pounded in his ears. His hands turned to ice. He would know that man anywhere! Balor was here, in the pub!

"Come on, we have to get out of here!" Timothy looked at Jessica. Her face was pale and her eyes wide in alarm. He stood, snatched up the paper, and, rounding the table, grabbed her by the arm. "There has to be a back way out."

Electra calmly stood, blocking Timothy and Jessica from Balor's view.

Timothy dragged Jessica to the back of the pub, toward the kitchen and restrooms, down a dark, narrow hall. He yanked open the first door beyond the bathrooms. A storage closet.

"Hurry!" he hissed.

Jessica kept turning to look over her shoulder.

Timothy grabbed her hand. It was slick with sweat.

There was one last door at the end of the hall. Timothy turned the knob. The door remained firmly closed. He could hear Jessica breathing behind him. Dropping her hand, he pulled at the door with both of his. The door gave. Stuck, not locked. Cold air bit his face as he dragged Jessica out onto the street. He took great, gulping lungfuls of air, as if he had been submerged.

Without speaking, Jessica held out her hand. Hers, too, was trembling. Timothy gripped it, and they ran, dashing through the dark side street, back toward the lights of the German Market. Timothy looked for the castle to get his bearings. His parents and Sarah would be waiting for them on the corner near the gardens. Next to him, Jessica's breath came in gasps.

Once they were on the main street surrounded by people and lights, Timothy slowed. Still without speaking they dodged between revelers, toward their meeting point. Timothy could see his parents and Sarah waiting on the corner.

Jessica broke the silence. "Do you think he saw us?"

"I don't think so, but I don't know for sure. I think Electra blocked us from view."

"But she doesn't take sides! She just observes, doesn't she?" Jessica asked.

"How was the Ferris wheel?" Mr. Maxwell strode forward to meet them. Timothy thought he saw a flash of envy in his father's eyes.

Sarah followed and linked her arm through Timothy's. "The dancing was great. Not at all like the Celtic dancers I've seen in the States. Why are you breathing so hard?"

Before Timothy could answer, his mother cut in.

"But poor Mr. McMorn had to leave in the middle of it. Some kind of family emergency." Mrs. Maxwell shook her head. "After he arranged for the outing and everything,"

"Let's not stand here talking in the cold. I'm ready to call it a night." Mr. Maxwell glanced at the sky. "The clouds seem to be gathering. Could be we'll see some of that rare Edinburgh snow."

✛ ✛ ✛

As soon as possible, Timothy, Sarah, and Jessica rendezvoused in the small bedroom. Timothy and Jessica interrupted each other as they described their encounter with Electra, seeing Balor, and the small progress they had made on the code.

That night Timothy slept with the map beside him under the covers. He didn't sleep well. In his dreams, he saw the Greenman, unable to move, frozen, while all around him the town of Edinburgh burned. But the fire was not hot; it was a freezing cold burn that caused buildings to explode and people to die in the streets.

# ICE STORM, DECEMBER 23

WHEN TIMOTHY AWOKE, he found that his covers were in a heap on the floor and he was curled into a small shivering ball in the middle of the lumpy sofa bed. He grabbed the blanket from the floor and wrapped himself in it. Then he looked out the window. The magic of what he saw hurt his eyes. Outside, the rare Edinburgh snow had not arrived. Instead, the world was coated in ice. It was a strangely beautiful and silent world. Every tree and light post glittered under a cold sun.

He watched as a red-faced man across the street tried to make his way down his walk. He stepped forward cautiously, one step, two, and then his legs flew up, and he was on his back like a beetle, legs and arms waving in the air. Farther down the street, a young woman bundled in a blue parka fared a little better. Hand over gloved hand, she pulled herself out to the street along the iron railing in front of her building.

"Looks like an ice storm!" Mr. Maxwell had come into the room so quietly, Timothy hadn't realized he was there. "And a doozy! We had them like this when your mother and I lived in the Midwest. Cars used to pile up in underpasses. They'd slide down and have no way to get themselves out." He rubbed his hands together. "Wonder if there's something wrong with the heat."

Mrs. Maxwell came out of the bedroom, yawning. "The radio says that there are car wrecks all over town and that no one should try to drive. Isn't the heat working? I'm going to make us some tea."

"Lucky there weren't any meetings today. Too close to Christmas, I guess." Mr. Maxwell stretched. "I'm going to take a look at the radiator."

Timothy had a sinking feeling in his stomach, heavy as wet cement. He remembered Electra's words: "The battle is about to begin." The ice storm paralyzing the city felt sinister, menacing. As if it had a purpose. "Won't the sun melt off the ice?"

"It's not supposed to get above freezing today," his mother called cheerfully from the kitchen. "It's beautiful out, don't you think? And we don't have to go anywhere."

But Timothy wasn't so sure. He was determined to return to the map store today, no matter what the weather.

✛ ✚ ✛

By midday the heat still wasn't working. Power outages were reported all over town. Mrs. Maxwell, wearing two sweaters and a stocking cap, hummed as she painted the view from the living room window. Sarah, Jessica, and Mr. Maxwell sat at the kitchen table with mugs of hot tea, heated on the gas stove. They played cards while Timothy tried to read. But his mind wouldn't stay with his latest sci-fi novel. The radio had reported that some stores and restaurants were open for business, and he wondered if Seaborg Cartographers was one of them. The temperature inched up slowly, and road crews had managed to salt the glittering streets. He dropped the book onto the floor and walked to the window.

"Goodness, Timothy, you're restless. You usually love having time to read." His mother frowned at her watercolor pad. "It's harder to capture winter light than one might imagine. Here, Timothy. Bring me another cup of tea, will you?"

He looked over Sarah's shoulder at her hand of cards, whispered a suggestion into her ear, and went to heat water on the gas stove.

"If only the place was heated with gas, we'd be set." Mr. Maxwell slammed his hand triumphantly on the table. "Nerts!"

"Not again! You've won two in a row! I admit defeat!" Sarah gathered up her cards.

The doorbell rang. "Who'd be out in this?" Mr. Maxwell rose from the table, but Timothy ran down the stairs and beat him to the door.

Mr. McMorn stood on the step, wrapped in a long wool coat, his arms full of shopping bags. His eyes raked Timothy's face, and a deeper cold forced its way into the room.

"McMorn, come in!" Mr. Maxwell spoke from over Timothy's shoulder.

Timothy led Mr. McMorn up to the main room.

"I worried you wouldn't have supplies to ride this weather out." He dropped the bags of groceries onto the kitchen table.

"That's so kind of you, Brian." Mrs. Maxwell wiped her hand across her face, leaving a streak of carmine red on her nose.

"Here, let me get that." Mr. McMorn reached into his pocket, pulled out a large white handkerchief, and wiped the paint away. Timothy's muscles tensed.

"I hope your family's okay." Mrs. Maxwell offered their visitor a steaming mug. "I was sorry you had to leave the dance recital."

Mr. McMorn undid the buttons on his coat. "Just my sister in a spot of bother." He reached for the mug and held it between both hands.

"I didn't know you had a sister in town. Have a seat. How'd you manage to get here?" Mr. Maxwell scooped the rest of the cards off the table, and Sarah slipped them back into the pack.

"You just have to go carefully. For those who don't know the right roads, it can be treacherous." He smiled at Timothy. Again Timothy felt the strange sensation of something crawling across his face. He brushed his cheek, and McMorn's smile widened. "I wouldn't recommend that any of you try going out."

"I was just thinking that I needed to finish up my Christmas shopping. I've seen people out walking," Jessica said.

Timothy was startled to find her standing by his side. He hadn't suspected she was thinking of anything but cards.

"I'm not sure that would be the best idea." McMorn turned his gaze to Jessica, and Timothy thought he saw something flicker in the tall man's eyes; it reminded him of a fish swimming just below the surface, a flash, and then it disappeared into the depths.

"Brian is right. I don't like the idea of you going out in dangerous conditions alone." Mrs. Maxwell frowned at Timothy and Jessica.

Surprisingly, his father took Jessica's side. "We appreciate your help and concern, McMorn, but we have ice storms in the U.S., too. And I'd agree with you about driving, but it's likely just slow going on foot."

Mr. McMorn's eyes glittered, but he merely shrugged. "I also want to extend an invitation for Christmas Eve." He spoke to them all but looked at Mrs. Maxwell with one eyebrow cocked appealingly.

"Oh, we've already accepted an invitation," she said.

"Nessa Daring's invited us for dinner," Mr. Maxwell added.

Again Timothy thought something almost swam to the surface of McMorn's eyes.

"Nessa Daring. She's rather odd—a fine colleague, knows her subject, but a bit eccentric . . ." McMorn let his voice trail off. His gaze circled the room. Timothy noticed Sarah brush a hand across her cheek. "Well, happy to see you're surviving the ice storm. Perhaps you'll consider spending some time with me on Boxing Day—that's what we call the day after Christmas. Oh, I've brought a few treats along as well." He handed a plump bag to Sarah. "Happy early Christmas to you." He stood, pulled on his leather gloves, and began buttoning his coat.

When the door closed, amid a chorus of thanks, Mr. Maxwell shrugged. "Sometimes he seems like a mother hen. Thinks we can't manage without him."

"Arthur, he's so kind! Just look at these groceries." Mrs. Maxwell began unpacking the bags. "And he's right. The kids need to stay in, where we know they're safe."

"What did he give you?" Timothy and Jessica had crowded around Sarah.

"A package of macaroons and some Scottish fudge to share. They're from some famous sweet shop."

"Macaroons! I love coconut!" Jessica began to peel open the package.

"Speaking of Christmas presents, Nessa gave me something for the three of you. I almost forgot."

"Mom, we need to go out. We still have presents to get. We'll be careful. Besides, we'll have our cell phones with us." Timothy tried to sound convincing.

"Lizzie, I think it's perfectly safe if they stay together. There won't be much traffic." Mr. Maxwell looked at his wife.

Timothy could hardly believe his ears. His dad hardly ever disagreed with his mom when it came to letting them go places.

"We *will* be careful." Jessica brushed macaroon crumbs from her pants. "We can check in every hour if you want."

Mrs. Maxwell crossed and then uncrossed her arms. She looked at Mr. Maxwell. "No more than two hours."

Timothy looked at his dad.

"You heard your mother."

All three hurried to get their coats before Mr. and Mrs. Maxwell could change their minds.

⊢ ⊹ ⊢

Walking was harder than it looked. Every step forward felt like two steps backward. Even the slightest incline was treacherous. Sarah laughed and clutched Jessica's arm as she slid, which sent Jessica straight into Timothy. They landed in a heap as they rounded the corner from Frederick onto Princes Street. At least here the street and sidewalk had been properly sanded. Stores were open, and the smell of food made Timothy's stomach growl. He carefully untangled himself from the two girls and rubbed his backside. Six arms and six legs could get hopelessly entwined, and somehow he always ended up on the bottom.

"It's going to be difficult on the stairs to Wynde Alley. I bet the sun can hardly peek between the buildings," Sarah said. "We'll just go slowly and—"

*Whomp!* Jessica's feet flew up, her mouth opened in a startled O, and her blue beret skittered across the pavement.

Timothy dove for the hat just as a boy a few years older barreled out of a shop door and sent Timothy sprawling sideways.

"Sorry, mate. Here, let me help you." He hooked an arm through Jessica's and lifted her to her feet.

Jessica beamed at him.

Timothy, beret in hand, was forced to scuttle sideways like a crab before he regained his footing. "Here's your hat, Jess."

She shot out one hand to grab the beret, never taking her gaze from the tall, ginger-haired boy at her side. "Thanks for rescuing me."

"Damsels in distress are my specialty, especially ones with big hazel eyes. My name's Tam."

Jessica giggled. "I'm Jessica, and these are my friends, Sarah and Timothy."

Timothy glared and then extended his hand. Sarah smiled.

"Americans, by the sound of it. Sorry to plow you over, but I'm in a bit of a rush. Spending the holidays in Edinburgh?"

"Our father's here for a conference, and we got to come along." Sarah folded her tourist guide and put it in her pocket.

Tam beamed as if the news delighted him. "Well, I've lived here my whole life and am an excellent tour guide. Why don't you give me your phone number? I'd be happy to show you around sometime."

Timothy was about to say that they were managing quite well by themselves when he saw Jessica pull out paper and a pencil from her purse.

"Here's my cell number. We'd love a tour."

"We've already seen the castle and ridden the wheel," Timothy interjected.

Tam laughed and adjusted the black wool scarf around his neck. "I know places you won't find in the guidebooks." He took the folded paper from Jessica's hand and put it in the breast pocket of his overcoat. "I'll keep it close to my heart, so I don't forget." He winked an amber eye. "Off to work, I go." And he ambled sure-footedly up Princes Street.

"I think he likes you, Jess." Sarah smiled. "We'd better get going before we all freeze."

Timothy didn't say a word.

# THE MAP AND
# THE HILL

A S SARAH PREDICTED, the steps to Wynde Alley were painfully slow going. An iron handrail set into the brick wall was the only thing that made the climb possible at all. They walked single file, each gripping the rail, with Sarah in the lead.

"There's no one out. I don't think the map store will even be open," Jessica said.

"Then why didn't you just stay in the apartment?" Timothy asked the back of Jessica's head.

Jessica shot Timothy a frown over her shoulder.

The going wasn't much easier on Wynde Alley. Sure enough, the sun hadn't yet looked in on the narrow, cobbled lane. Most shades were drawn, and as Timothy peered down the glittering alley, he worried that Jessica might be right. They might have made their way there for no reason.

"I feel like we're going into a tunnel. It's so dark." Sarah linked arms with Timothy. "Why don't we all walk together. We can hold each other up."

Jessica grabbed Timothy's other arm. He didn't look at her. It did feel better going down the alley together, even if they likely wouldn't do much good holding one another up. The crooked buildings loomed above them, shutting out most of the sky. Windows were shuttered; the milliner's was dark and closed up tight. But near the end of the alley, a faint light gleamed onto the ice-frosted cobbles. Timothy's shoulders relaxed; someone was in the cartographers' shop.

A small CLOSED sign hung on the door, and a shade was draped like a heavy eyelid across the large window, but a smaller window in the door shone with light.

"Now what?" Sarah asked.

"We knock anyway. We didn't slide all the way here for nothing." Jessica rapped on the wooden door. No one responded.

"I know they're in there!" Timothy, balancing on tiptoe, pressed his face to the glass just as the door swung open, and he tumbled in.

"We're closed." Then, as he recognized the threesome, Mr. Seaborg's tone changed. "Well, well, out skating on the streets. I guess you'd better come in and get warm."

Timothy picked himself up off the threshold, while Jessica and Sarah stepped past him into the warm shop.

Maggie Seaborg was perched on her stool, putting the finishing touches on a map. Today silver chopsticks held her white hair in a mound on top of her head. "What brings you out in all this ice? Must be something important."

"It is." Timothy unzipped his backpack and carefully removed the leather pouch.

Sarah caught her breath. "Are you sure—?"

Timothy gave a brief nod. "I've brought a map to show you. It's the one we were talking about the last time we were here. I was able to figure out—"

Here Jessica glared at him.

"Jessica and I," Timothy corrected himself, "were able to figure out a code that's written on the map. A tree code."

Mr. Seaborg had advanced, rubbing his hands in anticipation. If he had been a dog, Timothy thought, his entire body would have been wagging.

"The map with the colored illuminations?"

Timothy pulled out the cylinder containing the map and walked over to the long table where Maggie Seaborg worked. Without a word she moved pens and bottles of ink, clearing room for Timothy to unroll his treasure. Sarah and Jessica gathered close.

Timothy could hear Mr. Seaborg's intake of breath as the map unfurled. In the warm light of the cartographers' shop, the jeweled tones glistened deep and rich. Maggie peered intently through her silver spectacles, then tapped a cluster of bare trees with one blunt finger. "That's the code right there. I'd bet on it."

"It's fantastic. A marvel." Mr. Seaborg was chortling. "One of the best I've seen."

Then, in a hushed voice, Maggie Seaborg spoke in a language Timothy didn't recognize.

*"Cinnidh Scuit saor am fine,*
*Mar breug am faistine:*
*Far am faig hear an lia fáil,*
*Dlighe flaitheas do ghab hail."*

"What does that mean?" Sarah's eyes widened.

Maggie touched the Ogham running along the illuminated border.

*"The race of the free Scots shall flourish,*
*if this prediction is not false:*
*wherever the Stone of Destiny is found,*
*they shall prevail by the right of Heaven.*
*Except old seers do feign,*
*and wizard wits be blind,*
*the Scots in place must reign*
*where they this Stone shall find."*

She paused, then said, "I've heard that prediction since I was a child." She lowered her glasses. "You're looking for the coronation stone, are you? Who gave you this map?"

Jessica's glance flew to Timothy.

But it was Sarah who spoke up. "A friend in America gave it to us."

"Not just any friend, I'd wager," Maggie responded. Then she looked at her husband. Something passed between them, and she nodded. "It's a Pont's map. Drawn in the 1500s. North is to the east. Timothy Pont's maps are the oldest recorded maps of Scotland. Extremely valuable, but this one, well, this one is unlike any other. Look over there."

Mr. Seaborg led them to the back of the shop, where a few maps were in gilt frames. "Pont's maps, but notice that none of these are illuminated."

Timothy stared at the maps. They had the same intricate lines but none of the strange flowers or animals, no border of Ogham, no tree code.

"Yours is a Pont's map that has been illuminated, and a cipher added as well, for a special purpose," said Mr. Seaborg.

Maggie stood and drew a shade to cover the window in the door.

"It's a good thing you came here. A map like this shouldn't be shown to just anyone." Mr. Seaborg looked sternly at Timothy. "I suspect that there is much more to the story." Then he cleared his throat. "Maggie knows more about the legend of the Stone of Destiny than just about anyone. And I, well, I can tell you where this section of land is located." He removed one of the maps from the wall and carried it into better light. "There are similar features." His finger traced a river and then pointed to a hill. "Dunsinane."

Maggie shuddered a sigh. Timothy noticed that her eyes sparkled wetly. "So, it's Dunsinane Hill, Macbeth's land. And not far from Scone." She shook her head.

"Macbeth?" Sarah asked. "The one from Shakespeare?"

"Aye, he was real, all right. Had a castle on Dunsinane Hill in the Iron Age. Only a bit of rubble and a few walls remain. It's about an hour and a half from here. But the coronation stone's story begins long before Macbeth was king."

"So, this map is of a part of Scotland only an hour and a half from here?" Timothy felt as if he were shouting.

"That's right, son. See here?" Mr. Seaborg pointed to a river. "Scone Abbey was here by the bend in the river. Someone left out or removed all the labels, but it's as plain as plain can be to someone who has eyes to see."

"Why do you have this map?" Maggie Seaborg stood so close to Timothy that he could smell the tea on her breath. Involuntarily, he backed away. "Didn't steal it, did you?" Her eyes glittered.

"Like my sister said, a friend gave it to us for safekeeping."

"That's not the whole story. Why you?"

"Because I, ah, because—" Timothy felt like a beetle pinned to a board, and he began to squirm.

"Because," Jessica broke in, "we are supposed to find the Stone of Destiny." Her words dropped into the small shop like a rock might drop into a pond. Timothy could almost see the ripples traveling through the room.

Maggie Seaborg lunged toward Timothy. He swung sideways, but her thin arms were quick. She grabbed his head between her hands and kissed him on the forehead. Instantly, the tension in the room dissipated. "Oh, you sweet, sweet boy. It *is* you! You've come at last." And then she burst into tears.

Jessica relaxed her hands, which had balled instinctively to fists. Sarah looked from one Seaborg to another, her blue eyes saucers of surprise. Timothy stood frozen, his heart still racing, his legs still ready for flight.

"What does that mean, 'You've come at last?'" Sarah asked.

"Legends say that the Stone of Destiny will be returned. I believe you're the one to do it." Maggie looked at Timothy.

"Maggie's family have been Scots nationalists for hundreds of years," Mr. Seaborg explained. "In fact, her brother, Brian, was one of the four involved in stealing the stone from Westminster Abbey in 1950 and bringing it back to Scotland. Of course, it wasn't the real stone, not the Stone of Destiny; everyone just thought it was."

"You never could tell a story straight from beginning to end," Maggie said, wiping her eyes.

"We've heard some of the story at the castle," Jessica said. "We heard about it being stolen. That was your brother?"

Maggie nodded, now beaming wetly. "Brian was always the impulsive one, ready to take a risk. But it was the political statement that stealing the stone would make that he cared about." Her spare shoulders hunched. "We've always known it wasn't the real stone at all."

"The castle tour guide said the real one may have been hidden by monks."

"Scone Abbey was here." Mr. Seaborg again pointed to the bend in the river. "Scone was the ancient crowning place of the Scottish kings, on Moot Hill. If they hid it anywhere, it would have to be near."

"And what about the tree code?" Maggie asked.

"We're working on it." Timothy, his heart returning to its normal patter, was still reluctant to reveal what the code said.

"That's all right. You be cautious. But there are four other words in Ogham you should know: *cauldron, sword, spear,* and *stone.*" Maggie pointed to the four words.

"Those are the same as the pictures on the map!" Sarah exclaimed.

Jessica shot her a dark look.

Sarah lowered her voice to a whisper. "And they're the same ones Mr. Twig said Balor is looking for."

"Yes, and I'd wager you'll need them all."

✛ ✛ ✛

All the slippery way back to Frederick Street, Timothy was quiet. The map of Dunsinane on the Seaborgs' wall had given him an idea. If he was right, they would be much closer to solving the code. As soon as they were back in the flat, he pulled the girls into their bedroom and unrolled the map.

"Timothy, what do you know?" Sarah watched her little brother silently count trees.

"Look." Timothy bent low over the map, tapping the group of nine bare trees near the top of the map. "This last letter"—he pointed to the last tree in the group—"is the same as the last letter here and here." He pointed to the trees they had marked as spelling *the*. "An *e*." Then he smiled.

the            the

"So, what nine-letter words do you know that end in an *e*?" Jessica asked.

Timothy kept smiling.

Jessica pinched him. "What do you know?"

"Dunsinane. Remember the map on Seaborg's wall, when he told us this map is of Dunsinane, too? I saw how the name was spelled. It has nine letters and ends in an *e*."

"How can you be sure it's spelled that way?"

Timothy hesitated. "I can still see the way it's spelled in my mind. I think this word with the nine letters is Dunsinane." He wrote out each of the letters.

"If you're right, that will give us a lot more letters."

They worked together, taking each of the letters from *Dunsinane* and filling them in where they found identical trees.

"Okay, here's what we have so far." Timothy read the clue aloud, putting in blanks where they didn't know the letters.

On Dunsinane

Against the - - - - -

-u--ed stones to the - - a - -


"We have to climb Dunsinane," Sarah said. "We'll have to find someone to take us there."

"If Star Girl was right," Timothy said, "the code will have to give us some directions, since there is no compass."

Jessica squealed. "*Clock!* Against the *clock!* I remembered what Star Girl said. 'If there is no compass, something else must show direction.' I think it means we go counterclockwise!"

✛ ✛ ✛

A sharp rap on the door was followed by a whistle. Maggie Seaborg put the last strokes on a hunting hound and stood stiffly, her back tight after spending hours hunched over her work. There could be only one visitor now as this extraordinary day waned. Her brother stood on the icy step.

"Come in, Brian. The children were already here. Let me get you something warm." She moved slowly to the simmering teapot.

"It was a Pont's map," Newton Seaborg told his brother-in-law. Brian was taller and darker than Maggie, but the family resemblance was there: strong cheekbones, nose as sharp as an eagle's beak, spare frame, sinewy arms. You could always tell a McMorn.

# CHRISTMAS EVE

NESSA ĐARING'S HOUSE was buried in the woods. As the Maxwells and Jessica drove down the narrow lane in a rented car, the branches of giant elms touched overhead as if they were joining twiggy hands in a game of London Bridge.

"I expect it's lovely in the summertime, all leafy and green," Mrs. Maxwell said from the front seat. "But it's awfully isolated. I wouldn't feel safe out here all by myself."

Mr. Maxwell grunted in agreement. "And we may have trouble getting out of here tonight. This road can't be too good in snow."

A thick, flannel blanket of cloud had moved in to cover the moon. The weatherman on the car radio warned of snow.

"I like it all tucked away in the woods," said Sarah, who was tucked in herself between Jessica and her brother. "It reminds me of a cottage in a fairy tale."

Nessa Daring's house did look like an illustration from a fairy story. The roof was thick with thatch and the windows heavy lidded, as if sleepy eyes were looking out on the world. Knobbly skeletons of climb-ing roses framed a bright blue door. A tangled garden surrounded the house, and a large willow leaned like a friendly neighbor over the back-yard fence. "Look, there's even smoke coming out of the chimney!"

"Nessa's an interesting woman. She knows more about local lore than just about anyone," said Mr. Maxwell. "Her family's been here for generations, but she's traveled all over the world. She told me she'd break out all the Scots traditions for us. Might be some other guests, too."

But only Nessa's ancient white Morris Minor was in the yard when they arrived. As they waited on the step, arms filled with presents and loaves of Mrs. Maxwell's Christmas bread and cake, Jessica nudged Timothy. "There's rowan over the door." He looked up; a cluster of rowan berries hung from a bright red ribbon.

The woman who opened the door was tall and straight with bright blue eyes set deeply above a patrician nose. Her short black hair was streaked with gray, and her earlobes winked with rubies. She was not at all what Timothy expected a botanist to be.

"Welcome to my home! I'm delighted you came to spend Sowans Nicht with me." She ushered them into a small entryway. Sarah looked at Timothy and raised her eyebrows in a question. He shook his head. He had never heard of Sowans Nicht.

After Timothy's father made introductions, Nessa led them through the entry to the heart of the house. The family gasped with surprise. They stood in an expansive room with a polished floor and open rafters lit by a myriad of candles. Swags of greenery were tied to the beams with bright plaid ribbons. Every wall, every nook and cranny displayed some type of art: eccentric masks, finely woven baskets, fabrics, photographs, even musical instruments. The room was a museum, Timothy thought. But museums were usually only for looking at things from a polite distance. This room was definitely lived in. At one end of the open room stood a massive stone fireplace. A copper cauldron hung over a fire, while just beyond, an island separated the living space from a very modern kitchen. Double French doors led out to the garden.

"I know it's a bit of a contradiction, but I decided that having a traditional exterior didn't mean I should live without a comfortable interior. One large living area suits me best. I've got a little sleeping loft beyond the kitchen, and there's a guest room down the hall. Other than that, it's one big room." Nessa laughed, a surprisingly deep laugh. "I like to display finds from my travels, but I still keep to many of the traditional ways. That's a rowan log in the fire, traditional at Christmastime. And we're having a trifle for dessert. There's nothing more traditional than that on Christmas Eve in Scotland, unless it's a whisky toddy." She moved to fix drinks for the adults while the family stood taking in the eclectic mix of the room. "We'll eat as soon as my nephew arrives. He's single, and holidays can get a bit lonely for us singletons."

Timothy stood in front of a display of masks, each wooden face more gruesome than the last.

"Pretty, aren't they?" Nessa stood by his side, offering a cup of spiced cider. "They're African, designed to keep away evil spirits." She dropped her voice so only Timothy could hear. "But we know that it takes more than masks to keep the Dark at bay, don't we?"

Startled, Timothy searched her face, but her expression was blank. Still, her words about the Dark made Timothy's breath quicken. Nessa moved on to offer Sarah, who was examining a tapestry, a cup of cider.

"Just a replica of part of a very famous unicorn collection."

"You're a surprising woman, Nessa. I didn't know you had quite so many anthropological interests." Mr. Maxwell, his face rosy from both the firelight and the toddy, stood in the middle of the room, looking from wall to wall.

"Did you think I studied only plants, Arthur? 'This world is as wild as an old wives' tale,' and I don't want to miss any of it." She chuckled again. "That's from a poem by G. K. Chesterton, by the way. Do you know him?" She looked at Timothy.

He shook his head, his glasses winking in the firelight.

"Well, you should. He had a number of important things to say, especially in his fairy stories."

"Important things in fairy tales?" Jessica looked skeptical.

"Very important, my dear. I'm surprised a bright girl like you hasn't figured that out already. But I'm being a poor hostess. I should offer you all some smoked salmon and crackers. Smoked by my nephew himself."

As if on cue, the heavy front door opened, and a tall man wrapped in a long woolen coat and several bright scarves stomped across the threshold. A pair of brown eyes were the only visible part of his face. Crystals of snow clung to his dark coat and sparkled on his flannel cap.

"It's beginning to snow, Aunt Nessa!"

The voice was instantly recognizable. Timothy, Jessica, and Sarah each turned to watch Julian unwrap himself from the tangle of scarves. Then he unbuttoned his coat. A green kilt crossed with black and gold topped a pair of legs covered in long socks of the same design. Julian smiled at the open mouths. "I break out the family tartan on special occasions."

"MacArthur on my mother's side." Nessa beamed. "From the Isle of Skye. The clan were pipers to the MacDonalds, a hereditary position."

From behind came a clattering of toenails on the wood floor. Gwydon, his fur speckled with snow, padded into the room.

"I hope no one's allergic to dogs," Julian said.

Timothy, his heart thudding with joy, wanted to run forward and grab the great dog in a hug, but he glanced at his parents and then at Nessa.

His mother beamed. "What a beautiful animal!"

"His name is Gwydon, after one of our legendary shape-shifters."

A small squeal escaped from Sarah as she hurried forward and buried her face in Gwydon's fur.

Nessa gathered up Julian's wet coat and scarves. "And this is my nephew, Julian. A true Renaissance man—librarian, storyteller, historian, tour guide extraordinaire!"

Mrs. Maxwell was staring at the gangly man in the entryway, a thin line deepening between her brows. "You look so familiar. Have we met?"

Julian smiled. "I believe I was your tour guide at Edinburgh Castle."

"That's it!" And the room relaxed into introductions, while Gwydon, overcome by petting and chatter, retreated to the warmth of the fireplace and lay, head on paws, watching the party unfold.

Timothy's mind began to whir. It was wonderful to be with Gwydon and Julian again. But their presence could mean only that something was brewing. He remembered Electra's comment that a battle was about to begin. Here were his old friends and allies gathered in one place, a place not far from where the legendary Telling Stone might be hidden. He looked closely at Nessa. She was handing around a plate of food while talking with his mother about South American art. Her ruby earrings glittered in the firelight. "If you'll come to the table, we'll start with sowans. It's a traditional Christmas Eve dish in the region. I hope you don't mind that I've assigned you places at the table." Nessa herded her guests to the table in the manner a goose herder directed a gaggle of geese. He watched Nessa even more closely now, a slow assurance building.

Timothy found his name card, placed between Jessica and Julian.

"O'Daly is the family name, isn't it? Irish, but with ties to Scotland." Nessa looked at Mrs. Maxwell.

"Well, yes, however did you know?" And then she turned to her husband.

"Nessa asked me a while back if we had any Celtic ancestry in the family. I'm surprised she remembered."

"Oh, the name O'Daly has quite a bit of fame associated with it. They're part of a hereditary line of poets. Muiredach O'Daly, a renowned bard and Filidh, fled Ireland after a fight with a chief of the O'Donnells, who demanded he pay taxes. Poets never did pay taxes. He fled to Scotland, I believe, after splitting the poor fellow's head in two with a battle-axe."

Jessica pinched Timothy's leg under the table.

"My goodness, you know more about my heritage than I do." Mrs. Maxwell wrinkled her nose. "I had no idea there was such a dramatic and violent story associated with the name."

"Dramatic, yes, and part of a much longer story. But let me tell you about the sowans." Nessa ladeled bowls with a substance that looked very much like oatmeal. Oatmeal was not what Timothy was expecting for Christmas Eve dinner, but he was too excited about the mention of Muiredach O'Daly, the Filidh armed with a battle-axe, to complain.

"Sowans is made from oat husks and fine meal steeped in water. It's about as traditional a Scottish food as you can find. Don't worry; the whole dinner won't be porridge."

Timothy took a bite. It tasted like unsweetened oatmeal, and he was glad the portions were small.

"And, in keeping with tradition, as I said, that's a rowan log in the hearth. The Christmas Eve fire signifies that any bad feelings between friends or relatives have been put aside for Yuletide. A nice tradition, don't you think?"

"Lovely. Perhaps it should be done more than once a year." Mrs. Maxwell took a small bite of the sowans. "But I can see why the sowans is saved for special occasions."

Mr. Maxwell shot his wife a look. "And what about all these candles, Nessa? We burn candles in the States, too, of course, but usually not so many at once. And I can't say I've ever had oatmeal at Christmas."

Nessa scooped the last of her sowans from the bowl, wiped her lips with a red cloth napkin, and looked directly at Mr. Maxwell. "The candles are to hold back the Dark, Arthur. People seem to have forgotten that. On Christmas Day the Light comes into the world. On Christmas Eve, the Dark makes one last-ditch effort to win."

✝ ✝ ✝

Timothy didn't remember most of the rest of the meal. There had been salmon his parents exclaimed over, vegetables, breads, and potatoes, but all the while a spring had been winding tighter and tighter in his chest. It took every ounce of concentration just to remain in his chair. Ever since Nessa had mentioned the Dark, Timothy knew with a heavy certainty that the Dark was out there, just beyond the cottage walls, waiting. While the rest of his family talked and laughed, he pushed his food around on his plate, stealing looks at Sarah across the table and at Jessica by his side. He noticed that Jessica had gone pale and quiet at the mention of the Dark, but Julian on his other side was loquacious, a word Timothy admired, entertaining them all with the funny stories of a tour guide. Gwydon remained peacefully sleeping by the fire, and his presence offered Timothy some comfort against his growing fear.

When everyone had pushed back their chairs and exclaimed over the festive dinner, Nessa rose and stood at the head of the table.

"And now for my trifle and the lovely Christmas cake you brought."

Mrs. Maxwell rose to help Nessa bring in the desserts, and Gwydon wandered from his place by the fire to sit at Julian's left hand. The women returned with the trifle and cakes, and Timothy was pleased to see that the desserts did not resemble oatmeal in the least.

"I don't know that I can eat another bite, Nessa. You're a fine cook." Mr. Maxwell sighed with contentment as they finished dessert. The wind whiffled and murmured at the door. The flames in the fireplace flickered.

"It sounds like the wind's rising." Julian walked to the tall windows and lifted the drapes. "The snow's flying. I'm glad we're safe inside, Aunt Nessa."

Timothy thought he saw them exchange a glance. Then he noticed that Sarah was staring with a strange expression on her face at Gwydon. The dog, still at Julian's side, was sitting up straight and tall. His massive head was cocked, as if he were listening for something in the wind, and he lifted his muzzle like a coyote or wolf about to bay at the moon.

"He looks like he wants to talk."

Everyone's eyes turned to Gwydon.

"There's an old tradition of animals talking on Christmas Eve," said Julian. "Supposedly it's the one time of year they are no longer mute, as if a spell is broken. They prophesy."

"What do they say?" Jessica leaned forward, and her brown curls danced in the candlelight.

Mr. Maxwell laughed. "Every country has its peculiar traditions. It doesn't mean that they really happen. Perhaps we should be thinking about the weather and—"

The noise was a rumble at first, deep and throaty like a growl. Timothy felt the spring inside himself propel him from his seat. He stood, eyes riveted on Gwydon, who was moving his lips in a very peculiar manner. The growl changed to a series of strange, guttural noises.

At the head of the table, Nessa's eyes glittered.

The first word was half howl as the dog's mouth contorted into strange shapes. The sight was terrifying, an ordinary dog trying to form human sounds.

*"Five must stand. Three will go forth. One remain."*

"I've never seen anything like it! How did you teach him to count?" Mr. Maxwell's excitement shone in his face. "It sounded like he counted to five. Quite a trick!"

"That's funny." Mrs. Maxwell rested her chin in her hands and stared at Gwydon, who now lay quietly at Julian's feet. "That's not what I heard at all. It sounded like he was singing. Well, not really singing, but trying to, anyway. Something more than a howl."

"Now, Lizzie, you just weren't listening carefully enough. It wasn't very clear, but I believe the dog counted to five."

Timothy looked at Sarah and Jessica. "Did you—?"

"Yes, I think it was counting," Sarah cut in. "I saw a horse do it once on a TV show. He pawed the ground once for one, twice for two, and so on." She gave Timothy a swift kick under the table.

"He's a remarkable beast." Nessa's eyes were still gleaming. "Perhaps we should move over by the fire with our tea. I'd like to see if we can get a weather report on the radio."

Mr. Maxwell slapped Julian on the back and talked animatedly about animal tricks he had seen. Mrs. Maxwell helped Nessa clear the table.

"What did you hear?" Jessica's voice tickled Timothy's ear. "Didn't he say something about 'three shall go out'?"

"Five must stand. Three will go forth. One remain," Timothy recited without hesitating.

Sarah was at their side. "We must be the three. With Julian and Cerridwyn, we make five. Why do you think everyone heard something different?"

"We hear what we need to hear, when we listen," Nessa said as she passed by, a teapot in her hands.

With those words, Timothy was certain. All evening he had suspected it; Nessa was—

"Cerridwyn?" Jessica looked into Nessa's strong face.

"We are all more than we seem, love." And, teapot in hand, she calmly joined the Maxwells and Julian by the fire.

# THE BIRD

**T**HE RECEPTION ON THE RADIO was poor. "I don't have television out here. I find it a distraction. So this will have to do." Nessa adjusted the knob.

"Internet reception is down." Julian looked up from Nessa's laptop.

The wind continued to rise and beat the house like a drum. Timothy's sense of dread grew as Gwydon paced the floor. Knowing Cerridwyn was with them, too, offered some comfort.

"We've weathered fiercer storms, but I certainly wouldn't suggest driving in this." Nessa refilled cups of tea. "I've plenty of bedding if it comes to spending the night. I can put you all up out here and in my guest room."

"No, that would be too much trouble for you," Mr. Maxwell said.

"The roads won't be safe." Julian looked at Timothy.

"Don't you worry about being so isolated out here? Do storms usually grow so fierce so fast?" Mrs. Maxwell asked. Timothy could hear the rising tension in his mother's voice.

"I like the privacy. After working with people all day, it's nice to be alone." Nessa looked toward the window. "Midwinter storms can be the most unpredictable, though."

Mr. and Mrs. Maxwell exchanged a glance. Mr. Maxwell nodded.

"We'll take you up on the offer to stay over if it isn't too much trouble," Mrs. Maxwell said. "It probably wouldn't be safe out there."

Jessica stood and walked toward the window. "I noticed you had a sprig of rowan at the door."

Nessa looked at her with bright eyes. "Very observant. It's an old custom found throughout much of the world. Rowan offers some protection when the Wild Hunt rides."

"The hunt?" Mr. Maxwell sat back comfortably by the fire with an enormous mug of tea balanced on his lap. "Surely no one is out hunting in this weather."

Julian brushed the hair from his eyes. "Aunt Nessa is referring to the Wild Hunt. It's a legend throughout the British Isles that a hunt rides through the sky on Christmas Eve when the world is in darkness, the time when the world is most vulnerable."

Memories of white hounds with their blood-red eyes and slavering jaws made Timothy shiver. He had once been their prey as he rode through the sky on Gwydon, hunted and alone. He looked at Jessica, who stood very still, listening by the window, her back to the room, and wondered if she, too, was thinking of that night. Nessa's house felt like a world other than the brightly lit Edinburgh with its giant Norwegian

Christmas tree on the castle mound. But they were only miles from Frederick and Princes Streets decked with fairy lights and Yuletide decorations.

Sarah spoke in low tones with Nessa while Julian entertained Mr. and Mrs. Maxwell with stories of Scottish Christmas traditions. Jessica rejoined Timothy, and they sat on the couch, listening to the growing storm. Something in the wind changed. It no longer sounded like an impersonal force of nature battering the small house, but a person shrieking and wailing.

"Do you hear dogs barking?" Timothy asked. Jessica got up anxiously, walked to the French doors, and parted the curtains. A terrible shattering of glass knocked her backward to the floor. The thick limb of a tree had thrust through the door and into the room. Cold rushed in as the doors hung open on broken hinges, and with the cold came a bird.

The bird was large, black, and desperate. Like a ship caught by waves, it battered itself against one wall and then another. Mrs. Maxwell screamed. Nessa rushed to Jessica's side with Timothy close behind. Julian and Mr. Maxwell hurried toward the doors to assess the damage where snow blew in uninvited. But Sarah stood motionless, Gwydon by her side. She was listening to the bird's caw and to something just beyond the voice of the wind: the baying of hounds.

Blood trickled down Jessica's face where sharp twigs like fingernails had raked across her skin. Pieces of glass sparkled in her hair. She grasped her left wrist with her right hand and winced.

"Nothing too serious, from the look of it, thank goodness." Nessa helped her to her feet. "Though that wrist might give you some trouble." She used a napkin to wipe the blood from Jessica's face as she led her back to the couch, then hurried to the hearth.

Timothy sat next to Jessica and picked pieces of glass from her hair. He whispered in her ear, "Can't you heal it?"

"It's only for others. I can't heal myself."

Nessa filled a cup from the copper cauldron that hung over the fire. Vines and stars bordered its top.

"I think you'll find this soothing, dear."

"Thank you. I wish my mother could see your pot. It's beautiful. She collects all kinds of copper things."

"It's a cauldron," Nessa said. "A very old one."

A spicy fragrance rose from the steaming mug, and Timothy leaned in to inhale the steam. Jessica took a tentative sip and then another. As she drank, the pain in her wrist subsided.

Mrs. Maxwell joined them on the couch. "I think we should ice your wrist. Thank God that heavy limb didn't land on you."

The great black bird swooped low across the room, and Jessica threw up her uninjured arm.

"Let's get that thing out of here." Mr. Maxwell tried to drive it toward the gaping black doorway with one of Nessa's rainsticks. The beans inside the hollow cactus tube chattered like rain as he swung the musical instrument at the bird.

"Wait. Can't you see it's desperate?" Sarah looked out toward the night. "You can't send it back out there with them."

"What the devil are you talking about?" Mr. Maxwell looked at his daughter as if she had lost her mind.

"Didn't you hear what Julian said? The Wild Hunt will kill it. It always does."

The bird crashed into a mirror and thudded to the floor. Sarah ran to its side.

"Here, tender heart; let's put it in a box until it recovers." Nessa scooped the bird into a large file box and gently placed the lid on top. "There should be plenty of air coming in through the handholds."

Julian appeared from the basement, a saw in one hand, plywood in the other. "We have to seal up the doorway. I'm going to cut the limb."

A crest of snow had formed inside the room where the wind blew in like waves. The drape, torn from its rod, hung askew, and the gnarled limb reached at least four feet into the room. The cold settled in.

"There's someone out there!" Mr. Maxwell was at the open doorway, helping to clear away glass. He peered into the swirling dark.

In the box, the injured bird woke and beat its wings.

"I see a light moving."

Nessa hurried to join Mr. Maxwell and Julian by the door, while Timothy froze on the couch, remembering hounds and their red eyes that glowed in the darkness. The wind stopped its terrible shrieking, satisfied that it had found a way into the house. In that sudden stillness, Timothy could hear the clock ticking on the mantel, the bird struggling in its box, and even Jessica's soft breathing beside him. Everything was amplified as he waited to see what would come in out of the dark.

"Who would be out on a night like this?" Mr. Maxwell strained forward.

"Not all things in the dark should be invited in." Nessa looked at Julian. "Perhaps we should seal the door closed quickly."

Julian made the first cut into the thick limb, and Timothy was reminded of the trees who had fought so valiantly at the Travelers' Market. He was sure he saw the limb shudder. As Nessa went to retrieve a hammer and nails, a man carrying a small flashlight stepped up to the door from the dark.

Timothy's hand found its way into his pocket, but it was empty. If only he had the glass leaf given to him by the Greenman. Julian put the saw aside and stood blocking the man from entering. There was something familiar about him. Timothy stood and walked to the door, and Jessica, one wrist wrapped in a dish towel with ice, followed. She gasped. The figure in the dark was Tam!

"I'm so sorry. My car broke down, and this was the only light I saw. Why, hello." He stopped and looked from Jessica to Timothy. "We've met before. This is the strangest coincidence."

Nessa joined the group and silenced his chatter. "It's a strange night to be out. How can we help you?" Timothy noticed that she positioned herself next to Julian to block Tam's entrance into the house. Gwydon growled low in his throat.

"Oh, his name's Tam. We met him the other day in town." Jessica stepped forward.

"That's right, we did." Tam smiled directly into Jessica's eyes. "I still have your number in my pocket." Tam turned to Nessa. "I've been at a friend's for Christmas Eve dinner and must have taken a wrong turn in the storm. Drove right off the road. Now the car's good and stuck, and I can't get any reception out here." He held up his cell phone, clicked off the flashlight, and shivered.

Timothy noticed that his thin jacket was iced in snow. He wore no hat, only a pair of driving gloves and boots. White flakes stuck to his sandy hair and eyelashes.

"Come in and get warm!" Mrs. Maxwell, her face taut with alarm, joined her husband.

Tam quickly stepped in through the damaged door and stomped the snow from his boots. It formed small puddles on the wood floor.

Julian and Nessa shared a glance. Again Gwydon growled, low and ominous. Julian silenced him with his hand.

"Yes, come in and have some hot tea. Let me take your wet things. We've no phone reception here at the moment, either," said Nessa.

"Very kind of you." Tam pulled off a sopping glove and shook hands first with Mr. Maxwell and then with all the adults. "Looks like you've had a bit of trouble yourselves."

Suddenly Jessica remembered her hurt wrist and clutched it, rather too dramatically, Timothy thought. "The storm crashed a tree through the glass doors, and I was standing right next to them when it happened." Jessica continued the story while Mrs. Maxwell poured tea. Nessa brought a blanket, and Julian and Mr. Maxwell finished boarding up the door.

Only Sarah, Timothy noticed, hung back, Gwydon by her side. She watched Tam closely. The bird continued to struggle in the box. She lifted the lid and soothed its feathers with her hand. "There, there, poor bird. We're going to have to splint that leg before we turn you loose." She turned to Timothy. "I think it's broken. It's hanging at a strange angle."

"Let me take a look." Tam walked over to the box. All at once, the bird, who had finally settled under Sarah's touch, cawed loudly, beat its wings, and flew up. Startled, Sarah dropped the box. The bird flapped in desperate circles, its broken leg dangling. It circled the room once, crashing into a window. This time when it fell to the floor, its head hung sideways.

"Oh, dear. The poor thing." Mrs. Maxwell bent over the lifeless form.

But Timothy wasn't watching the bird. He was watching Tam and thought he saw the ghost of a smile on the boy's face.

"Oh, I must have startled it! I should never have come near." He looked at Sarah from under his ginger curls.

"I'm sure you didn't mean to—it was injured, anyway." Sarah flushed. "Hush, Gwydon." She put her hand on the great dog's head. "He's not always good with strangers."

Timothy wanted to interrupt. What was Sarah talking about? Gwydon was *excellent* with strangers. She was talking about him as if he were a mere dog.

"Perhaps we should put him in the basement?" Nessa turned to Julian.

And Julian obediently led the still-growling dog out of the room.

Had everyone lost their minds? Timothy looked at Jessica. She was holding Mrs. Maxwell's Christmas cake in her good hand. He thought of Julian's warning that the Dark was most powerful at this time of year and looked speculatively at Tam. There was something not quite right.

"You must be hungry," Jessica offered.

"How'd you end up spending Christmas Eve with two of the bonniest girls in Scotland?" Tam turned to Timothy.

Mr. Maxwell laughed as if Tam had said something terribly clever; Timothy scowled. The storm and the Dark seemed forgotten as they again relaxed into the warmth of the room. The fire burned brighter, and Mr. Maxwell began a funny story that Timothy had heard at least a hundred times before. He watched the contented scene by the fireplace. Tam sat on the couch, wrapped in a blanket, next to Jessica. Julian added more wood to the fire. The plate of cake was nearly empty, and Nessa had gone to the kitchen to refill it.

Yet Timothy was not at ease. It was eleven o'clock. Well past the time his parents usually stayed up. His eyes felt sleepy and heavy. Suddenly the room was too warm. He had an intense desire to step out into the cold night air. If only he could crack open the front door. The night was a presence, breathing all around him. It was crouched, a cat waiting for a mouse. He remembered his house after it had been searched, and Mr. Twig looking frail in the white hospital bed. He thought of the map hidden safely in his backpack. He glanced at it hanging on a hook by the door. Whatever had come hunting for the map at home was here now in Scotland. He could feel it. Suddenly he wanted the map by his side. He crossed the room, grabbed his pack, and stuffed it next to him in the leather chair.

Nessa and Julian showed off her collection of unusual musical instruments gathered over many years of travel, starting with the rainstick Mr. Maxwell had swung at the bird.

"This is a didgeridoo," Julian explained. "They're made—at least the early ones like this are made—from the trunk of a eucalyptus tree. Ants have eaten away its inner cells, so it makes a buzzing noise like this." He picked up the long instrument, which looked to Timothy like an elephant's trunk, and blew. A strange noise somewhere between a vibration and a buzz filled the room.

Mr. Maxwell snored open-mouthed in the chair closet to the fire, but Mrs. Maxwell smiled with interest.

As Timothy watched, Tam nudged Jessica and pointed up to a low beam. Timothy looked up. A sprig of mistletoe dangled from a gold ribbon. When Jessica turned her face up, Tam kissed her lightly right on the lips. Jessica laughed in surprise. No one else noticed.

Timothy balled his hands into fists. He looked away, his heart racing.

"Could we play some Christmas music?" Sarah asked, looking from Julian to Nessa. "We could try some of the instruments." She eyed the small drum Nessa had called a bodhrán.

"Despite all these instruments you see, I don't play anything but the piano, and I don't even play that very well. But we could sing Christmas carols, and you could each have a go at an instrument if you want," Nessa said, smiling.

Something was wrong with her, Timothy thought. The sparkle was missing from her eyes. The wind shrieked around the old timbers of the house.

"No one carols anymore, do they?" Tam asked lightly. "But I know some modern stuff I could bang out on those drums, if I could get an accompanist."

The slightest furrow appeared between Sarah's brows. "Carols are wonderful. It's all right to be old-fashioned on Christmas."

Timothy watched Tam's face and thought he glimpsed a flash of anger before it was smothered by his natural charm. "Well, how about the one you Americans like about the reindeer?"

"No, that isn't a real Christmas carol at all." Sarah held her ground.

Timothy felt as if he were watching the growing drama from a great distance. The rest of the players seemed to fade into the background. His father woke with a snort, and he and Mrs. Maxwell exclaimed about the time.

"Let me show you to the guest room." Nessa led Mr. and Mrs. Maxwell to the other side of the house.

✛ ✛ ✛

Jessica sat just a little too close to Tam. She couldn't keep her eyes off him, Timothy thought in disgust. In contrast, his sister and Tam stood out in sharp relief, their battle of the wills pitched over something as silly as Christmas carols.

Sarah continued in her crusade to persuade Tam. "I mean, a carol like 'Silent Night' or 'Joy to the World'—you must know those, even in Scotland." She closed her eyes and began to sing the first lines of "Joy to the World."

"Ewh!" Tam pressed his hands to his ears. "I can't stand your voice!"

Timothy had never heard anyone say anything like that to Sarah before. Unlike Timothy's, her singing was always praised. She narrowed her eyes and looked, Timothy thought, like a cat about to spit. "How could you say such a thing?" she gasped.

But Tam paid no attention at all. His hands were pressed to his ears, and his face was contorted as if he really were in pain.

"Oh, just stop, Sarah! Stop showing off." Jessica put her hand on Tam's shoulder and turned her back on her friend. This was so much like the old Jessica that Timothy winced.

Sarah, silent now but with eyes still flashing, retreated to a corner of the room. Timothy tried to catch her eye.

The scream of the wind was becoming deafening. Julian added more wood to the fire. The room grew uncomfortably warm as the hands of the clock pushed slowly toward midnight.

# FINULA

**W**ITH A SHARP CRACK, the newly hung plywood board separated from the French doors. Bitterly cold air again rushed in, and with it came another stranger: a woman leading a white stag. Blood dripped from the trembling animal onto the wood floor. It was immediately clear that the animal was mortally wounded. But it was the woman who commanded the room.

With her came the remembrance of something lost, something you wanted to find more than anything else. Everything in the room stilled. In that stillness, Timothy heard the front door slam, but he dared not tear his eyes from the woman.

Her hair was a portion of the night sky framing a face of solemn white. Even in the bitter cold, her pale arms were bare and muscled. Later no one could agree on what she'd worn. Jessica said she was dressed in green like the woods, but Sarah swore she wore blue. A musky scent of moss and lichen filled the room, as if the forest had stepped inside.

Julian was the first to speak, and it was in a voice Timothy had never heard him use before. "One of the Daoine sídhe, here in the house. I never thought to see one."

The stag's legs shook. Without speaking, the woman helped the stag to lie on the floor. It was a beautiful creature, gleaming like frost, with a terrible red gash that laid open its chest and flank.

"This room is thick with a spell called glamour." She shook her head, raised one long arm, and swiped it through the air.

Immediately, Timothy felt lighter. His lungs expanded. It was as if a too-warm mist had cleared from the room. Nessa returned, her usual, placid smile replaced by a keen, pointed gaze.

Now unmistakably Cerridwyn, she stood tall. "The Daoine sídhe use glamour to deceive. It is one of the oldest forms of enchantment." She looked pointedly at the stranger. "Why are you here? Since when are the Good Folk, the Daoine sídhe, concerned with the affairs of humankind?"

"*I* have used no glamour tonight, nor would I. And you are right, your affairs do not often concern us. I am Finula. Tonight I have come asking help." She looked down at the stag. "Orisis, one of the few remaining stag people, was pursued and injured by the Wild Hunt. The power of our people fades each day, just as our numbers do. But there is someone in this room who I believe can help." She turned to look solemnly at Jessica, who had pivoted toward the front door.

But Jessica cried, "Tam's gone! He'll never survive out in this storm!"

With all the strange happenings, Timothy had forgotten completely about Tam. But now, as he looked about the room, he realized that Jessica was right. The front door had slammed, and Tam was nowhere to be seen.

"It is the darkest hour. He will survive, though it would be better for all if he did not," Finula replied.

"How can you say that?" Jessica crossed her arms across her chest.

Finula ignored her question. "Word has spread among the Daoine sídhe that a Healer has arisen with power that reaches beyond our own. Orisis has been mortally wounded by one of Herne's hellhounds. At any other time, my own strength could heal him, but tonight, when the powers of the Dark are at their peak, I do not have the strength. By tomorrow, it will be too late. Heal Orisis, and the best of the Good Folk will be in your debt."

Julian and Cerridwyn remained quiet as the Daoine sídhe spoke. Timothy noticed that Jessica was standing taller now, her hand clutching the red stone at her throat.

"It is your choice." Cerridwyn looked at Jessica. "But to have the Good Folk in your debt is no small thing."

Jessica paused. Then she knelt by the silent stag. His breath was shallow and fast. When she raised her face questioningly to Cerridwyn, Cerridwyn nodded. Slowly, Jessica ran her hands along the length of the gash, and Timothy held his breath.

As her hands traveled the wound, Jessica's face grew paler. The stag's flank was laid open wide, and it was obvious the animal had already lost a good deal of blood. Little by little the flesh drew together, and the gash began to close. Jessica's arms trembled with the effort, and her face grew not only pale but taut. No one spoke or moved.

The stag's breathing deepened. The animal began to twitch. White beads of foam flecked its muzzle as the wound, so raw and red, became but an angry scar. When Jessica rose shakily to her feet, Julian hurried to her side and supported her arm. Timothy finally exhaled.

"You've performed a great service for our people. And for that service, we are in your debt." The sídhe's presence filled the room. Again Timothy could smell the musky scent of moss and pine needles. "I have come with another concern as well."

This time her pale eyes sought out Timothy. He found it impossible to return the look without faltering.

"Word also has spread among the people that you have come to find one of the ancient treasures." Her eyes searched his face.

Timothy knew that under that gaze it would be impossible to lie. His legs that had felt so heavy now trembled like frail sticks. His friends ringed the room: Sarah, Julian, Cerridwyn, and Jessica. He thought of Gwydon's words: *Five must stand.*

"I have come for the map." She extended her hand toward Timothy. "Why should a mere boy be trusted with it?"

Timothy's words tumbled over one another. He was breathing very fast, as if he'd been running. "The map leads to the Telling Stone. I need the map to find it. I can't give the map away. If I don't find the stone, the Dark will rule. There won't be peace. The old stories will be lost."

"The perils of humans are as fleeting as grass, here today and gone tomorrow. However, humans will outlast these perils. In one form or another, you will even outlast the Daoine sídhe. That is something the old stories say. Until then, my people, the sídhe, should keep the stone."

Timothy spoke again, surprised by his own words. "But if the Dark finds it before I do, all the true stories will be lost. The future will be built around the Dark's lies."

Silence stretched taut across the room. "Humans have already forgotten what is true," Finula said. "There is little difference between those who serve the Dark and the Light. Each wants power. If my people have the stone, we will see that it is kept from the Dark and from humans who seek to use it for their own advantage. And I will not lie. The Stone of Destiny will protect the Daoine sídhe until it is time to pass it to a true Filidh. Give me the map, or I will take it."

Her advance on Timothy was like the rushing of the wind. The room blurred, and Timothy was enveloped in the scent of the forest. He had very little breath left. "I'm to be the keeper of the stories." Timothy's voice sounded frail and pompous even to his own ears. "I'm the true Filidh."

"By whose design?"

"The Greenman."

At that name, the sídhe shuddered. "The Daoine sídhe have been caretakers and co-creators for years out of mind. Then man came. I believe it was a great mistake to loose humans upon the earth, but it was not my decision. There will come a time when what remains of the earth will be left to humankind." Her voice was filled with sadness. "The Greenman understands this. His power is greater even than ours." Her pale face softened. "And above all, the Greenman is good."

Across the room Cerridwyn's eyes gleamed, and Julian's gaze never wavered.

"And we are to help him." Sarah stepped forward, and Jessica stood by her side. For the first time that night, Timothy felt happy.

Finula's gaze traveled over the three. "You are an unlikely trio. Older and wiser people have failed at this task. But if you are truly sent, you are not alone." She paused. Orisis rose and snorted restlessly by the fire. "There have been rumors that a new Filidh has arisen. If that is so, then you know that the stone is only one of four ancient treasures, lost so long ago. All four will be necessary for a true Filidh to rule. One is kept safe by my people . . ." Here she paused and looked at Jessica. "The Spear of Lugh, or Light. The spear was forged by the smith of Falias, the city of the gods, for High King Lugh to use in his fight against Balor the One-Eyed."

At the name Balor, Timothy winced as if he were pierced in the side. The pain was so sharp that he almost doubled over. He looked for Julian. But Julian remained sitting in the shadows, looking down, so Timothy couldn't read his face.

"I see the name Balor is not new to you. For many centuries he has sought the Stone of Destiny himself, and he will do everything possible to block your way."

"He tried to kill Timothy once," Jessica said.

"I have said I am in your debt." The Daoine sídhe smiled at Jessica, and even the smile held something of sadness. "I cannot interfere in your quest, but I can put one of the four treasures at your disposal when the time comes. Another is already in this room tonight: the god Dagda's Cauldron, which never empties and also has power to heal." She looked toward the fire, where the copper cauldron hung.

Nessa put a thick mitt on her hand and reached into the hearth, lifting out the small cauldron. "Fire cannot burn it, nor can cold destroy it. You can see it already worked well for you tonight," she said, as she gestured toward Jessica's wrist. "It is only given to a Healer. You must guard it well." She extended the pot to Jessica. "It won't burn you. Take it."

Jessica hesitated before extending her bare hand and grasping the handle. "Why, it's not hot at all!" she exclaimed. Then she added solemnly, "Thank you."

Timothy was pleased to see that Jessica spoke again like the friend he knew and trusted. And with excitement he remembered the Ogham words Maggie Seaborg had translated from their map: *cauldron, spear, sword,* and *stone.* They now had the first of the treasures.

"It is the middle of your Christmas Eve, and soon the Light will come into the Dark. Orisis and I must go about our business in the time we have left."

Before Timothy could speak, Finula mounted the white stag. Together the woman and stag made a fearsome pair. Orisis arched his gleaming neck as if he were ready to be off. Timothy longed to know more about the stag and the fairy folk. Finula looked down at Timothy. Her voice was a whisper. "Once you know the true nature of something, you know its weakness. Remember that, Timothy James." Then the stag and rider moved to the door. As quiet as that whisper, the Daoine sídhe was gone.

Outside, the wind had stilled. Timothy walked to the doors. *True nature*. What did it mean? No more snow was falling. The moon had parted the clouds and looked down implacably from a sky dizzy with stars. Jessica and Sarah joined him.

"It's beautiful!" Sarah stood looking out at the silver world. "And it's Christmas morning!"

Julian, who had gone back to the basement, returned with Gwydon by his side and another sheet of plywood. "And we could all use some sleep. But first I'd better repair the door again."

Timothy looked at Jessica and Sarah. Jessica was gripping the cauldron with both hands, just as if her wrist had never been injured. "We've got the first treasure: the cauldron."

"And Finula said she could help us with one other," Sarah added.

"Isn't it strange that Tam left as soon as Finula arrived?" Jessica asked. "It's funny, but I can hardly remember anything about his being here."

Timothy wondered if she remembered the kiss.

# CHRISTMAS DAY

ESSICA AND THE MAXWELLS returned to the Edinburgh flat on Christmas Day. Timothy, Sarah, and Jessica had only a few hours of sleep at Nessa's in the early hours of the morning. By late morning the roads were passable again. The snow and ice had become slush and melt.

When they arrived, Timothy found his old Christmas stocking from home hanging from the foot of the sofa bed. His parents must have filled it before leaving for Nessa's. Very sneaky. It was lumpy with small gifts and candy, the seams stretching as if they would burst. He grabbed it and hurried with the girls into their room. At the foot of each bed hung a plump stocking.

"Merry Christmas!" Mr. and Mrs. Maxwell beamed.

For the next few minutes there was a flurry of tearing paper and exclamations as candy and presents were tossed onto the beds. Mr. and Mrs. Maxwell sat down to watch the excitement.

"This is the exact leotard I've been wanting." Sarah unrolled a V-necked, deep blue leotard and held it up. "Perfect!"

Timothy wondered for the millionth time how his sister could get so excited about clothes. Fortunately, his stocking didn't contain any except a long gray-and-charcoal-striped wool scarf. It did, however, have something that he'd been waiting for, the latest sci-fi book by his favorite author.

Jessica shook her gifts out on her lap. The new CD she'd been wanting, a silk scarf, and a pair of dangly silver earrings made a small pile. "There's something still in there!" She stuck her arm into the stocking and pulled out a thin box wrapped in red tissue with silver lettering. "'*Merry Christmas with love from Mom and Dad*,'" she read out loud. "I think I know what this is!" She ripped off the paper. She held up the slim red phone triumphantly.

"That's the newest model!" Timothy eyed the phone with envy.

Jessica plugged it in to charge. "Both of you, I have something for you!" She rummaged under her bed and triumphantly pulled out two bright packages festooned with dust bunnies. "Open them!"

Sarah unwrapped a pair of red lacquered chopsticks.

"They're for your hair!"

Timothy wasn't sure what to expect as he unwrapped his gift. At first he thought it was a pocket watch. He opened the small brass disk. Inside was a compass with filigreed hands.

Timothy smiled at Jessica. "This is amazing!"

Jessica preened. "I thought you'd like it. And who knows? It just might be useful."

"This is the best gift ever. Thanks, Jess. Where did you get it? It looks really old."

"Wynde Alley. When you were in the map store. There was this funny little place that looked like a junk shop."

"We have something for you, too." Sarah reached under the bed and drew out a small, carefully wrapped box.

Timothy held his breath, hoping Jessica would like it. Jessica deliberately undid the ribbons and paper. Inside was a snow globe with the Edinburgh Ferris wheel inside. Jessica turned it upside down and watched the snow fall. She didn't say a word.

She thought it was stupid, Timothy worried.

"Thanks. It's perfect!" Jessica's smile included them both.

Timothy sighed with relief.

"We have something for you, parents! The three of us went in on it together." Sarah pulled a box out from under her bed and handed it to her parents.

"You open it, Elizabeth," Mr. Maxwell urged.

Mrs. Maxwell carefully undid the ribbon and opened the box. Inside were two items wrapped in tissue paper. The first was a framed photo of all of them at the pub the first night they arrived in Edinburgh.

"Remember? Jess asked Mr. McMorn to take it. Then we had it framed," Timothy said.

"It's wonderful!" Then Mrs. Maxwell unwrapped three carved wooden Christmas ornaments.

"They're from the German Market," Sarah explained.

"I think this may be our best Christmas yet!" Mr. Maxwell exclaimed.

"I'm sure it's one we'll never forget," Timothy said.

As Sarah sucked contentedly on sour lemon drops and Jessica flipped through the pages of Timothy's book, Timothy sighed again. Somehow Christmas with his family and friends always made him feel this way. *Replete*, thought Timothy. Nine points and a good word, even if the point value was low.

# DUNSINANE

S SOON AS HIS PARENTS left the room, Timothy said what he'd been thinking all along. "It's time to plan the trip to Dunsinane and the search for the Telling Stone."

Jessica looked at the Dagda's Cauldron at the foot of her bed. It would be a gift for Jessica's mother, Nessa had told the elder Maxwells. "It's hard to believe this pot is so important," said Jessica. "But the cauldron's on the map."

"*'Daoine sídhe'* is what Mr. Twig said in the hospital. The fairy folk must be the Good Folk." Sarah clasped her arms around her knees. "Finula didn't seem like any fairy I've ever imagined!"

"And what happened to Tam? All of a sudden he was gone! He didn't even say good-bye!" Jessica sounded a little too disappointed to Timothy.

"He is possibly the rudest boy I've ever met!" Sarah began to tug a brush through her tangled hair. "And he killed that bird!"

"He did not. He was just looking at it. And I guess I was pretty rude, too. Sorry, Sarah."

"Oh, it's all right. You were just enchanted by him."

"That's exactly what I've been thinking!" Timothy burst out. Both girls turned to look at him. "Don't you remember that when Finula arrived, she said the room was full of glamour?"

"No." Jessica looked puzzled.

"Well, she did. And then she moved her arm across the room, and things became clearer. Tam left. I heard the door slam. There's something suspicious about him. Do you really think it was a coincidence that his car broke down near Nessa's house?"

"I think he was just stalking Jess." Sarah twisted her hair up into a bun and stuck a red chopstick through it.

Jessica laughed, looked pleased, and changed the subject. "We need to look at the map. We need to find that hill the Seaborgs mentioned."

Timothy scooped up his presents from the foot of the bed. The feeling of repleteness had vanished. He put the compass in his pocket and went to get the map. They did need to look at the map so they could plan out their next move. But he seemed to be the only one who suspected just how dangerous that next move might be.

When he returned, they spread two maps across the foot of Sarah's bed, comparing them side by side. One was a touring map of Scotland and the other the map cipher from Mr. Twig.

"Here's Dunsinane Hill." Timothy pointed to a location to the northwest of Edinburgh. "According to the scale, it looks like it would be about an hour and a half away, just like the Seaborgs said."

"How are we going to get there?" Jessica tapped a pencil thoughtfully on the paper. "We could say we wanted to go sightseeing, but what's there?"

"Don't you remember what else they said?" Sarah stuck her finger between the pages of the guidebook she was reading to mark her place. "I knew I'd heard of Dunsinane even before the Seaborgs told us. It's in the Scottish play. 'Not till Birnam Wood come to Dunsinane.'"

"That's from *Macbeth*?" Timothy asked.

"Don't say the play's name aloud; it's bad luck. Everyone knows that. But, yes, this book says that's where his castle might have been, and that's what the Seaborgs said, too."

"I thought they might be wrong about that. I never thought he was real. I thought he was just a character Shakespeare made up for a play," said Jessica.

Sarah shook her head. "No, he really was a king from the Iron Age, just like the Seaborgs said. The guidebook says there are some ancient ruins there but that it's not a big tourist draw because there's not too much to see."

"Well, it's going to be what we want to see most of all. We can say it ties in to school," said Timothy.

"Hot chocolate or tea, anyone?" Mrs. Maxwell appeared in the doorway, smiling. "Then we're heading into town to hear the choir at Saint Giles' Cathedral." She paused in the doorway, looking at the maps. "Are you making plans?"

"Oh, we're just checking out all the best sights." Jessica pointed to the guidebook. "After all, how many times do we get a trip to Scotland?"

✛ ✛ ✛

Electra had watched through the long dark night as the Wild Hunt rode, as the Dark gathered itself into a relentless storm and battered the stone city with cold. She had seen the ginger-haired boy first at the house in the woods and then, in the earliest hours of the morning, on the High Street, shivering. She had watched as he huddled miserably against the wall of a pub, waiting. Finally, the pub door swung open. A tall man with golden curls and a woman with long dark hair emerged, pausing only long enough to speak with the boy. Electra had seen the woman before. She was one of the Daoine sídhe but not the one who had appeared at Nessa Daring's. As Electra watched, the man spoke to the boy. When he heard the boy's answer, the man angrily raised his arm. The boy cowered. And as the arm was lowered, the boy collapsed, writhing on the sidewalk. The man and woman had continued on, arm in arm, into the snowstorm.

Now in the sun of Christmas Day, Electra stood outside the cathedral. She watched as the Maxwell family, chattering happily, joined the throng of people waiting to enter the tall wooden doors. The glittering world of ice had melted, leaving the city gleaming like polished stone.

"Did you see her?" Jessica asked.

"See who?" Timothy was busy looking up at the stone arches framing the entry. The enormity of the cathedral made him feel very small.

"Star Girl, Electra. I'm sure I saw her on the corner across from us when we came in." Jessica looked over her shoulder. But the corner was empty now. Timothy turned to look. "If she was here, she's gone now."

"Why do you suppose they made cathedrals so big?" Jessica craned her neck to follow Timothy's gaze.

"To reach up to God," Sarah answered.

"I think," Timothy said, "it's to remind us of how very small we are."

The rest of the day was quiet. Mr. McMorn had promised to drop by on his way home from dinner at his sister's house. So when the doorbell rang, Timothy, who had had enough of reading, was ready for a diversion. Brian McMorn stood in the doorway with a bottle of Scotch and a tin of cookies in his hands.

Again Timothy had the strange feeling of an insect crawling over his skin. He froze, searching the man's face, one hand on the door. Whenever Mr. McMorn smiled, it seemed to cost him a great effort, Timothy thought. Then he noticed the tremor in the man's hands. Was he nervous?

"Well, are you going to invite me in?"

"Oh, sorry. Come in, and Merry Christmas!"

"Happy Christmas to you, too!" He held up the bottle of Scotch. "Arthur, some Christmas cheer and a tin of my sister's shortbread—the best in Scotland!"

Mrs. Maxwell served them all the shortbread. They sat around the table, eating and talking.

"Tomorrow is Boxing Day. I promised to take you all somewhere. Have you any special plans in mind?"

"Boxing Day? Does everyone fight?" Sarah asked.

"No, Boxing Day traditionally was when rich folks would box up their leftovers for the servants. Today it's just another bank holiday, one more day to exchange gifts. Don't want to miss the torchlight procession later this week, either. People carry wax torches through the streets. Scottish pipers and drummers accompany the crowds. On top of the hill, we burn a Viking longship, and at midnight there are fireworks."

Now, that was exactly what Timothy wanted to see, and for a minute he completely forgot about the map and Dunsinane, but Jessica wasn't so easily distracted.

"Well, there is a place we want to see, and it isn't the kind of tourist attraction that will be closed. It's Dunsinane Hill, where Macbeth's castle was," she said.

Mr. McMorn put down his fork. "I know Dunsinane. There were some archaeological digs there a few years back. They found two buried chambers, an ancient torque, or metal collar, and some human remains, I believe. No one is sure that it was Macbeth's seat, but then, I'm sure there's still much to discover." He looked at Timothy from under his heavy eyelids. Again Timothy noticed something in McMorn's glance. Was it fear?

"But your mother and I have been invited to the Gladstones tomorrow. He's one of the major backers of the conference. I'm afraid we can't get out of it." Mr. Maxwell shrugged.

"I'd be happy to take them, Arthur," Mr. McMorn said.

"Oh, we wouldn't want to inconvenience you on your day off," Mrs. Maxwell countered.

"No inconvenience at all. I'd like to see the place again, see what I missed the first time. And to have young people so interested in one of our historic sites . . ." Mr. McMorn's voice trailed off.

Go with Mr. McMorn without his parents? Timothy wasn't so sure. McMorn didn't feel like a person he should trust. He looked at Sarah and Jessica. Sarah looked as alarmed as he felt, but Jessica didn't hesitate.

"That would be great! Thanks so much! I have to write a paper on a Shakespeare play in the spring. I could do *Macbeth!*"

Timothy recognized her manipulative tone, but this time Jessica might not know what she was getting them all into.

# BOXING DAY

IN THE QUIET MORNING of Boxing Day, John Ahearn rapped on the shop door. It took a little while before he heard the lock turn, and then Newton Seaborg, still in a bathrobe, cracked open the door.

"I've come for me map."

Newton looked the burly customer up and down. His tweed jacket strained across broad shoulders, and his thick neck rose into a gray-streaked beard. A preposterous hat, as tall and wide as a chimney, sat on top of his unruly crop of hair. His shoes were thick brown brogues, well scuffed. Newton shuddered. He had a particular fondness for shoes and never liked to see them treated poorly. This fellow in his ridiculous hat annoyed him.

"It's Boxing Day. We're closed."

"I've come for me map. Name's Ahearn. John Ahearn."

Then Newton heard a clicking, the sound of toenails on cobbles, followed by panting. Two hunting hounds with strange, pale eyes circled Ahearn's thick legs.

"Who's at the door?" Maggie Seaborg, wrapped in a fuchsia silk housecoat, pulled the door wide. She eyed the man and his dogs. "Mr. Ahearn. The map's been ready for several days now. I believed you were in a hurry for it." She looked at him severely.

"Pressing business came up, but I'm here now." A string of drool dropped from one of the hounds' jaws onto his shoe.

Maggie was displeased. She didn't like to be rushed in her work, and she had rushed for this Mr. Ahearn. On the other hand, he had paid handsomely for the illuminations, and they could use the money. "Why don't you come in? As you can see, we're barely up and about. I'm afraid your dogs will have to remain outside."

Mr. Ahearn hesitated. "Stay." The dogs whined and dropped to sit on the cobbles. He ducked his head to enter through the low door but did not remove his coat or hat.

As Maggie went to get the map and Newton poured tea, her mind ticked. The children had mentioned a fellow named Herne, and she had suspected something then. Now, when John Ahearn returned to her shop wearing the same exceptionally tall hat he had worn on his last visit, she was curious. He was hiding something under that hat—she was sure of it. It was no coincidence that the children had come with a map to find the coronation stone, and now this Mr. Ahearn showed up with his hunting hounds. There was a connection. She could feel it in her bones, and her bones were rarely wrong. Could Timothy really be the new Filidh they had waited for? If the old myths were walking the streets in broad daylight, things must be very close to the prophecies indeed.

She walked over to her worktable, where the map lay finished. Hopefully, the children had gone to Dunsinane straightaway. The sooner the stone was found, the better. "Mr. Ahearn, take a look at the finished work."

He met her at the table and traced her intricate drawings of hounds and prey with a hairy finger.

"I hope it is satisfactory?"

"Aye." He nodded. "More than that."

Maggie thought fast. Why would Herne, the Master of the Hunt, be busy after Christmas? Traditionally this was the time of year when the Wild Hunt rested, though it could be summoned to seek out traitors.

"What keeps you busy on Boxing Day?" Maggie asked.

He looked at her with an eyebrow half cocked and drew his hand across his mouth as if he'd just tasted something good. "I've been told there's some interesting prey about."

╬ ╬ ╬

On Boxing Day morning, Mr. Maxwell disappeared into the bedroom and returned with three very small packages wrapped in white tissue with red ribbons. "Last week Nessa gave me Boxing Day presents for the three of you. She was very particular that I save them until today. I almost forgot." He started to randomly hand each of them one of the small gifts. "Wait. It seems there's a name on each one." He redistributed them according to their tags.

Sarah undid her red ribbon as she finished her breakfast muffin.

"Look. It's a lovely stone." She held up a cut, polished rock with deep blue concentric rings. "It's beautiful!"

"It's an agate. Must have come from one of her botany excursions." Mr. Maxwell ran his fingers over the smooth surface. "Funny she didn't give you them on Christmas Eve."

Jessica's gift was also a polished and cut stone, the color of rust with rings of white. "Open yours, Timothy."

He wiped his fingers and hoped his stone would be something impressive to add to his collection at home. But the stone he unwrapped was a flat gray-blue, and a hole ran through the middle of it. It wasn't polished. It definitely wasn't an agate. It was something he could find anywhere, except for the hole in the center. He tried not to let his disappointment show.

A small gift tag was attached to the package. "It says it's a fairy stone, and the hole was made by a brook tumbling onto it." He held the stone up so everyone could see it and then continued reading. "'Legend says if you look through a stone with a naturally bored hole, you can see what others can't. You can see the true nature of things.'"

His mother reached for the stone. "What an odd idea, but the stone is lovely!" She turned it over in her hands, running a finger around the hole. "What a thoughtful gift, a piece of Scotland to take home." She handed the fairy stone back to Timothy.

Timothy held the rock up to one eye and looked at his mother through it. For a moment the light caught her in just the right way to reveal how healthy and happy she was. He waited, but she didn't change. What had he expected? He didn't see anything that anyone else couldn't.

"How do I look?" she asked.

"Good. You look like my mother."

She laughed.

He slid the stone into his pocket. He liked the smooth feel of it. Poking his little finger through the hole in the center, he wondered why he hadn't received an agate instead of just another Scottish superstition.

✛ ✛ ✛

Timothy was forced to take the front seat with Mr. McMorn on the long Boxing Day drive to Dunsinane Hill. The girls had conspired against him and bolted for the back. Timothy sat close to the door and hoped he wouldn't have to do much talking. But he didn't have to worry. McMorn kept up a monologue about bits of history and geology as they drove through the foggy countryside.

Trees rose like wraiths from the white fields, as if the car were traveling through a dreamscape. The temperature had risen, and rain now turned the snow to patches. This early on Boxing Day the roads were almost empty. Timothy hardly listened to a word McMorn said. His thoughts were consumed with plans for searching out the Telling Stone. He and the girls had spent hours going over the map again and working on the cipher. Then they tried to come up with a plan to distract Mr. McMorn. But every plan had a flaw. Now Timothy was relying on improvisation and serendipity to see them through, which he found quite unsatisfactory.

They drove the A9 to Perth, stopping briefly for hot drinks and a bathroom break. The fog grew denser on the road to Collace, a town just north, according to Mr. McMorn, of Dunsinane Hill. The heater was turned on high. Timothy fought to keep his eyes open. When the car stopped on the side of the road, he jerked awake.

"What are we doing?" Sarah's sleepy voice from the backseat held a note of alarm. Timothy was immediately alert. His hand felt for the door handle and rested there.

"I thought a bit of history about the hill might be useful." Mr. McMorn paused, his eyes, fastened on Timothy, glittering like a snake's. He cleared his throat. "I happen to be a member of the Society of Antiquaries of Scotland."

Timothy wasn't sure how to respond to that pronouncement, so he kept silent.

"Chalmers, one of our historians, claims that King Macbeth reigned for seventeen years from a castle *near* the Britons' fortress on Dunsinane Hill."

"Dunsinane was a British fortress? Not Macbeth's castle?" Jessica leaned forward from the backseat.

McMorn held up a pale, black-haired hand. "Dunsinane Hill was the place King Macbeth hid many of his valuables. It was really a fortress, built in the Iron Age by the Britons. Macbeth ruled from a nearby castle with a view of the famous Birnam Wood." McMorn's voice became melodious, and with one hand he stroked his long chin. "'*My flyttand wod thai callyd ay, That lang tyme aftyre-hand that day.*'" When Macbeth saw Birnam Wood move, he was really seeing the approach of an invading army led by Malcolm, son of Duncan. Macbeth's army was defeated. But Macbeth didn't die then; three years later, in 1057, he was murdered."

The car was silent as the word *murdered* hung in the air.

"What was that other part you said?" Timothy asked, his mouth gone dry.

"'*My flyttand wod thai callyd ay, That lang tyme aftyre-hand that day,*'" McMorn repeated and then continued. "Like any experienced general who sees an approaching army, Macbeth gathered his forces. The battle between the two opposing armies was brutal. In the end, Macbeth was defeated.

"'I will not be afraid of death and bane till Birnam Wood come to Dunsinane.' That's *Macbeth*, Act Five, Scene Three. I looked up references in the play to Dunsinane last night," Jessica added smugly.

*That's all very interesting,* Timothy thought, *but we're here to find the stone.* Silently he willed McMorn to hurry and get them to the hill.

The sun was winning its battle against the fog. Gradually the world emerged from a flat, white canvas. Hills appeared, and outcroppings of rock. Color bled its way back into the landscape. Mr. McMorn cracked his window; steam cleared from the glass.

"That's Dunsinane right ahead of us."

A craggy hill rose out of the patchworked miles of farmland. It looked like a nothing-special kind of hill, Timothy thought.

"But there's nothing on it!" Sarah's voice held an edge of disappointment.

"There's a great deal on it. But you have to be on the hill to discover its secrets."

"Well, what are we waiting for?" Jessica had already opened the back door of the car.

"Wait! We need some sort of plan." Timothy looked at McMorn. They needed to get away from him. He couldn't know about their quest.

"A wise idea. There are several paths to the top, but I suggest taking a farm trail that begins in that field." McMorn pointed toward a fenced field where a few cows grazed.

"Can we just go through someone's field?" Timothy asked.

"Walking paths are open in Scotland. Anyone can cross another's property," Mr. McMorn answered.

+ + +

Timothy slipped on his backpack and zipped his jacket with shaking hands. They were so close to everything he had been searching for, but they couldn't lead McMorn to the Stone of Destiny. The man made him uneasy. How could they get away from him?

The air was damp and chilly. Timothy shivered. The soft ground squished underfoot as they approached the farm's gate. White patches of snow still lingered in the fields like discarded papers. And cows appeared to float in a sea of fog. McMorn pushed open the wooden pole gate and gestured at a narrow, muddy track running across the field. "Stay on the walking path. It looks like we're the only adventurers this morning. When we get through the field, there's a reader board with some information about the fortifications at the top."

Timothy set out across the field, the two girls and Mr. McMorn right behind. At the far end of the farmland, the trail disappeared into copses of heather as the field met the foot of the hill. Timothy walked as quickly as he could, hoping to leave McMorn behind. Sticking his hands into his pockets for warmth, he found the smooth rock with a hole in the center. He ran his fingers over its slippery sides. It was almost as soothing as the glass leaf from the Greenman. Nothing had happened when he looked through the stone's hole before, but if he was lucky it might tell him something about McMorn. He drew it from his pocket and held the stone up to one eye.

Just as he turned to look at McMorn, Sarah screamed from behind. "Timothy— look out!"

# THE BULL

STARTLED, TIMOTHY jerked his head up. From across the field, an enormous black shape with horns was eyeing him and pawing the ground. A bull! He shoved the stone back in his pocket. The fence and safety were at least a hundred feet off. Timothy urged his cold legs to run. But before he could move, the bull charged. With a burst of adrenaline Timothy sprinted for the fence, slid mid-stride, and landed hard on his side. Cold mud smeared his jeans. He scrambled to get up. His hands were slick with mud. His lungs wheezed for breath.

With one slippery hand, Timothy grabbed the sturdy gatepost, steadied himself, and swung both legs over. He landed with a jarring thump on the other side of the fence. The bull trotted to a stop and snorted, so close that Timothy could feel its hot breath. It was not a glorious way for a Filidh to start his quest. At least the map was still safe in the pack on his back.

The bull then turned its attention to the small group still in the middle of the pasture. Mr. McMorn, Sarah, and Jessica stood frozen.

The animal blocked their way to the gate. It cocked its head to take in the new threat, snorted, and pawed the ground.

"Don't worry about getting to the gate. Just get over the fence any way you can. Move slowly." Mr. McMorn's voice was tight and low.

Timothy dropped his pack and looked for a rock to throw. With luck his arm wouldn't fail him now. He moved several yards down the fence line.

Still the bull stood, its eyes fixed on the girls.

Jessica kept her gaze fixed on Timothy rather than the bull. She took one tentative step in his direction. The bull moved its head to follow her.

"No, Jess. Don't come toward me. Go toward the gate!" Timothy called out.

At the sound of his voice, the bull turned its massive head, but only briefly. It snorted, and its breath formed a white cloud in the cold air.

Then Timothy shouted. He lobbed the rock he'd found toward the beast. It smacked the animal's flank with a thud. The great animal swiveled its head again to look at Timothy, then took a few steps toward him. Now to keep its attention. Timothy flapped his arms and yelled, "Run now!"

Jessica, Sarah, and McMorn dashed toward the gate. With every stride, Timothy could see their feet slip. The bull charged toward them. Timothy ran to swing the gate open. Jessica careened through and Sarah and McMorn slid right behind.

Bending forward, Jessica rested her elbows on her knees.

Timothy shoved the gate closed just as the bull's lowered head crashed into the wooden rails. Sarah screamed. The fence shook but held.

Jessica sank down onto the muddy ground. The bull, with a satisfied snort, shook its head and walked back into the field.

"Quick thinking, lad." McMorn looked closely at Timothy. "You saved us all. I didn't know of a bull or see it in the fog, or I'd never have taken you this way." His voice was warm, but the eyes that met Timothy's were bleak. The group rested for a few minutes, catching their breath as the bull trotted across the field.

The farm track now became an upward trail winding through heather. In the distance, woods and hillsides changed the landscape. As Mr. McMorn promised, there was a small reader board with information about the site. Timothy was the only one who stopped to look at it.

"That's Pitmiddle Wood. Not far from here is the Long Man's Grave." Mr. McMorn's strides were brisk.

"The Pitmiddle was on the sign, but it didn't mention a grave," Timothy said. With every step his cold, muddy pants clung to his legs.

McMorn nodded. "It's an unmarked stone slab right below the cliff of the Black Hill. Supposedly he was an exceptionally tall man, a horse trader, who regularly visited an annual fair. One year, after the fair was taken down, the long man's tent remained, but no one ever saw him again. The stone was placed where his tent had stood."

McMorn stopped, and Timothy, following closely on the narrow trail, was forced to stop as well. Patches of fog still clung like cobwebs to the ground. Timothy could hear the girls' chattering just behind them. McMorn lowered his voice.

"Some believe that is where the original Stone of Destiny was buried when it was stolen and taken to England. You've heard of our famous stone, no doubt?" Timothy found it difficult to swallow.

"It's nonsense, of course. The Stone of Destiny is not in the Long Man's Grave." McMorn turned his back on Timothy and continued the climb.

✢ ✣ ✦

The path wound upward now between heather and gorse frosted with white. They walked in silence, McMorn slightly in the lead, with Timothy, then Jessica, then Sarah behind. Each time Timothy slowed his pace in hopes of speaking privately with the girls, McMorn matched his stride. The countryside mirrored their silence. The snow had mostly melted, but the air was damp and sharp. No birds called in the cold morning.

Dunsinane Hill was bare of trees. Heather softened the hill's flanks, while tussocks of grass and hummocks covered the summit. Just like the lumpy head of a bald man, Timothy thought. The fortress was located, according to McMorn, on a little green knoll on the narrow summit of the hill surrounded by a series of terraces. As the way grew steeper, Timothy felt winded. A large puddle seeped across the path. And he was glad when McMorn stopped, squatted, and cupped some of the clear water in his hands. "Macbeth's well." He lifted his hands to his mouth and took a long swallow.

"That's a well?" Jessica looked skeptically at the puddle as the girls came up from behind.

"It's a natural spring, and it never runs dry."

Sarah squatted next to Mr. McMorn. "Is it really Macbeth's well? Did he really drink from here?"

"That's what tradition says. Tradition isn't always the truth in fact, but it's often the truth in essence." He stood and wiped his mouth on his sleeve. "Was Lady Macbeth really unable to wash the blood from her hands? Not in reality, but in essence it's true." He pointed up the hill. "The remains of the lower fortification are just ahead."

Timothy knelt down, pretending to drink from the spring. "Here, Sarah, try it."

"But it's in the mud." She wrinkled her nose.

"Stay here a minute," Timothy whispered. He glanced up to make sure McMorn was out of earshot. "You've got to do something to let me get away and explore. McMorn won't leave my side. Keep pretending to be interested in Macbeth."

"Okay, I'll try."

Timothy straightened up and wiped his mouth.

Jessica looked back over her shoulder. Sarah came from behind, passing Timothy and Jessica to gain McMorn's side. "Tell me about the fortifications. Have there been any recent excavations?"

It was his chance. Timothy skirted past Sarah and McMorn, who had paused to answer her questions. The melting snow had made the ground soft in places. In others, rocks pushed through the soil like bones. The hill had the feel of a living thing, and somewhere, here on this hill, was the very Stone of Destiny that he was meant to find. But so many people had hiked here before him; how could the stone remain hidden?

He was above the fog now. It lay in thin blankets on the valleys and farmland. He could hear McMorn's voice from below, explaining to Sarah in great detail about the lower fortifications. Timothy paused behind a hummock, slid off his pack, and pulled out the Pont's map.

✚ ✚ ✚

Electra watched from the bottom of the valley as the three children and the tall, dark man climbed the treeless hill. There was a lonely farm near the flank of the hill, and a woman came out of the stone house, wiping her hands on her apron. The door banged, and a boy carrying a milking pail followed her out. Across the field, cows and a bull munched on grass. The sound of a car headed to Collace broke the stillness. Two hikers appeared at the bottom of the trail, one a ginger-haired boy and the other a girl, thin and long-legged.

Electra watched all this in silence. The world was hushed and white with fog. There was no sign that Christmas had passed, that the Light had once again, as every year, triumphed over the Dark. This time, Electra knew that much still hung in the balance. And once again a strange rawness filled her. What would happen to the children?

# THE GUPPED STONES

I GUESS I WAS expecting more." Jessica looked across the summit of the hill. She had caught up with Timothy while McMorn explained early excavations to Sarah. "You know, walls and pieces of fort. But this all just looks like lumps of earth on a hill to me." Her voice was wistful.

Timothy, too, had trouble imagining King Macbeth's castle. He realized, though, that the location was perfect for defense: There was an unobstructed view in every direction. To the northeast the rugged face of Black Hill loomed over them, and to the southeast the trees of Pitmiddle Wood rose like spires through the fog. An invading army would have little chance of mounting a surprise attack. "Quick, Jessica, before McMorn climbs up here."

They bent over the map, while Jessica read the tree code aloud:

*"On Dunsinane . . .*

*Against the clock . . .*

*Cupped stones to the Black . . .*

Remember, *against the clock* means counterclockwise, so we need to start walking around the top of the hill looking for cupped stones."

"They're somewhere on the west wall of the defenses." Timothy pulled out the compass and opened it. "Over this way." Then Timothy started to laugh.

"What's so funny? And how do you know that?" The wind whipped the words from Jessica's mouth. She hunched her shoulders against the cold and frowned at Timothy.

"That reader board at the bottom of the hill. It said there are ancient cupped stones on the west side. They're even older than the Iron Age fortress." He rerolled the map and zipped it back into his pack.

"Cupped stones to the Black," Jessica muttered.

Timothy could no longer hear the drone of McMorn's voice. "We've got to hurry. Where are those cupped stones?"

They were moving along the rimmed earth forming the western wall of the defenses, looking carefully at each stone. The old walls were only slightly raised, and the ground was pocked with depressions. Within the stone wall, the earth was soft, and in several places it had caved in where the soil was especially wet. *Hummocky*, Timothy thought, twenty-four points. The perfect way to describe the lumpy hilltop.

From somewhere just below, Timothy heard McMorn's voice again, lecturing. "There are three concentric lines of defense around the summit of the knoll. The innermost is a massive stone wall that's been pillaged over the years. Within the walls were circular stone huts."

His voice was getting closer. Why couldn't they find the cupped stones? Timothy slid behind one of the many large rocks so that he was out of sight.

"Get down, Jess. They're right below us."

McMorn's voice drifted up. "Where have your brother and Jessica gone? I prefer that we all stay together."

"I'm sure he's just up ahead. I think I saw them go this way," Sarah offered.

Timothy couldn't see which way she pointed, but he hoped it wasn't in his direction. If Jessica had any sense, she was hiding now, just like he was. He counted to twenty, resting his head against cold stone, and listened carefully as the voices faded. Then he peered over the rock. The top of the rock dipped in. A depression in the middle was smooth and hollowed like a . . . like a cup! "Jess, over here! I think I've found it." He didn't dare raise his voice above a loud whisper. He called again. "Jessica!" In moments, she was at his side. "See here? This rock is hollowed."

Jessica ran a mittened hand over the top of the rock. She moved to the slightly smaller stone nearby. "This one, too—it's cupped on top! Timothy, we've found them!"

Success tasted good. Timothy's face broke into a smile. "The Black.

That's got to be the Black Hill." They both looked at the dark mountain that loomed over Dunsinane to the east.

"Okay, then, we go directly east from here. You'd better check the compass."

Timothy could hear the excitement in Jessica's voice. "Yeah, the Black Hill is directly east." He stuck the compass back into his pocket. Impulsively, he grabbed her hand. "Come on!"

Keeping low to the ground, they scurried straight east across the grassy mounds toward the far side of the inner wall and the Black Hill. As they crossed into the center of the old fort, the ground became even softer and wetter. Mud squished over the top of Timothy's shoes. The fog was spreading again; damp white tendrils crawled up the side of Dunsinane.

"Timothy, Jessica, where are you?" McMorn's voice boomed out impatiently. He was too close. There wouldn't be any time to look. Timothy looked at Jessica. She grinned as if she could read his mind, droplets of fog sparkling on her curls. She dropped his hand and ran in the opposite direction.

"I'm over here," she called out.

Crouched low behind a hummock, Timothy smiled. That was one of the things he liked best about Jessica; you didn't have to explain everything to her. She understood right away. She was giving him the chance he needed by leading McMorn in the wrong direction. But he wouldn't have much time.

"Where *is* Timothy?"

Timothy heard McMorn, but he couldn't catch Jessica's low reply. It didn't matter; he knew she would find a way to stall the man. Timothy was moving now, crablike, toward the eastern part of the interior. His hands were sticky with mud, his pant legs thoroughly soaked. The damp seemed to inhabit him. If only he could stand up and look around, but it was too risky. He crept sideways and paused. He'd have to run the next few feet; there were no hummocks to give him cover. Over the top of a green mound, he could see McMorn's profile and the two girls. Sarah was pointing at something in the distance.

Still keeping low, Timothy ran, but the muddied ground was slick. He slipped and slithered into a crater, his pack bouncing on his back. The depression was about four feet deep, and Timothy scrabbled against the slippery sides to pull himself out. Snowmelt had collected, leaving the bottom a soupy mess that covered his shoes. Timothy grabbed at a tuft of dried grass to pull himself up. It came loose in his hands, and he fell back. With a sucking sound, the earth beneath him gave way. Timothy clawed at the muddy grass as the earth swallowed him.

He hadn't fallen far, no more than another six feet, when he hit dry ground. He was somewhere below the surface of Dunsinane—in a chamber deliberately lined with stone!

Timothy stood up. In the semidarkness, he felt rough-hewn stones. He reached up and could touch the ceiling of the space with his hand. He spread his arms. The place was about six feet wide and just under that in height. The light was very dim, seeping in like drops of water from the ragged opening above him. On every side, the chamber melted into shadows. He shuffled forward a few feet until his shin collided hard with a loose rock against a wall. *Ouch!* Still running his hands along the wall, Timothy crept forward. The chamber opened into a narrower tunnel, and the tunnel led into darkness.

"Timothy!" Sarah's voice was anxious and far away.

✢ ✢ ✢

Electra watched as the two new hikers made their way to the top of the hill. The ginger-haired boy and the thin girl stood watching the other three. The fog was coming in fast. Too fast. It was not a natural fog, she thought, but a fog of purpose, sent to obscure. She thought again about the thin, dark-haired girl. And she recalled that when she had last seen her, the girl was walking with Balor, arm in arm.

✢ ✢ ✢

Timothy should have had time by now to look for the Stone of Destiny at the east side of the fort, Jessica thought, but not much. She had done her best, but McMorn had been impossible to distract. Then two things happened that worked in their favor. The fog, which had all but disappeared earlier, came rushing back into the valleys, climbing up the hill to meet the lowering clouds. Visibility had dropped. Now she could see only a few yards into the distance. Good cover for Timothy, but it made McMorn more nervous. He repeatedly called for Timothy, as did Sarah.

Two hikers emerged out of the fog. And they weren't just any two hikers. The first one was Tam. Jessica's heart raced, and blood flushed her face as she remembered his kiss under the mistletoe. How had he found her here? This couldn't be another coincidence! Mr. and Mrs. Maxwell must have told him where they were. Now she'd have a chance to ask him how he'd managed to get home in the ice storm.

Then she noticed the person with him. His companion was a girl, a tall, thin girl with long dark hair topped by a purple wool cap. She was Tam's age or a little older. Jessica felt her words of greeting die on her lips as the girl slipped her arm through Tam's and laughed. The damp chill from the fog crept up Jessica's legs and settled deep in her bones.

"What a surprise, running into you again!" Tam raised his eyebrows as if he were indeed surprised to see them.

"Oh, come on. Who told you where we were? That's way too many coincidences for me." Sarah pulled her knit hat down over her ears.

Tam held up his hand. "Okay, I confess. I did go looking for all of you this morning. I wanted to apologize for leaving so abruptly on Sowans Nicht, but I was desperate to get the car fixed. Your folks told me where you were headed today." He looked over at Jessica and smiled. She tried to smile back, but it felt as if her face were frozen. "And this is my big sister, Morgan. Home visiting for the holidays."

Jessica felt the smile thaw on her face.

"This is Sarah and Jessica and—" Tam looked in Mr. McMorn's direction.

For the first time, Jessica noticed that Mr. McMorn had not said a word. In fact, he looked positively threatening. *If looks could kill,* she thought.

"Brian McMorn." He didn't extend a hand.

"Nice to meet you," Jessica said to Morgan, and she meant it now that she realized the girl was Tam's sister.

"But where's Timothy?" Tam looked from side to side as if he expected him to pop out from behind a hillock.

"We were just looking for him," Sarah explained. "He's disappeared in the fog. He likes to explore on his own."

"Well, I think we should help, don't you?" Tam looked at his sister. "It isn't safe to be wandering in this fog. Morgan and I will go this way." He gestured east, in the direction Timothy had gone. "Why don't the rest of you split up and—"

"I don't believe we need your help." Mr. McMorn had not moved, but his voice seemed to have dropped an octave.

Why was he being so rude? Jessica looked at Sarah, who stood frowning with her hands jammed in her pockets, pale streamers of hair lifting in the wind.

"Just trying to help. Don't want the kid to get lost." Tam shrugged. "Come on, Morgan, we'll walk this way."

"I think not." Then, from inside his Burberry trench coat, McMorn drew forth a sword.

Jessica turned to Tam, but where he had been there was nothing but a quivering in the air, the scent of smoke where he had stood. And then he was there again, but his skin had erupted into welts, as if he were diseased. Each welt burst into a scale. Tam's arms fused to his sides. His legs twisted, melding into one thick body, while a forked tongue flicked from his smiling mouth.

Sarah screamed.

Jessica opened her mouth, but no sound came out. Her stomach heaved, and her legs took over. Before she could think, she ran.

She ran blindly through the fog, her heart pounding in her ears, over the hillocks toward the east, where she knew Timothy had gone. But the girl, Morgan, was right behind, her thin legs pumping furiously, her black hair streaming. Jessica ran until her lungs could barely draw air. She knew that if she slowed, one of Morgan's skeletally thin arms would reach out and grab her.

The ground was soft, the grass wet. Fog had now enfolded the summit of Dunsinane. It was no good keeping up this pace. She couldn't see the terrain, couldn't judge where the hillocks were. Her feet slithered in the mud. She fell onto her side, sliding down a grassy knoll. That one misstep was all it took. Before she could stand, Morgan was on her, her long legs straddling Jessica's chest. Her white hands had a stranglehold on Jessica's neck.

✛ ✛ ✛

Even in the swirling fog, the sword was bright. For an instant McMorn held it high over his head, and then he sliced it downward toward the serpent. Sarah watched, openmouthed, as the serpent gathered itself up and readied a strike at McMorn's unprotected chest. She looked wildly for a rock or anything else that she could lob at it. McMorn's stroke missed by inches as the snake swiveled away from the blade. Thick tongues of fog roiled and curled. Now Sarah groped blindly for a rock on the cold ground.

The serpent struck, but McMorn was nimble and dodged sideways, his dark coattails flapping behind. But it wasn't McMorn the beast wanted. As soon as the man no longer blocked the serpent's way, it oozed forward, the long body traveling east. Again McMorn struck. This time the sword sliced through the serpent's flesh, severing the tail. The serpent stopped. It eyes sought out McMorn as it hissed. Sarah held her breath, a rock finally clenched in her fist. But the snake did not strike. Its wound glistened wetly as the tailless body disappeared into the fog.

# STONEWORK

TIMOTHY CAREFULLY MADE his way down the tunnel, guided by the rough stone wall. Underfoot, the tunnel floor was smooth, dry dirt, an underground passage that led from the chamber and was obviously manmade. His fingers traced the fitted stones on each side— about three to four feet wide, he guessed. At one point the left wall receded, creating a small alcove. He stopped to take off his pack. Inside was a small key-chain flashlight, but a light could be dangerous. Who knew what else might be in this underground tunnel and attracted by the light?

Timothy looked up. The stone ceiling rose a few feet above him. He could just make it out in the dim light. Ahead, the ground sloped gently downward, and the passage widened. It was darker here, away from the hole where he had fallen in, but the tunnel wasn't musty-smelling like an unused basement or a cave. A fogou, Timothy thought. He had read about chambers and passages like this in a book about knights. They were used to store food but also as hiding places when Iron Age villages were raided.

A thrill shot through him. This would have been the perfect place for the monks of Scone Abbey to hide the Telling Stone when they heard the English were coming. He would have chosen a place just like this himself. Here, in this underground chamber, there were no sounds, no rustle of wind, no far off birdcall, only the sound of his own footsteps, the beating of his own heart. The dark and silence had swallowed him. Despite his fear of being seen, he decided to risk the flashlight. Its beam of light was small but comforting. Without it, he might miss the stone if it was hidden here.

Each step was a soft thud on the soft earth floor. Timothy had read that fogous had more than one entrance. There had to be another way out, and he was determined to find it as soon as he found the Stone of Destiny.

✛ ✛ ✛

Timothy held the flashlight in his mouth. Despite the small circle of light, he extended both his arms in front for protection. Finally, his fingers met rough stone in three directions. He grabbed the light and played it over the rough walls. A dead end. No exit here, and if the Stone of Destiny was hidden in the fogou, he hadn't found it. It was too easy to imagine the walls closing in on him, and he fought back a rising sense of panic. Even several deep breaths didn't steady him. Leaning forward, elbows on knees, Timothy made a decision. He would be methodical, like Sherlock Holmes, covering every inch of the passage and chamber in hopes of finding the coronation stone, no matter how desperate he felt. There had to be something about this particular stone to make it stand out.

As Timothy walked back the way he had come, he heard a soft scraping. He paused, straining to hear better. It was a whisper in the dark, something large being dragged across the dirt floor. He turned off his flashlight and held his breath. The sound of breathing. Something was in the chamber with him! It was between him and the only opening he knew to the outside world.

✛ ✚ ✛

There had to be another way out! Timothy turned the light back on and cupped the beam with a hand as he shone it across the rock ceiling, searching for a way of escape. Nothing. He turned off the light and pressed into the small alcove, hoping he hadn't given himself away. Cautiously, he peeked out. A thick darkness was gliding toward him along the chamber floor. It glided across the ground without legs. A giant snake! His fingers dug into the rock wall. He had no doubt that the creature was coming for him. The alcove was small, just a jag in the tunnel. It wouldn't offer any protection. What he needed was a way of escape.

Directly ahead was the stone where he'd scraped his shin. It was dimly backlighted from this direction, and Timothy could see it was a rectangle about a foot wide, raised about two feet off the floor by two smaller stones. All three must have fallen from the ceiling, first the smaller stones dropping, and then the larger rock falling to rest on them. Maybe, with any luck, there would be an opening left where they had dropped or at least a ledge where he could hide.

Any place would be better than here, waiting like a mouse for the slithering snake. He would have to walk toward the serpent to get to the rock and find any opening above it. His legs shook as he inched forward. The snake raised its head. Timothy shone his light into the beast's face, hoping to blind it, but its eyes were set high on the sides of its head. The nostrils were raised holes, and the mouth a wide slit in shiny skin. So, this is where stories of dragons began, Timothy thought dizzily. Would he be swallowed whole like a rat, or was this the type of snake that would squeeze the life out of him?

The snake caught his scent. Its head shifted from side to side as it searched. Its forked tongue flicked out, tasting the air. Timothy pressed himself against the wall and turned off his light. Cold stone cupped his shoulder blades. The long body coiled, then struck, but it overshot its prey and passed Timothy. This was his chance! He ran to the raised stone, keeping it between him and the snake. The snake was quick to turn its head and strike again. Timothy dodged, but the snake was faster. It caught and tore the edge of his pants. The smell of burned cloth filled the fogou.

Before it could strike again, Timothy jumped up onto the raised rock, praying for an opening in the low ceiling. His muddy tennis shoes landed with a smack on the stone. The fogou shook and rumbled. A terrible groan rose from the depths of the earth, as if something ancient had been wakened from sleep. The noise reverberated through the chamber.

Timothy's hands flew to cover his ears. The note vibrated up his legs, playing his body like a tuning fork. The snake rose, prepared to strike. Stones rained from the ceiling, and dust billowed. Timothy crouched and covered his head with his arms, trying to balance as the stone swayed and rocks tumbled around him. Would he be buried alive with the snake?

An explosion ripped through his head. Colors, words, and sounds rushed at him. Strange information filled his head: lines of poems, bits of stories, histories he had never learned. Here in a dark underground chamber, his mind had run amok, and that was even more terrifying than the snake. Again the ground shook; he could no longer keep his balance.

Timothy tumbled from the stone to the ground as more rocks rained from the ceiling. The snake coiled around itself. Timothy covered his head. The stone rocked from its support and dropped with a thud onto the floor of the fogou. The soft earth drew it in, and the stone where Timothy had stood disappeared from view.

⁜ ⁜ ⁜

The chaos in his mind quieted, but every part of his body ached. Timothy struggled to take a deep breath of air and coughed out dust. He lay on his back. Overhead, he could see the stone ceiling. He was still alive and still in the tunnel. Or was he? Sitting up slowly, he cradled his head as it throbbed with pain. Where was the snake? Where was the rubble? Around him, light flickered. Timothy looked up. Above him was the stained-glass window with the girl who looked very much like Sarah, the window in Saint Margaret's Chapel at Edinburgh Castle. And he was not alone.

A company of men and women stood in a silent ring around him. Perhaps he was dead. Timothy bit one of his fingers. It hurt the way it would in real life. In the stillness he could hear the soft breathing of the assembly, see their very human faces in the candlelight.

"Welcome to the Society of the Stone." A silver-haired woman spoke. Her voice, whispery as old leaves, was gentle, but her eyes were fierce. "We have waited a long time for you to come."

A murmuring of assent filled the room.

Timothy looked at the faces, a mixture of young and old, of various races. Most were unfamiliar, but two he recognized.

"Julian! Professor Twig!"

A man stepped forward from the crowd. He was old but as straight and tall as a younger man might be. His hooked nose rose from a face as lined as a walnut shell. White hair braided with feathers and beads hung to his shoulders. Timothy knew this face, too. He had seen it somewhere before, but he couldn't place it. "This assembled group are the Stewards of the Stone. We have been tasked to protect the Stone of Destiny and the Filidhean for generations."

Timothy looked past the older man to Julian. "You knew where the stone was all along?"

"None of us knew where the true stone was hidden. That knowledge has tempted Stewards in the past. The Dark pays well for information. Our task has been to help you find it," Julian said.

The white-haired man stood over Timothy. "Stand up; you are chosen."

"But why me?"

"Filidhean, male and female, are chosen because of who they are, the gifts they are born with. But this is not the time for questions. That will come later."

And Timothy, in his ripped pants and muddy tennis shoes, stood. In the back of the crowd was another face he recognized. Mr. McMorn lounged against a wall, his face partially hidden by shadow.

"Filidhean arise at the great turning points of history, the ganglions of time." The old man's thin beard quivered as he spoke.

"Where am I?" Timothy asked.

The woman answered. "Time out of time. The fogou was a portway to us. But let us begin."

The circle drew tighter. Timothy swallowed. His mouth was as dry as dust. Where were Sarah and Jessica? Were they all right?

The white-beard spoke again. "As Filidh you are keeper of the word, repository of knowledge." He touched a knotted finger to Timothy's forehead. And at the touch, the madness came rushing back like a wave, tumbling Timothy over and over while he gasped for air. Words, histories, lineages assailed him; there was no end.

Each person stepped forward and, one by one, placed a hand on him, filling him with the knowledge of their lives. Years passed, armies marched, songs were written and sung. Timothy crumpled and fell to lie like a babe in the old woman's arms.

⊹⹊⊹

Sarah and McMorn tracked the snake that had been Tam as best they could in the thickening fog. Sarah could barely see her own fingers at arm's length. She stayed close to McMorn by watching the gleam of his sword. Every now and then she caught a glimpse of something moving, or McMorn would call out to her as if they were players in a deadly game of Marco Polo. They moved eastward.

"The snake must not find your brother before he finds the stone!" McMorn whispered.

And then she heard the noise, an inhuman cry. It ran up the ridge of her spine and lodged at the base of her skull. Her teeth rattled. "What is that?"

Slowly, McMorn dropped to one knee, raising the sword above his head. A smile nudged its way across Sarah's face. Timothy had found the Stone of Destiny; she was certain now. Timothy had found it!

McMorn's voice rose through the mist. "The stone cries out! I do believe we're hearing the voice of the Stone of Destiny."

Sarah felt as if a terrible weight had lifted from her chest and dissipated into the fog. Timothy must be alive, and he had found and stood upon the coronation stone! Two more steps and her foot thudded against something soft and large. She bent toward the ghostly shape. She had stumbled on a body.

# THE SPEAR OF LUGH

**S**ARAH TOUCHED the damp curls, the felt hat. The body trembled. *Jessica!*

"It's okay, it's me, Sarah. What happened?"

Jessica continued to shake. Sarah wrapped her arms around her. She called out to McMorn, "I've found Jessica, and she's hurt!"

Mr. McMorn was quickly by her side. Together they searched for a wound but found nothing. McMorn removed his black Burberry and tucked it around Jessica. "She has no visible injury, but she may be in shock. We need to keep her warm. Stay with her while I try to find out where the serpent has gone."

"You need to find my brother, too." Sarah was miserable, cold and damp. She crouched over her friend, trying to warm her with her own body heat.

"I believe if we find one, we'll find the other." McMorn straightened, turned, and ran into the fog.

A blue flame flickered in the mist.

"What's that?" Sarah pointed toward the blue light, which moved closer. She drew her body into a tight ball around Jessica. Her friend would not be able to protect herself.

As if a curtain parted, Orisis the stag stepped out of the fog. On its back was Finula, and across her chest was strapped a spear that glowed with a blue light.

"The Daoine sídhe, Finula," Sarah breathed. There could be no mistaking the woman who had appeared in Nessa Daring's home just two nights ago. Today she wore crimson, and her black hair was beaded with drops of fog.

"The Good Folk pay their debts," she said from high on the tall stag's back. "It is an old agreement from the time when the mortals and Good Folk walked together. Even today, in a just battle, we will fight side by side with mortals." As the stag bowed its front legs, she slid from its back. "I have brought the Spear of Lugh." She drew the long blade from a scabbard and held it aloft. It glowed in her hands. "It has not been used in battle for many years, but now the time has come. It was forged for the mighty Lugh to use in his fight against Balor."

Sarah's heart lurched as the name of their old enemy was spoken.

"It shall fight against him again today. But as legend says, it is a stone that will fell him. The spear will burn anyone who is not destined to wield it. It's for the warrior girl." And her green eyes beamed at the girls.

Sarah looked at Jessica. Her limbs were slack, her face pale. She was in no shape for battle. Her weak arms would not even be able to hold a sword. "Jessica has been injured. She—"

"She is not who must take the spear."

Perhaps the Daoine sídhe was mistaken. Sarah knew she was no warrior. She recalled when Timothy was pursued by the Wild Hunt. Cerridwyn had given her a bow and arrows and said something about being more than meets the eye.

"That is your gift, Warrior." Finula's gaze never wavered.

*Warrior?* Sarah straightened her shoulders, trying to stand a little taller.

"Take it, child." The Daoine sídhe's face was solemn and her voice a command. "Though it burns blue-hot, it will not harm the one who is intended to use it."

Sarah closed her eyes, held out her arms, and cringed when the spear met her flesh. But it didn't scorch her. The metal was warm, and the spear trembled like a living thing in her hands. "What do I do with it?" Her voice was little more than a whisper.

# MORGAN'S KISS

WHEN TIMOTHY OPENED his eyes again, he lay curled on his side on the dirt floor of the fogou, swallowing dust, stones heaped around him. They were on his shoulders, his legs. Every inch of his body hurt. The earth was still. He carefully lifted his head. Coughed. From under a pile of rock several yards away, something hissed. The snake! How could he have forgotten about the snake? His muscles clenched. He pushed up to his forearms.

The pile of stones shifted as the snake slithered out. Timothy held himself very still. He had nowhere to go. No way to move fast in all the debris. He sat up slowly, shedding rocks and dust. The snake was still within striking distance. Timothy grabbed the largest rock he could hold and stood.

Immediately, the snake's full attention was riveted on Timothy. The serpent drew back. Its mouth gaped open, two white fangs poised like gatekeepers. Timothy drew back his arm, prepared to release the rock. But what he saw was not the snake's head. Instead, it was the face of the ginger-haired boy. Tam.

Timothy's mind whirred. Pictures flashed. He saw things he'd never witnessed, knowledge passed from the guardians: Balor walking with a dark-haired girl called Morgan; Tam, bewitched by the same dark-haired girl that he now knew as one of the sídhe, but a malign one. He saw the girl whisper plans into Tam's ear, and the boy's outline grew fainter. And he knew the boy's name, a name now told in legend: Tam Lin, the boy enchanted by the queen of the fairies.

Then Timothy recalled his own memories: Tam bumping into Jessica on the icy sidewalk, and Jessica's laugh when Tam asked her for her phone number; Tam at Nessa Daring's house, the room thick with glamour.

The snake moved to strike. With the rock still clutched in his hand, Timothy spoke. He called the boy by name. "Tam Lin," he said, and the snake froze, mid-strike. What was left of the boy inside the creature trembled at his true name.

"There is still time," Timothy whispered. "Balor is not true. The sídhe, the fairy girl Morgan, works with him."

The boy in the snake shrank smaller. Almost nothing of him remained.

The snake hissed. From outside the fogou, a whistle split the air. The effect on the snake was immediate. Its body dropped as if all the fight had leaked out of it. Timothy remained frozen, rock in hand. The snake glided past him in the direction from which it had initially come. Slowly, Timothy exhaled. Why was the snake retreating? As the snake slithered through the dust and rubble of the fogou, Timothy trailed behind, just out of striking distance. It was that or stay in the partially collapsed fogou. The snake was his chance of finding a way out.

Crawling now where fallen stones made the passage narrow, Timothy tried not to panic. He thought of math, he thought of codes, anything but the dark, close space around him. Gradually more light filtered into the darkness, a dim light filled with particles of dust. Timothy coughed and scrubbed the dust from his face. He stood at a crouch. With each step, his breath whistled and wheezed. His lungs screamed for fresh air. He wanted to see Jessica and Sarah. And that wanting was stronger than anything he had ever felt before.

Light! It pierced the dimness, forcing Timothy to blink. Overhead was a narrow opening in the ceiling of the tunnel. He couldn't tell if it was the hole he had fallen through. It didn't matter. It was a way out. The snake slid over the rubble and debris, wound its way up toward the narrow opening, and disappeared into the light.

Timothy climbed onto a loose pile of rocks. The hole, just within reach when he extended his arms, looked large enough to wedge his shoulders through. He took great gulps of fresh air, grabbed on to the loose soil, and tried to pull himself up. His fingers curled into wet soil aboveground. But his arms weren't strong enough to lift his body out. He braced a leg against the rock wall and tried again. Damp, cool air bathed his face. But before he could clear the opening, his foot slipped, sending down a shower of small stones. He dropped back into the fogou.

Winded, he looked up at the small patch of light. "Help!" he called. His arms shook.

A voice answered. Someone was right outside! Again he braced a leg on the rock wall and pulled himself up. This time his head and shoulders cleared the opening.

Strong, sinewy arms grabbed Timothy and pulled him the rest of the way out. He blinked in the foggy light, wiping the dust from his eyes.

Timothy stared into the face of a girl with eyes like black full moons. "Who are you?"

In response, her fingers dug into his arms, and one strong hand encircled his throat. As she pressed on his windpipe, he struggled for air. A small whistle hung from her neck. Had it produced the sound that had summoned the snake?

"I have you now, stone seeker."

The snake was coiled around the girl's legs, like a dog at the feet of its master. Her face was close enough that Timothy could feel the puff of air each word made against his face. "Where is it?" she asked in a voice as thin and sharp as a cold wind.

Timothy tried to make sense of the scene before him. And then he remembered: She was a friend of Balor, one of the sídhe—but, unlike Finula's, her heart was dark. The long history of the Daoine sídhe spread out before him like a road he had traveled. Their love for the world, the mountains, hills, and streams, their distrust of man and the great sadness that filled them as the number of humans increased and their own numbers decreased. He knew all this as quickly as a thought.

The girl continued to stare at him, unblinking, her black eyes wide and flat. "I have come to take what my people should have been given, even if I must kill to get it." He also knew exactly what she wanted: the Stone of Destiny, the one thing he couldn't give her, for he had no idea where it was anymore.

The girl's pale lips almost touched him now. Timothy could smell her breath, mossy and damp like the forest floor. Her death-cold fingers loosened on his throat. "I can suck the air from you in one breath. I can freeze your heart until it stops beating. Once we have the Stone of Destiny, we will diminish no more. Men will not rule. You will tell me where the stone is."

Old lore, knowledge long forgotten, bloomed in his mind. Iron could overcome the sídhe, but he had none. Even his small flashlight had been lost in the collapse of the fogue. Where was Jessica? Sarah?

Timothy's head tumbled with images he had never known before. Most of all, he knew he should be afraid. The snake's body slithered over his shoes. This time no words surfaced in Timothy's mind to save him. The girl pressed her lips to his face. Cold peeled the flesh from his cheek. Timothy writhed in agony. She covered his lips, sucking the air from his lungs. He sputtered. He had no breath to call for help.

But help came. It came through the fog. The shape that emerged was not the Greenman, or Cerridwyn, or even Gwydon, but Sarah. And she held a terrible spear. Behind her emerged the shadowed figure of a stag bearing two shapes on its back.

The Spear of Lugh. The bits of history that mysteriously floated in his brain arranged themselves into an order. The spear in Sarah's hand was another of the four treasures of Ireland kept safe by the sídhe through the long ages.

At the sight of the spear, the dark-haired girl hissed. She drew her lips from Timothy, but she did not loosen her grip. He sputtered for air, as if he had just risen from a lake with his lungs full of water. His cheek burned.

The sídhe spoke to the rider on the stag. "Would my own sister use this spear against me? Would you be traitor to our race?"

Finula answered from the back of the stag. "It is you, Morgan, who is the traitor. Our race was never promised immortality in this world. These lands, these hills, belong to the race of mortals. You have aligned yourself with a lie. The stone is for the Filidh."

"Sister, you are the fool. Man isn't fit to be a caretaker of the earth. His time will pass, and we will remain." Almost delicately, Morgan's fingers stroked Timothy's face, and each stroke seared his flesh.

"It's too late. The new Filidh has been chosen." McMorn's voice rang out across the hill. In his hand was a sword, the Claíomh Solais, Sword of Victory, which once belonged to Nuada, a great warrior of

Ireland who lost his hand in battle. Even as Timothy recognized the sword, cold crept down his neck and toward his heart, while Morgan's fingers continued to stroke his skin.

"Not too late, if he dies." Morgan's hair brushed Timothy's face, one hand still on his throat. The snake, now doubled in size, tightened around his legs as a blast of wind sliced through the fog.

# THE HUNT
# RETURNS

TIMOTHY HEARD CRIES in the distance. At first they sounded like the far-off call of geese, but quickly they grew loud enough to be recognized as the baying of hounds. The hounds came swiftly, with a terrible baying in the milky white sky. He turned his face skyward.

Again McMorn's voice rang out. "The Wild Hunt rides. And the hounds seek out a traitor."

Finula also looked skyward and then turned her gaze toward her sister. "Morgan, the Wild Hunt rides out of season for only one purpose, to seek a traitor. But there may still be time to redeem yourself."

But Morgan's face remained set.

A thunderclap punctuated Finula's words. Hounds bayed overhead and broke through the fog. Morgan dropped Timothy to the ground. The hounds descended in a wild clashing of teeth. Their baying was deafening. Behind them on a dark horse rode Herne. He lifted a brass hunting horn to his lips and blew. The note was as fearsome as the baying of the hounds. Timothy covered his ears. Morgan, stumbling, began to run over the hummocky ground. The lead dog descended with its teeth bared. Even through covered ears, Timothy heard Jessica cry out. He lifted his eyes. With a great snapping the hound had Morgan by one arm and lifted her from the ground. She managed to wrench herself free and lurch a few more paces, her arm hanging at a strange angle. Then the hounds were upon her again and carried her off into the air.

"Timothy, look out!" Jessica shrilled.

The snake tightened its thick, scaled body around his legs, making it impossible for him to move. The terrible mouth opened wide. Its head drew back to strike. This time Timothy saw no trace of Tam at all, only snake.

McMorn stepped forward, but from behind, steel whistled by Timothy's ear. Sarah had plunged the Spear of Lugh into the open mouth of the serpent. She then thrust it upward, the blue blade exiting through the top of the snake's skull. Timothy fell to his side as the snake unwound itself. It thrashed. The body flailed back and forth. As its mighty length beat the ground, Dunsinane shook, but the spear stuck fast in the snake's head. Thick mucus drained from the open mouth. Sarah fell to her knees. The reptile twitched and was still.

With a long shudder Finula spoke in a voice hollowed with pain. "It is done. There are laws that cannot be broken." For a long moment no one spoke. Finula looked into the distance. "Once, Morgan was brighter than the North Star, more joyful than a summer afternoon. My sister, firstborn. Balor promised her immortality; she gained death."

The sound of her wail pierced the fog, and the fog split until they could glimpse the sky. The wind answered with its own voice.

Timothy threw his arms protectively around his sister as she sat sobbing in a weary heap. "It wasn't just a snake. It was Tam, and I—"

"There was nothing left of Tam. He was consumed. Sarah, you saved me and destroyed only what was already lost."

Jessica, wrapped in McMorn's long coat, dropped from the stag's back and joined Timothy and Sarah. "Look."

McMorn turned. Timothy, one arm still around his sister, looked up. There on the treeless hill stood a man, and by his side was Star Girl. As he moved closer, Timothy could see that the man wore a loose coat with many pockets, a coat Timothy had seen once before, when a stranger had entered his house to gather whatever lamplight he could. He remembered the man's words: "The light will draw him to me." The man's face was pale, but his eyes were eyes Timothy could not mistake. He stood in his pauper's coat next to Finula as she grieved, and the voice that filled Dunsinane Hill was a voice Timothy would always know: the voice of the Greenman. It was full and strong, and as he spoke, the last of the fog turned to tatters, and the tatters faded. "I am sorry. Morgan was made for better things."

"Greenman? Is that you?" Sarah's voice was still thick with tears.

"Yes, child. But it is the time of my waning. When spring comes, I will again be as you knew me, part man, mostly tree." He drew her to her feet, and Sarah buried her face against his chest.

Electra spoke. "I have witnessed a change in history. The coming of the new Filidh."

Finula turned to Timothy. "Today we have honored an old alliance made when men were caretakers of the earth, to stand with humans against the Dark."

The stag bowed low, and she climbed onto his back. Longing pierced Timothy as he watched the stag bear the sídhe down the hillside. It was like losing the memory of a song he loved.

The Greenman stood by his side. "You have the knowledge of the Filidh. You are the keeper of the word and memories. The stories and histories have passed from the Stone of Destiny to you, just as they have done to all true Filidhean throughout history."

Timothy looked down at his torn jeans and gingerly touched his scarred cheek.

"He doesn't look different at all to me," Sarah said.

"Very little of who we truly are shows on the outside." The Greenman turned to the lifeless snake. "Tam Lin looked like a boy for a while and then like a snake, when no boy remained." With a jerk he withdrew the spear from the snake, wiping its blade on the thin grass.

"But what happened to Tam?" Jessica asked in a small voice.

"Morgan's accomplice? Morgan enchanted him to help her," the Greenman answered. "Surely you've heard the stories of the sídhe enchanting humans? Tam was beguiled by Morgan, and soon there was none of his true self left. Not all the Fairy Folk honor the old alliances.

There are those who have sided with Balor and seek to destroy man. Morgan and Tam failed in their task. Balor will try another avenue."

Brian McMorn had walked a short distance away from the group and stood looking down from Dunsinane to the valleys beyond. He didn't turn when the Greenman spoke.

Timothy felt a cold deeper than the surrounding damp wash through him. Why did McMorn keep his distance and not acknowledge the Greenman?

"Despite our mourning, this is also a time of celebration. Today there is a new Filidh among us. The Stone of Destiny has spoken, and its voice has been witnessed." The Greenman bowed toward Electra.

Timothy noticed a wolf bounding up the hill with two hikers close behind: a young man with a walking stick, long hair peeking out from under a deerstalker cap, and on his arm a woman, Nessa Daring.

The Greenman's next words rang across Dunsinane. "It is time we returned to the Market."

# THE FILIDH
# RETURNS

**A**T THE THOUGHT of returning to the Travelers' Market, Timothy's heart surged. He could picture the bright caravans, the jugglers, people he had come to know as friends.

The Greenman, Nessa, Julian, McMorn, and Gwydon drew close around the three children. Timothy felt Gwydon's wet nose against the back of his hand. He was pressed shoulder to shoulder with Sarah and Jessica, and somehow Jessica's cold, small hand found its way into his. Timothy grabbed Sarah's hand, too. Every time they had traveled before, there had been a portway, but where was it here?

The Greenman spoke. "This hill contains a portway that is older than Macbeth's fortress, one that has been used for time out of time. But we will not all travel together. There is one among us who may not come."

Puzzled, Timothy looked at the Greenman and then from face to face.

"I'll wait here for the children to return and then see them home."

McMorn stepped back from the circle. He slipped the sword back under his coat.

The Greenman led them to the largest of the cupped stones. "We must each place a hand on the stone."

Timothy noticed that Julian hung back to speak with McMorn. Why wasn't McMorn coming, and why was he keeping himself apart from the group? As he watched, McMorn handed the sword to Julian.

Jessica's hand tightened in his grip. He placed his other hand on the cold, rough surface of stone. Julian returned and reached out to touch the stone just as the familiar lurch began. It started somewhere deep in Timothy's gut and radiated out toward his fingers and toes. The world readjusted, as if he were caught inside a kaleidoscope.

They landed with a very real thump on a wooden dais. Timothy looked out over a sea of expectant faces. Beyond the farthest heads, he caught glimpses of wagons and twinkling lights. They stood on a raised platform at the edge of a forest. New snow, like fine lace, draped ash and fir trees.

Jessica squeezed his hand. Timothy glanced at her, then looked again. Her mud-spattered jeans were gone. They had been replaced by a long purple skirt made of a velvety fabric and a short cape of the same. Her curls were caught up in a silver net, and the ruby necklace sparkled at her throat. It was a Jessica he hadn't seen in a very long time, as if the girl she truly was had stepped out through her skin. He shot a glance at Sarah, who also had undergone a transformation. She wore a garment made, it seemed, from the blue of her eyes. Her blond hair was studded with pearls and wound in a braid around her head. She looked so beautiful and so fierce, so grown-up, that Timothy had to look away.

Half afraid he would still be in his mud-soaked pants, Timothy looked down. His pants were a soft green, and his wet sneakers were replaced by pale leather boots. Standing a little taller, he tried to pick out individual faces in the crowd, but the folk of the Market were difficult to recognize under stocking caps and shawls. Finally, his gaze settled on a familiar face, Fiona, Peter's mother. But where was Peter?

The sound of approaching footsteps on the dais made Timothy turn his head. A tall, rangy boy approached. He smiled from ear to ear with the delight of someone meeting long-lost friends. In a familiar gesture, he rubbed one finger down the side of his nose. Timothy felt Sarah stiffen by his side.

✛ ✛ ✛

Peter looked older than just a few months should account for. Suddenly Sarah had no words. Everything she could think to say fled.

"Peter!" Jessica rushed forward and threw her arms around him.

He hugged her and then turned and grabbed Timothy's hands in both of his.

Still, Sarah hung back. She didn't know where to look. She felt color flame in her face.

Peter stepped forward. "Hello, Sarah. I knew you'd return." His gaze included all three of them, but Sarah felt it settle on her.

She swallowed and looked at the ground. Why couldn't she say anything?

Peter drew a silver medallion on a chain from around his neck and slipped it over Timothy's head. Then he dropped to one knee.

The crowd roared its approval.

A deep voice, the voice of the Greenman, boomed from behind. "Today we crown a new Filidh, a new Master of the Market, a new lord of the Travelers. The Stone of Destiny has spoken, one prophecy fulfilled. And it has returned to hiding until a future Filidh is summoned."

Again the crowd roared.

✚ ✚ ✚

The Greenman they knew and loved stood at Timothy's side. In traveling to the Market he had transformed once more into the tree man, and in his twiggy fingers he held a crown, Timothy's crown with the single gold leaf. With a rustle, the Greenman stretched his knotted limbs, flexed the bark of his branches, and placed the crown gently on Timothy's head. "There are some things better not left at home." A smile split the bark, and his eyes shone merrily. "With the crowning of the Filidh, the long-promised treasures are returned. A cauldron for the Healer to mend the injuries of the people and teach kindness." He placed the Dagda's Cauldron from Nessa Daring's at Jessica's feet.

Nessa herself stepped forward, but she was no longer only Nessa Daring, the botanist. She was transforming quite rapidly into Cerridwyn, with flaming red hair and broad shoulders.

"The Spear of Lugh for a warrior who fights for truth and justice."

And with gloved hands Cerridwyn handed the glowing spear to Sarah.

"And the Claíomh Solais, the lost Sword of Victory."

For the first time since arriving in the Market, Timothy noticed Julian. He now held the sword McMorn had carried. He no longer looked like the librarian of Timothy's world, or like the Market's Storyteller, or like Nessa Daring's nephew in Edinburgh. His clothes were finer, a thick cape with a silver clasp and polished boots. Gwydon stood quietly by his side. Julian was someone, Timothy realized, to be reckoned with.

Julian stepped forward and presented the sword to Timothy with a slight bow.

For a moment, Timothy hesitated. Gwydon nudged his hand with his cold, wet nose, and Timothy reached out to receive the sword. It gleamed in his hand. Timothy bowed his head.

"The Filidh, as keeper of the word, must guard the old stories and see that they live to transform new generations. The best stories always involve great cost." Julian's voice was sure.

With a rustle of leaves, the Greenman turned his solid trunk toward Peter. "Peter, as Steward, has served the Market well with civility and justice while you were gone." Timothy heard Sarah's faint intake of breath and noticed that her eyes were wet. What was wrong with her?

The moment was interrupted by a great rushing, as if a winter wind was arriving in a blast. But there was no wind. Still the rushing grew and, with it, a terrible thumping. Timothy looked out across the crowd. His grip on the sword tightened. But it wasn't warriors he saw on the move; it was the forest. What had woken the trees? Adrenaline surged through his body.

"It's the trees! They're on the march again!"

Timothy felt the same mixture of fear and delight that he heard in Jessica's voice.

"Will there be a battle?" she asked.

"They've come to join the celebration, just as the old stories foretold." Cerridwyn spread her arms wide as if welcoming them all.

The silver-haired willows, the firs in capes of snow, the bare-armed oaks—all of them were coming to the Market. From somewhere in the crowd, music started up: fiddles and drums, then the whine of bagpipes. People danced, and even Sarah lost her pinched, bewildered look as Julian swung her in a circle. There was nothing, Timothy thought, like a party that involved dancing trees.

✚ ✚ ✚

It was just before nightfall. Timothy sat near Peter and finished off a plum tart. They were watching the dancers. And not far from them, another watched as well. Electra sat in a tree, observing the merriment. She smiled and hummed along with the music, and her bare feet swung in time.

Timothy noticed a flock of white moving through the revelers. A small man drove them with a stick. His cap was set at a jaunty angle, and he carried a flagon of drink in one hand.

"Nom!" Timothy cried and jumped to his feet.

"Of course it's me. What did you expect? Someone still has to keep things in order while others are off gallivanting." The little man nodded in Cerridwyn's direction.

"It's so good to see you." Timothy hurried to Nom's side.

"Well, I never thought I'd find meself talking to a Filidh. Here now, Master Tristan, behave yourself." He tapped his long herding stick against the neck of a smallish gander that had inched closer to an ear of corn held carelessly in a reveler's hand. "And you, the one always asking too many questions." Nom shook his head, looking at Timothy. "But look where it got you. I always knew it. Knew you'd make good." And Nom nodded, as if he was responsible for the way everything worked out.

"And you were right!" Jessica, face flushed and eyes merry, paused from dancing with a sapling. "We're all proud of him."

Timothy felt, well, he didn't know exactly how he felt. Flattered. No, *humbled*, he corrected himself: fifteen points. He looked at Jessica. Her cheeks were very pink, and her curls, as usual, sprang out in every direction. Then he found himself doing something completely out of character.

"Jessica," he asked, "would you like to dance with me?"

✠ ✠ ✠

Timothy, dancing! And with Jessica! Sarah smiled. She sat on a log just outside the circle of firelight. For the first time since returning to the Market, she was alone. Nearby, Julian talked in a low voice with the Greenman. Gwydon padded to her side and lay near her feet. Absently, she ran a hand through his fur.

"Sarah, it's good to have you back."

She started at Peter's voice. He approached from behind and sat next to her on the log.

Absurdly, her heart hammered in her chest. "Thanks," she mumbled.

He sat in silence.

Sarah shifted her feet. Crossed and uncrossed her legs. "How did you become Steward of the Market? You look older now."

"Time passes differently here. It's been two years since you were last at the Market. I'm seventeen now. After the battle, when the three of you left, the Market was a mess. No one was in charge anymore. Tristan was a goose, and the Animal Tamer was gone. Even a bad ruler makes people feel more secure than no ruler. The Greenman asked me to stand in, just until Timothy returned." Peter paused. "Or in case he didn't."

She felt those words suspended above Peter's head, hovering like a dialogue balloon.

Peter continued. "I guess it wasn't easy finding the Stone of Destiny."

Sarah shook her head. And suddenly her words returned, tumbling over one another, as she told the story of finding and searching Dunsinane. But when she got to the part about the spear, her words deserted her again. She would not cry, not here, not now. Blinking, she looked up at the sky.

"Then what happened? How did Timothy get away?"

"I killed the snake with the Spear of Lugh. And the snake . . . had once been a boy named Tam."

Finally, she did cry, and Peter stroked her hair. And for the first time since all the fury at Dunsinane, Sarah felt at peace.

# PARTINGS

**D**AYS AT THE MARKET passed in swift succession, filled with new duties and friends.

"It's almost like we've always been here at the Market," Sarah mused aloud. "I can remember life at home, but it seems so very far away. I wonder if Mom and Dad are missing us, or if it's like it's always been, and time doesn't pass."

Timothy cleared his throat, and the girls paused. His eyes were downcast, and he fidgeted in his seat. "Last night I spoke with the Greenman."

"He's back?" Sarah asked quickly. A few days after the crowning celebration, the Greenman had disappeared with Julian, though Cerridwyn and Gwydon remained.

"He was just here for a short time. Remember when he said that a Filidh needs to keep the old stories alive? It's time for us to go back."

"Go back!" Jessica looked up in alarm from a sketch she was making for new banners. "When?"

"Soon," Timothy said quietly. "Tonight."

"But you're the Filidh. The Market needs you. We can't leave all of a sudden!" Sarah's voice sounded indignant.

"The stories aren't just for the people of the Market. Peter did a good job as Steward. He'll do a good job again . . ." Timothy's voice trailed off. "There's a portway opening tonight. It will take us back to Edinburgh. It will be like we've just been gone for the day. Mr. McMorn will meet us and take us back to the apartment."

"It's already afternoon. Why didn't you tell us sooner? There are people I need to say good-bye to!" Jessica's eyes flashed.

Sarah remained quiet.

"This is how the Greenman asked me to do it. Maybe he thought that if we worried too much about it . . ." Again Timothy's voice trailed off, and he bit his lip. "We'll be back. I *am* Master of the Market."

"If the Greenman says we're supposed to go, then we have to." Jessica's voice was quieter now, assured. "Tell us what to do."

✛ ✛ ✛

Sarah needed to tell Peter they were leaving. For a few minutes she allowed herself to imagine Peter going with them, riding the bus with her to high school, staying at her parents' house. But that would be impossible. Peter was of another place. They had separate lives. He was needed at the Travelers' Market, and he, well, he wouldn't fit in at home. There were no other options.

The clear winter sky slowly turned to navy. Tonight the moon would be only a rind among the stars. Sarah searched for Peter in all the familiar places but didn't find him. The shadows grew longer and her thoughts heavier.

In the end, Peter found her. She was standing outside Julian's old caravan, ready to give up and return to Fiona's bakery, when Peter came up to her, whistling.

"Sarah! I've been looking for you!"

"No, I've been looking for you. I've got something to tell you."

He looked down at his hand and stuffed something quickly into his pocket. "Sit down and tell me about it." He indicated the steps up to Julian's door.

She shook her head. It would be better to tell him her news and leave quickly.

"No, I insist." He grabbed her hand and dragged her to the steps.

Reluctantly, Sarah sat next to him, realizing how much she would miss his company.

"Well, what's your news?"

Even though she had rehearsed the words and her quick exit, it was difficult to summon them. Again she shook her head.

"Let me guess, then. You're leaving tonight."

Sarah narrowed her eyes. "How did you know that?" And, worst of all, he didn't look at all concerned.

"Ah, well, Timothy isn't the only one who has conversations with the Greenman." He reached into his pocket. "I've made you something." He extended his hand and opened his palm. In it lay a small perfectly carved wooden caravan about two inches in length.

"See? The door even opens."

Sarah inspected the realistic little carving. The tiny door swung open on a minute metal hinge. She held it up to her eye to look inside. "It's beautiful, but it's so dark, I can't see inside."

Peter nodded. "We can't see very far, Sarah, but the story isn't over yet. There's more to come. I'm sure of it. Just wait until you see what I have in mind." And for the very first time, Peter kissed her.

✦ ✦ ✦

In the dark of the Market, when the lights in the caravans were out and that rind of moon rode the sky, Timothy led the girls to the same oak where Sarah and Jessica had watched the ferret-legging competition. *We'll miss seeing the first blossoms on the wild cherry trees*, Timothy thought, and *we'll miss spring opening day, when the Market is said to be at its finest.* He drew in a deep breath of the woodsy night air. Somewhere overhead a screech owl hooted and with a flapping arced through his line of sight. With longing almost as sharp as a knife, he knew it might be a long time until he returned.

"There are so many more stars here," Jessica whispered, as if she didn't want to disturb the night. "I can't imagine being back in school again as if nothing ever happened." Then she stopped. "What about the cauldron and the sword and the spear?"

Timothy shook his head. "They belong here in the Market. Peter will keep them safe. After all, what happens in one world can affect what happens in another. Mr. Twig told me that. They'll be here if we need them." He hoped he sounded more certain than he felt. "It's time. Take my hands."

Sarah and Jessica each took one of Timothy's hands, which had grown larger and rougher. A cloud sailed in front of the moon, and in that moment they were plunged into darkness. A sharp crack split the bark of the oak, as if it had been struck by lightning.

"Follow me." Timothy ducked his head and stepped through the layers of rippled bark into the heart of the tree, the girls close behind.

✛ ✛ ✛

The fog had faded from Dunsinane, leaving the hillocks, hummocks, and Pitmiddle Wood in the distance shining. The sun was low in the west. Arms crossed, Mr. McMorn leaned against the car, watching the children as they descended the hill. It was hard going for the girls in long skirts and sandals. The portway had not turned their clothes from the Travelers' Market back into twenty-first-century jeans and tennis shoes. Timothy's pale leather boots grew thick with mud as they carefully skirted the bull's field, his pack still on his back.

There wasn't much to say. Too much had happened. Timothy felt that his brain was full to bursting. He had no idea how life would play out now. What did it mean to be a Filidh in this time and place? Who was he now? And what had happened to the coronation stone?

McMorn was the first to break the silence as the little group straggled up to his car. "A fine sight you three look." He shook his head. "It's time we were on the road. We want to be back in time for the burning of the longship."

Jessica looked down at her dress. "We'll have to do something about these clothes before we get back, won't we? And how long have we been gone, anyway?"

McMorn looked at his watch. "It's four o'clock, and the festival on the castle mound begins at five."

Four o'clock. Timothy couldn't reconcile the time. He knew that time out of time was different, but this was too much. They'd been at the Travelers' Market for days and days. As they piled into the small car, McMorn started the heater. Timothy asked his burning question. "What happened to the Stone of Destiny? Is it still there in the fogou?"

McMorn backed the car out slowly. "The Stone of Destiny has fulfilled its current purpose. There will be other Filidhean until the day when they are no longer needed, when the stories themselves come to life. Until then, the stone waits. If you looked for it now, you wouldn't find it, but it is there when it's needed."

He looked at Timothy, who again had the strange sensation of something moving across his skin.

"What was that?" he asked, and then wondered if he should have. McMorn once again seemed aloof and incomprehensible.

"The truth touch. It's one way of knowing." And McMorn shot him a piercing look. "It helps me know how sincere a person is. It's an ability I've had since I was a child."

It was miles before the heater worked properly, and when it did, Timothy found his eyelids drooping. He yawned broadly. In the backseat, Jessica's head bounced on Sarah's shoulder.

The car bumped its way onto a narrow street in Edinburgh. It was no more than an alley, and no vehicle wider than McMorn's would fit between the stone buildings. Timothy started awake as they parked in front of the steps to Wynde Alley. "Why are we stopping here?" he asked, stretching.

McMorn didn't answer. Instead, he raised a pistol and pointed it at Timothy's head.

# 41

# BALOR

ELECTRA WAITED for the children to return from Dunsinane. She had watched as they climbed the hill, heard the stone cry out, and then watched as Herne and his hounds hunted Morgan through the fog. She watched McMorn drive the children to this narrow street. Now Electra knew it was almost time for her to leave; she could feel it. It would be time to return to her sisters, the Pleiades. But she was reluctant to leave the children. There was one more task before she was free to leave, one more event to witness in this long history of the coronation stone. Quietly, she climbed the stone steps to Wynde Alley.

✛ ✛ ✛

"Get out of the car, and bring your things." McMorn kept the gun pointed at Timothy, but he spoke to all three of them.

"What're you doing?" Jessica asked, the first to recover her voice.

McMorn made no answer. Timothy stepped out of the passenger door, his movements slow and clumsy, his eyes drawn like magnets to the gun pointed at his head.

As the girls climbed from the back, McMorn indicated the alley. "We're going to the map shop. Timothy will lead the way."

Wynde Alley was deserted. The entire town had gone to the celebration on the castle mound. Timothy's thoughts raged. Why hadn't he seen this coming? When McMorn hadn't gone to the Travelers' Market with them, when he had failed to turn at the sound of Greenman's voice, he had known something was wrong. He'd never completely trusted McMorn, with his strange "truth touch."

Behind him, McMorn and the girls' footsteps echoed in the alley. No one spoke. A thin band of light shone from under the door of Seaborg Cartographers.

"Open the door." McMorn prodded Timothy in the back with the gun.

Newton Seaborg stood when they entered, his bald head gleaming in the lamplight.

"I was beginning to think you'd changed your mind, Brian." His voice was high and eager.

"Where's Maggie?"

McMorn looked up. A rusted birdcage hung from a beam in one of the dim corners of the map shop. Inside, a gray mouse shivered.

McMorn let out a sigh of relief. "He hasn't come yet?"

Newton shook his head. Tears leaked from his eyes and glittered on his round cheeks.

It took several seconds for Timothy to process what he was seeing.

The mouse in the cage—could that be Maggie? He was sure he knew who "he" was without being told. The name coursed through his bones like a disease. Balor.

"What happened to her?" As Sarah looked up at the cage, the mouse thrust a twitching nose between the narrow bars.

"No speaking." McMorn's eyes were flat black disks. His nostrils flared.

Timothy and the girls huddled together, so close that he could smell the scent of Jessica's shampoo and feel Sarah tremble against his side, but from fear or anger, he couldn't tell. A sharp wind whistled up the alley and pushed its way into the room.

McMorn closed the door. He kept his eyes and the gun pointed at Timothy, even though he spoke to Newton. "Take the map from him."

Newton rubbed his hands down the length of his thighs. Then he walked behind Timothy and fumbled with the zipper on his pack.

"He finds the stone, we get the map, and the children go home and tell a story no one will believe." Newton spoke as if he were reciting a plan. His breath came in eager gasps as he pulled out the pouch with the map. "Oh, my pretty little thing," he crooned.

"The map won't do anyone any good; Timothy's already stepped on the coronation stone." Sarah's voice held that stubborn note Timothy had known all his life.

"What?" Newton's voice trembled. "The boy stepped on the stone?"

His voice dropped. "What will happen to Maggie now? He threatened she'd be raptor food!"

"It isn't just the map. *This* is the prize Balor wants." McMorn pointed at Timothy with one blunt finger. "The boy of the stone. I give Balor the children, and he has what he wants. But first I make sure he returns Maggie to her right form," McMorn said.

Overhead, the mouse shrilled.

"Everything I've believed in, everything I've fought for, will be gone. The world will be a different place." McMorn's voice rumbled into silence.

Timothy thought he had never seen eyes look so bleak. He said nothing. His mind sifted through years of information about Balor, about the ways of the Dark. All the things he had learned when he met the Society of the Stone.

The bell on the door tinkled. Expecting Balor, Timothy tensed. Instead, Electra entered silently in her long dress and bare feet and pushed the door closed behind her.

Newton Seaborg began to sputter. He clutched the map to his chest, breathing in shallow gasps.

"The star girl, is it?"

Timothy noticed a tremor in McMorn's voice.

"Get out."

"I have come to bear witness."

"Then you shall witness a great unmaking."

Wind rattled the windows. The door crashed open, and a man in a black woolen coat and scarf draped over a tuxedo entered. He wore fine leather gloves; his golden hair shone. And on his shoulder was a bird with a charcoal hood of feathers and blue-gray wings that formed a cape across his back.

"Have I arrived too late? Ah, Brian, Newton, I see you've been waiting for me. You can see I brought a guest, a peregrine falcon. He's very hungry."

The skin on Timothy's scalp tingled. If he had been a cat, the fur would have risen on the back of his neck. Every inch of his being reacted to the finely dressed man in the doorway.

Newton blanched and glanced up at Maggie in her cage. Jessica stuck out her chin.

As if he had swallowed something distasteful, McMorn grimaced. "You can see that I brought you what you wanted." He lowered the gun.

Balor drew off his gloves slowly and tossed his scarf onto a chair. Each movement was theatrical, exaggerated, for the captive audience. "You have brought me *exactly* what I want. And we even have a witness to your deed." He looked pointedly at Electra, who stood silent and watching. "Did you know that the peregrine prefers rodents to all other food? He swoops down and crushes his prey with his talons."

Newton began to sweat. Timothy could see shining rivulets run down the sides of his face.

The falcon cocked its head.

Despite being gifted with the long history of the Dark, despite being a Filidh meant to rule the Market, Timothy felt powerless. There was no one piece of knowledge that came to mind to help him in this situation. He was sure Sarah and Jessica expected him to know what to do. All three of them were weaponless, trapped by a man Timothy had thought could be trusted, once he knew him to be a member of the Society of the Stone. In desperation, he thrust his hands into his pockets. Empty, except for the heavy fairy stone given to him by Nessa Daring.

"So now you're a Filidh. You've found the Stone of Destiny." Balor's voice was light but his eyes hard when he turned them on Timothy. "Make no mistake, I have known generations of Filidhean before you, and to their displeasure, they have known me. A true Filidh is a problem. The last one was your great-great-uncle Edward. But he was easy—willing to trade his title for great wealth. You don't seem as easy to convince."

As he paced the room, a smile, thin as a thread, crossed his face. Timothy couldn't draw his eyes away from the falcon's talons that clutched Balor's shoulder.

"There can be only one ruler. One mind to control what people know, the stories they remember." Balor turned back toward Timothy. "Edward was intelligent enough to understand this. Every story has more than one version." He raised his neatly arched eyebrows. "Who is to decide what version they hear, you or me?"

"But there *are* true stories," Sarah interrupted. And then she looked startled, as if the words had surprised her.

"Which truth? Your truth, my truth? You are not so naive to think that there is only one truth, are you?" When Balor shook his head, light reflected off his curls. "With the right words you can make any man, no matter how noble, change sides, eh?"

McMorn cocked the gun. "Return my sister, or you lose the map. I'll burn it."

"You're willing to trade all you believe, even bring me the Filidh, to protect your sister? And if I don't play fair, you'll destroy the map? Pah! Why do I need it now? The stone has been found."

"The map contains more than the location of the stone." McMorn's words settled over the room.

More to the map? Timothy's mind whirred.

"What else does the map tell?" Balor asked, clearly surprised.

In the silence, the falcon ruffled its feathers and flew to a beam just above Maggie's cage. Jessica cried out.

Balor turned to her. "Great power requires great sacrifice. The Light breeds servants. I make kings."

Jessica spat.

With a swift movement Balor slapped her face with such force, she dropped to her knees.

Timothy lunged toward Jessica.

"McMorn, shoot him if he moves again. In the leg. Just to disable him. The Light loves martyrs, Timothy, but I won't let him kill you. I can always use a puppet."

The mouse scrabbled at the cage. The falcon fixed it with a bright eye.

Balor looked up. "McMorn, you've known this day was coming ever since I called you from the dance concert and explained the way I wanted things to go. You've had plenty of time to bring me the boy, yet you've kept me waiting."

Timothy gripped the stone in his pocket. A fairy stone, Nessa had called it. If you looked through the naturally bored stone, you could see what others couldn't. But there was more. And he remembered Finula's words: *And once you know something's true nature, you know its weakness . . .*

Slowly, he drew the stone from his pocket, but Balor noticed the movement.

"What's in your hand?" His voice was deceptively light. "I think you should give it to me."

Instead, Timothy raised the stone to his eye, but before it could get there, McMorn grabbed for it. Knocked from Timothy's fingers, the stone hit the floor and rolled to rest near Electra's bare feet.

"Get the stone, McMorn." Balor's voice was a command.

Sarah's voice was sharp with disappointment. "What good is that? It's only a rock!"

McMorn hesitated and looked at Electra. She smiled.

"Get it," commanded Balor. "Don't worry about her. She is here as a witness, and she can't intervene in the affairs of men. If she acts, the consequences will be great. She will never return to earth again but remain fixed forever in her constellation."

McMorn stepped toward Electra and bent to retrieve the stone. As his fingers closed around it, Electra lifted her foot and placed her bare toes on McMorn's hand. He screamed. The touch of her skin seared his skin. He grabbed for his burned flesh with his other hand. The gun clattered to the floor.

Timothy dove for the stone. Sarah scrambled for the gun. She picked it up and held it in two hands, pointing it first at McMorn, then at Balor. The falcon shrilled a harsh *kak* and clicked its beak.

Newton Seaborg moaned. The mouse shivered.

Still on his hands and knees, Timothy lifted the stone to his eye and looked through it at Balor. And Balor froze like a pinned insect. Timothy saw a great emptiness, a deep blackness, and at its very center a small and twisted thing, strutting and posturing. It was no bigger than a finger puppet. The thing he had feared so long was nothing in the light of truth. Timothy laughed.

A line appeared on Balor's smooth forehead. The line widened, revealing a flap of skin.

"Timothy, watch out. It's his Evil Eye!" Jessica called out.

"The stone—throw the stone!" McMorn's command filled the room.

As the flap lifted, in one swift motion Timothy hurled the fairy stone straight at Balor's face. With a satisfying *thwack*, the stone struck

Balor in the open eye. The smooth mask of his face began to crack, first one small fissure and then a larger one, until what had been his face slivered into shards, which splintered onto the floor. The shards dropped with the sound of ice pelting a window. The fissures spread throughout his body. Cracks split his neck, his hands. And with one massive tremor, Balor's entire body collapsed. A coat, a tuxedo jacket, and pants lay crumpled and slack on the wood floor as if the owner had discarded his clothes in a hurry. And where Balor's body should be, there was nothing.

McMorn, clasping his injured hand, stared, slack-jawed. His eyes, dark under beetling brows, darted from what had been Balor to Timothy.

Sarah still held the gun, pointed now at McMorn. Footsteps rang out from the alley, footsteps and the sound of toenails clicking over cobbles.

Newton's face blanched. The noise grew closer.

The door swung open.

Newton Seaborg closed his eyes and rocked back and forth. A man appeared in the doorway. He wore a thick cloak with a silver clasp, and on his head was a silver circlet. In his hand he held a spear, the Spear of Lugh. Gwydon stood by his side.

"Julian?" Jessica's voice was unsure.

It was Julian but not Julian. The man in the doorway filled the room.

"Lugh Lamfada, champion of the Tuatha Dé Danann, one of the high kings," Electra announced.

"The myths are walking. Don't let him near me!" Newton pleaded as Julian strode closer. "I only did what I needed to save my wife!"

Timothy felt as if his heart would burst with joy, as if something familiar, something long awaited, had arrived at last.

Julian's voice rang with authority. "Brian McMorn, a member of the Society of the Stone! You of all people should know that bargaining with the Dark is always futile. Balor wouldn't hesitate to enslave Maggie for all time, just as he did Edward, even if you delivered Timothy. Or he'd kill her while you watched. Do you think he'd give up his power over you?"

McMorn's eyes were red-rimmed. "I've been a fool."

"Not completely. You knew the old prophecy that Balor would be felled by a stone, and you told Timothy to throw it. You saved the Filidh. And Balor's power is diminished."

"You mean he's not gone for good?" Jessica asked.

"No, the battle between the Light and the Dark isn't over yet. But the Dark has been set back for a time." Julian took the gun from Sarah's hands.

"You're Lugh?" Sarah asked, puzzled. "So the Spear of Lugh was forged for you?"

Julian nodded. "But tonight, thankfully, it was not needed. And the falcon will go hungry."

Timothy glimpsed a movement from the corner of his eye; Newton

Seaborg was climbing onto the chair, reaching for the cage. "You're safe now, Maggie."

The falcon lunged its hooked beak toward Newton's hand but stayed settled on the beam. Gwydon growled.

Newton climbed down, cage in hand, and turned to Julian. "You can turn her back, can't you?"

"She can be returned, but not by me. Even though Balor's power is diminished now, what he has done must still be undone by a power greater than mine."

"But I thought . . ." Newton began.

"Open the door, Sarah," Julian said. Then he raised the spear and circled it in the air. With a harsh *kak* the falcon flew out the door and into the night.

"The Greenman will tend to your wife, Seaborg." Then Julian turned to Timothy. "Your first act as a Filidh seems to have been successful." He smiled. "I think it's time to reclaim the map and for you and the girls to find your family. I need to have a conversation with a certain star."

# A NEW CHAPTER

IN THE DISTANCE a ship burned.

"We've made it in time!" Sarah panted as they ran between revelers up Calton Hill.

The sky crackled with flames and rousing music from bagpipes and drums.

"My goodness, you were gone a long time!" Mrs. Maxwell exclaimed, giving them each a hug and also a puzzled smile. "I was getting worried, but I was sure that Mr. McMorn would take good care of you. And where did you get the costumes? They certainly fit right in with the celebration."

Sarah linked arms with her mother and hijacked her questions. "There was so much to see, all kinds of history!"

"At least you've made it back before the fireworks. Where is McMorn?" Mr. Maxwell searched the crowd.

"An emergency called him away," Timothy said.

"The man seems to lead a complicated life." Mr. Maxwell looked at the throngs of merrymakers threading their way through the night streets and yawned. "We'll be leaving the day after tomorrow. I'm about ready for my own house and bed."

*He has no idea just how complicated McMorn's life was,* Timothy thought. Although he had longed to see the Viking ship burning, it felt anticlimactic now. How could it compare to the adventure they had just experienced? How could anything?

The streets surged with tourists and locals; many wore kilts, and others were dressed in costumes as if it were Halloween at home. Timothy stepped aside to avoid a man taking pictures. A small boy with a snow cone bumped into him. Ice sloshed down the side of his pants. Didn't anyone watch where they walked?

"Good evening." One of the merrymakers, a gangly man with a large dog at his side, nodded as he walked past.

"Wasn't that Nessa's nephew and his dog with the funny name?" Mrs. Maxwell asked.

"Julian! Gwydon!" Timothy cried out. But too late—they had already melted into the crowd. Jessica squeezed his arm. Suddenly he was very glad to be right where he was.

In the distance, the lights of the Ferris wheel rotated against a black sky. Timothy looked up at the stars. "Do you think she's up there?" he whispered to Jessica, thinking of Electra and searching for the Pleiades.

"I hope so." Jessica slipped her hand into Timothy's. "I like to think of her watching over us."

"She did more than watch this time." He turned to Sarah. "What happened to the gun?"

"Julian took it. I don't think I could have used it, anyway. What do you think happened to Mrs. Seaborg?"

Timothy shook his head. "I don't know. Julian pulled me aside and said he would take care of things. I don't even know what comes next, where the story goes from here."

"I don't think we ever do know the whole story. I never knew that Julian was one of the high kings. What did Electra call him?"

"Lugh Lamfada, one of the Tuatha Dé Danann. They're a race of kings that have battled the Dark for thousands of years," Timothy said.

Jessica wrinkled her nose. "How do you know that?"

"It comes with being a Filidh. I know all kinds of things now that I didn't know before. But there are plenty of things I don't know, too."

He tucked Jessica's hand into the pocket of his jacket. *Stupendous*, Timothy thought. Only thirteen points, but enough. He looked at Jessica and his family. More than enough.

# EPILOGUE

J ANUARY. SCHOOL. Timothy grabbed his books and slammed his locker door. Apparently being a Filidh and knowing all he did didn't help him at all with science tests. He looked down the hall. Jessica was laughing, surrounded by the usual group of admirers. Timothy would have to pass right by her to get to class. If he looked straight ahead, maybe she wouldn't notice him, and he wouldn't have to face being ignored.

Hefting his backpack over his shoulder, he walked in her direction, eyes on the ground. He was almost clear of the group. Then her voice rang out.

"Timothy, wait." He stopped and looked up.

Jessica broke away from the crowd and walked straight toward him. "I was hoping I'd see you." She leaned over and kissed him on the cheek. "Will you walk me to class?"

THIS ENDS BOOK TWO OF THE  ADVENTURE.

# THE TREE CODE

In this book, Timothy, Jessica, and Sarah decipher the tree code embedded in a fifteenth-century map. While their particular map might not exist, there is a history of map ciphers, codes hidden in plain sight through patterns on a map. A tree code relies on the number of branches on a tree to correspond to a particular letter of the alphabet. Because the trees look like simply a geographical feature on a map, the message can easily be disguised. As you read the book, you can solve the tree code along with our protagonists! Clues are provided in the text. See if you can figure out which letters each of the forty-eight trees represents. You will find some letters are used more than once.

# MYTHIC GLOSSARY

Many of the characters in the Time out of Time series have their beginnings in ancient British, Welsh, and Celtic mythology. I have used legendary names for some of my characters and kept many of their mythological traits. However, I have ignored other traits that did not fit my story. So, while the characters aren't completely true to their mythology, none are completely foreign to it, either.

**BALOR:** He is often called "Balor of the Evil Eye." He's an evil warrior god found in Celtic-Irish mythology, and stories of his deeds originated in western Ireland. He comes from a race called the Fomorians, who were giants. Balor is a powerful magician who is able to strike people dead with one glance from his Evil Eye. Sometimes he is described as having one "normal" eye in the center of his forehead and one "evil" eye, covered, on the back of his head.

**BATTLE OF THE TREES:** This is from a fourteenth-century Welsh manuscript, the *Book of Taliesin*, which contains the poem "Cad Goddeu." The battle begins when the Welsh god of agriculture, Amaethon, the brother of Gwydon (or Gwydion), steals a dog, a lapwing, and a roebuck from Arawn, king of the otherworld in Welsh mythology. Arawn had been keeping the animals prisoners in his kingdom under the earth. Gwydon, the enchanter and master storyteller, awakens the trees, who have been sleeping for hundreds of years, and calls them to battle. In the poem and in Irish legend, each variety of tree has its own personality and role in the battle. The warrior trees correspond to characters in the Druidic alphabet known as Ogham. Gwydon and the trees win the battle when Gwydon guesses the true name of one of Arawn's men, Bran.

**CERRIDWYN:** She is a Welsh goddess of inspiration and wisdom. In myth, she is closely associated with Gwydon. She also symbolizes death and rebirth. In the Time out of Time series, parts of Cerridwyn's character are also borrowed from Artemis, the Greek goddess of the hunt, both a huntress and protector of wild animals. Both Cerridwyn and Artemis are associated with the moon and with deer and wolves. I've also used some of the traits of the pagan goddess Brigid for Brigit/Cerridwyn, so my Cerridwyn is a composite character. One Welsh myth states that Cerridwyn gave birth, through an unusual series of events, to the famous poet Taliesin.

**FILIDHEAN:** Filidhean were Irish poets and scholars. Their role was important in Irish society, and Filidhean were revered. They kept and passed on knowledge, mostly through the oral tradition. The position of Filidh was an inherited rank passed down through specific Irish families.

**FOUR TREASURES OF IRELAND: THE YELLOW BOOK OF LEGAN:** This book, from the fourteenth century, tells of the four magical treasures brought by the Tuatha Dé Danann to Ireland. The Lia Fáil, which is at Tara, is a stone said to cry out under the feet of a true king. The Sword of Victory glows as brightly as a torch, and no one can escape from it. The Spear of Light (or Lugh) triumphs in every battle. And the Dagda's (the "good god," of earth and treaties, ruler over life and death) Cauldron never empties until everyone is satisfied.

**GREENMAN:** The Greenman is a pre-Christian symbol found from Ireland to Russia, with the earliest examples dating back to classical Rome. The origins of the Greenman are still a mystery, but many researchers like to guess. Perhaps the Greenman portrays the interdependence of nature and man. Carvings in stone and wood are found in churches throughout the British Isles and Europe. Some folklorists believe that his foliate head has remained in churches as a symbol of resurrection, that it helped illiterate people understand the concept of rebirth.

**GWYDON (OR GWYDION):** He is a son of Welsh mother-goddess Dôn from one of the four branches of the Mabinogi, royal families of Welsh mythology. Gwydon, sometimes translated as "born of trees," is associated with poetry, magic, and music. He's also a warrior, shapeshifter, and trickster. He is best known for stealing the otherworldly pigs of the king Pryderi, starting a war, and being turned into various animals as a consequence for his bad behavior. He also has the ability to turn other people into animals and is known for tricking them to get what he wants. Some researchers believe that the same stories that were once told of Gwydon are now attached to the name of King Arthur, for their tales follow many similar paths. Other sources say that Gwydon fab Dôn is the best storyteller in the world. In *Beyond the Door* and in *The Telling Stone*, Gwydon, the shape-shifter, remains in the form of a wolf. His association with King Arthur is mentioned in Book I, *Beyond the Door*.

**HERNE:** Herne is one of many horned god figures found in various mythologies and is always associated with hunting, forests, and wild animals. In all stories, he has antlers sprouting from his head. Herne the Hunter is the Britons' version of this figure, while Cernunnos is the Celtic version. Herne was one of the keepers of the Forest of Windsor and was known for his hunting skills. There are many versions of his legend, including how he came to hunt in the night sky. Herne is said to still haunt the forests of Britain, leading the Wild Hunt, where he travels with his pack of white hounds, sometimes called Gabriel or Yell hounds. A sighting of Herne is said to predict a national disaster of some sort. Chaos, noise, and excitement are associated with the Wild Hunt, which usually occurs in the fall on Samhain, signaling the end of the harvest season and the beginning of winter, or the "darker" half of the year. Other mythologies connect Herne with Dionysus, the Greek god of the grape harvest, wine, and revelry.

## MORRIS DANCING (FOUND IN BOOK 1, *BEYOND THE DOOR*): Morris

dancing is an ancient tradition in Britain, but no one actually knows when it started. Even the name "Morris" has unclear origins. It may come from "Mary's men" or from exotic, "Moorish" dancing, or even from the Latin *mores*, meaning "customs" or "folkways." Historians believe that the tradition is anywhere from eight hundred to three thousand years old—earliest written records date from 1477—and it is still practiced today! Morris dancers performed for many festivals at the release of new, church-brewed ales, for May Day celebrations, and for village fetes. It was a way of celebrating life's richness and joy.

## OGHAM: This was a system of writing developed in Ireland in the

fourth century. It looks like a series of hatch marks crossing or joined to a central line. These marks form the twenty letters of the Ogham alphabet. The straight hatch marks were easy to carve on wood or stone, and that's where Ogham is usually found. You can still find stones in Ireland, England, Wales, and Scotland carved with Ogham letters. The marks read in the same way that a tree grows, from bottom to top.

## PLEIADES (OR SEVEN SISTERS): The Pleiades are star sisters said to be

companions to Artemis, goddess of the hunt and the moon. Although they have individual stories in Greek mythology, I did not use these. Instead, I gave one sister, Electra, the characteristics, impartiality, and invariability of the moon—a constant observer who waxes and wanes with the seasons.

**PONT'S MAP:** Timothy Pont was a Scottish cartographer and topographer who made detailed maps of Scotland from the late 1580s through the 1590s. Seventy-seven of his maps survive. The maps are known for their astonishing detail and accuracy, and many have tiny drawings of buildings of the period. The maps are considered key historical documents, and the surviving ones are kept in the National Library of Scotland in Edinburgh.

**PORTWAYS:** Secret passageways to other locations, times, and sometimes other worlds are common in myth. In Ireland, fairy mounds are said to lead people into the underworld. Pagan Celts and, later, early Christians described thin places where the boundary between the physical and the spiritual world disappeared. Time portals, often caves and tunnels, allowed travelers to move backward and forward in time. The two thousand miles of ancient Roman roads that still crisscross Britain are often thought to be the site of magical events.

**TAM LIN:** The legend of Tamlane was first seen in *The Complaynt of*

*Scotland* in 1549. The story tells of a young Scotsman who fell from his horse while hunting. He was taken captive by the fairie queen and enchanted. His enchantment could be broken only when a young maiden held him in her arms as he shape-shifted through all manner of creatures, including a newt, a snake, a bear, and a lion. If she managed to hold him, the spell would be broken. But if the enchantment was not broken, he would be given as a tithe to Hell. A young woman named Janet broke the spell. In *The Telling Stone*, Tam is not rescued but diminishes until there is nothing of him left.

**THE TELLING STONE:** The Telling Stone is actually called the Lia Fáil, or coronation stone, also the Stone of Destiny, and its story has as many twists and turns as a suspense novel. It is a real stone on which the ancient kings of Ireland and Scotland were crowned. Myth says the stone cried out loud whenever a true king placed his foot on it. Myth also says the stone was brought to Ireland by the Tuatha Dé Danann.

But if the stone started as a coronation stone for the kings of Ireland, how did it get to Scotland? The oldest Scottish document to discuss the stone, Rhythmical Chronicle, was written at the end of the thirteenth century. Supposedly the Lia Fáil was taken from the hill of Tara in AD 500 by the High King of Ireland, Murtagh mac Erc. He lent it to his brother Fergus (later known as Fergus the Great) for the latter's coronation in Scotland. It remained in Scotland at Scone

Abbey, was renamed the Stone of Scone, and was used to crown the kings of Scotland until the late thirteenth century. And the stone still cried out for a true king!

In 1296, Edward I of England decided he would have his army take the stone by force as a souvenir of his victories over the Scots. The plan was to place the stone in Westminster Abbey in London.

Here is where things get interesting. Many people believe that the true Lia Fáil was never taken by Edward's men, that the monks of Scone buried it on Dunsinane Hill, and that the stone Edward's men took was a fake. A letter to the editor of the *Morning Chronicle* of January 2, 1819, states:

> *On the 19th of November, as the servants belonging to the West Mains of Dunsinane-house, were employed in carrying away stones from the excavation made among the ruins that point out the site of Macbeth's castle here, part of the ground they stood on suddenly gave way, and sunk down about six feet, discovering a regularly built vault, about six feet long and four wide. None of the men being injured, curiosity induced them to clear out the subterranean recess, when they discovered among the ruins a large stone, weighing about 500, which is pronounced to be of the meteoric or semi-metallic kind. This stone must have lain here during the long series of ages since Macbeth's reign.*

The story of the stone doesn't stop there. The stone, or the fake stone, was stolen from London by four Scottish nationalists early on Christmas Day 1950. They took the stone to Arbroath Abbey and left it on the altar. The stone was returned to England two years later.

Finally, on Saint Andrew's Day, November 30, 1996, the British returned the stone to Scotland, and, amid much pomp and ceremony, it was installed with the Honors of Scotland (symbols of national identity) in Edinburgh Castle. Historians in Scotland examined the stone on its arrival and pronounced that it was "probably" the original stone, but no one knows for sure. The stone has been quiet since its return.

## TUATHA DÉ DANANN ("PEOPLE OF THE GODDESS DANU"):
This is a mythic race who allegedly arrived in Ireland by ship or in a dark cloud. Skilled in art and science, poetry and magic, they brought the Four Treasures of Ireland (the Dagda's cauldron, the Spear of Lugh, the Stone of Destiny, and the sword Claíomh Solais) with them. They are said to have invented the Ogham alphabet and are associated with fairies and supernatural powers. Their arrival in Ireland supposedly unsettled the existing tribes and resulted in at least three battles for control of the country. Eventually the Tuatha Dé Danann were defeated and driven into the underworld. However, legend says they are still present as fairies, the Daoine sídhe, and they will still fight beside mortals in just battles.

**WILD HUNT:** This is traditionally led by Herne the Hunter in much of Britain, but also by King Arthur in southern England and France. White Gabriel or Yell hounds with red-tipped ears and eyes accompany Herne throughout the sky, often riding on the festival nights of Halloween, New Year's Eve, and Beltane (May Day). The Irish have their version of the hunt, when fairy folk, the Daoine sídhe, ride on horses through the sky. Farm animals and pets are kept inside when the hunt rides so that they are not stolen, driven through the sky, and run to death. Sometimes the hunt is said to sound like geese in the night, and it is always accompanied by strong winds and turbulent weather.

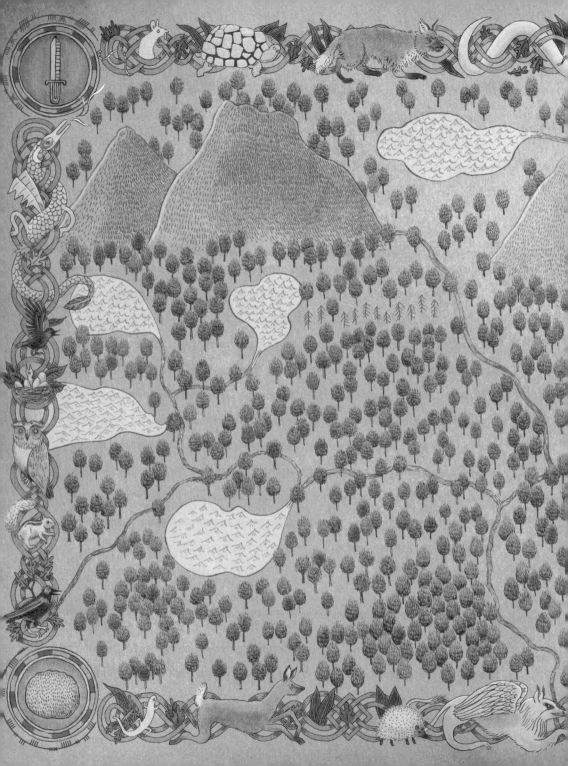

# ACKNOWLEDGMENTS

**Very special thanks** to Andy at www.stravaiging.com, an online guide to Scotland. Andy is an avid mountain biker and photographer. In 2008, when I was trying to envision hiking Dunsinane Hill, I asked this complete stranger if he was willing to take pictures of Dunsinane for me to better imagine Timothy's search for the stone. He sent me nineteen photos! Any errors in description are mine!

Thanks to Jeff and Steve, for making me more dangerous, and to Debra Murphy for her keen eye and early support. As always, profound thanks to my excellent editor, Howard Reeves, who reminded me that, in myth, evil can never cross a threshold until invited in; my agent, Sandra Bishop, who works so hard on my behalf; and to family and friends who cheer me on. Thanks to the great cloud of mythmakers who came before me.

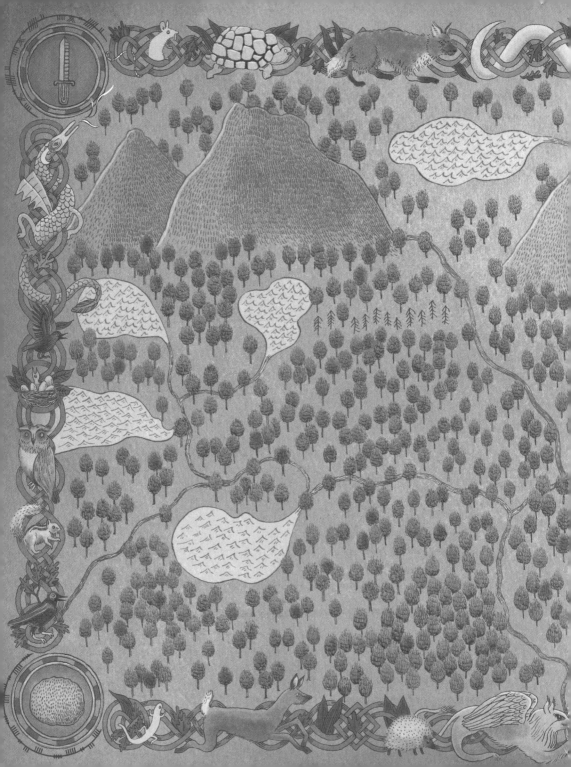